WAYNE STINNETT

FALLEN

HONOR

A JESSE MCDERMITT NOVEL

Caribbean Adventure Series

Volume 7

2015

Published by DOWN ISLAND PRESS, 2015
Travelers Rest, SC
Copyright © 2015 by Wayne Stinnett

Library of Congress cataloging-in-publication Data
Stinnett, Wayne
Fallen Honor/Wayne Stinnett
p. cm. - (A Jesse McDermitt novel)
ISBN-13: 978-0692489512 (Down Island Press)
ISBN-10: 0692489517

Cover Photo by Ruth Peterkin
Graphics by Tim Ebaugh Photography and Design
Edited by Clio Editing Services
Proofreading by Donna Rich
Interior Design by Write.Dream.Repeat. Book Design
This is a work of fiction. Names, characters, and incidents are either the product of the author's imagination or are used fictitiously. Any resemblance to actual persons, living or dead, businesses, companies, events, or locales is entirely coincidental. Most of the locations herein are also fictional, or are used fictitiously. However, I took great pains to depict the location and description of the many well-known islands, locales, beaches, reefs, bars, and restaurants in the Keys, to the best of my ability. The Rusty Anchor is not a real place, but if I were to open a bar in the Florida Keys, it would probably be a lot like depicted here. I've tried my best to convey the island attitude in this work.

FOREWORD

I'd like to thank the many people who encouraged and helped me write this novel. As always, my deepest thanks go to my wife and the many ideas she gives me. She is a great blessing in my life.

My motivation for the character Coral came from the Kenny Chesney song, "She's From Boston." A few real people were fictionalized herein and you know who you are.

A special debt of gratitude is owned to the many writers and professionals of Author's Corner, for all the great ideas, encouragement, and counsel. Colleen Sheehan did a fantastic job formatting this book. Much appreciation is owed to Dawn Lee McKenna, who makes a guest appearance as a character in this work. Thanks also to Shelley Kinsman for graphics materials.

A special thanks to beta readers Dana Vihlen, Alan Fader, Debbie Kokol, Mike Ramsey, Charles Hofbauer, Marc Lowe, Joe Lipshetz, Tom Crisp, and Russ Komp. Your input has been extremely valuable in making this book better than it was.

With a great deal of humbleness, I must thank two specific fellow authors. Contrary to popular belief, we're not competitors, but one another's greatest cheerleaders. The only way we could compete with each other is if we were able to write as fast as our readers read. We help one another with prose, promotions, and dozens of other intangibles.

Michael Reisig is the author of the *Road to Key West* series and the *Caribbean Gold* series. After reading one another's books, which are decades apart in their respective settings, Michael and I realized we had a lot in common, not the least of which is a Jamaican character named Rufus. Michael graciously agreed to allow me to make my Rufus, who is much older than Michael's character, a bit more like his quirky Rastafari mystic, depicting his Rufus as an older and perhaps wiser character in this and future novels. I hope my readers, and Michael in particular, like what I've done with him.

Sincere appreciation is given to fellow Marathon, Florida author Steven Becker. I'm a big fan of Steve's *Mac Travis* series, which shares not only the same location as my books, but the same time period. Knowing Marathon and the surrounding area as we do, Steve and I agreed that there just couldn't be any way that his characters wouldn't at least be acquainted with mine. Both Mac and Wood make guest appearances in this novel, and Jesse will be appearing in Steve's next novel, due out this summer.

This interaction and exchange of ideas with these and other authors has been a whole lot of fun and hopefully beneficial, as well.

DEDICATION

*Dedicated to my late father, Earl Talley Stinnett.
Growing up, I don't remember a time when he wasn't
working.*

*Whether it was on one of his construction sites, or just
"piddling around the yard," a teenage boy notices these
things and tries to emulate them.*

*I owe my work ethic to his example.
Throughout my novels, there are a
sprinkling of Earlisms.*

"On the whole, it is better to deserve honors and not
have them than to have them and not deserve them."
Mark Twain - 1902

If you'd like to receive my monthly newsletter for specials, book recommendations, and updates on coming books, please sign up on my website:

www.waynestinnett.com

Jesse McDermitt Series
Fallen Out
Fallen Palm
Fallen Hunter
Fallen Pride
Fallen Mangrove
Fallen King
Fallen Honor
Fallen Tide (November, 2015)

Charity Styles Series
Merciless Charity
Ruthless Charity (Winter, 2016)
Heartless Charity (Fall, 2016)

The Gaspar's Revenge Ship's Store is now open. There you can purchase all kinds of swag related to my books.
WWW.GASPARS-REVENGE.COM

FALLEN
HONOR

MAPS

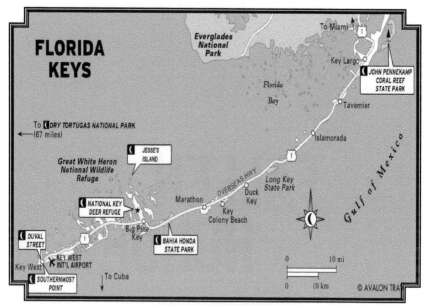

The Florida Keys

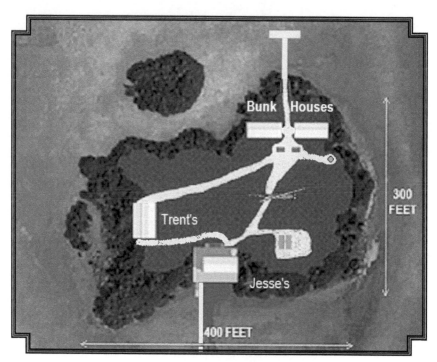

Jesse's Island

CHAPTER ONE

During late July, in the southernmost city of the United States, taking a breath is an exhausting chore. More so if you aren't used to the steamy tropical climate of South Florida. The very air seems to carry a massive weight, pressing down on this island town at the end of the road, flattening it. Here, the term "hot and humid" loses all meaning. The air is so saturated and heavy with moisture it feels as if you can cut it with a knife. The sun is like a blast furnace, searing into exposed flesh. Stifling and still, the air shows not even a hint of the slightest breeze. The sun bears down without mercy, heating the already hot air and evaporating any moisture lying on the surface of the land. Being surrounded by the ocean, there is plenty of moisture and little land.

Standing on the corner of Duval and Caroline Streets waiting for traffic to clear, a man stood restlessly shifting his weight from one foot to the other. A beat-up old Chevy pickup blocked the crosswalk, its exhaust adding

to the heat and misery. Feeling like he was standing on a bed of charcoal, the man waited. Stepping out in traffic was ill-advised on the crowded and narrow streets of Key West.

The few seconds of respite the fidgeting afforded his feet didn't really help much in his new flip-flops. The pavement only heated up the rubber soles. Late July and the man was sweating profusely, his new tropical-looking shirt already sticking to his skin after only five blocks of walking. Even in shorts, he could feel the sweat dripping down the backs of his knees. The temperature and humidity both hovered near the one-hundred mark, and any cooling breeze that might have come off the sea wasn't quite making its way down to street level.

A native of Pittsburgh and on his first-ever trip out of the Alleghenies, it was like Michal Grabowski had crossed into a new dimension when he'd stepped off the Greyhound bus late the previous night and encountered the sights, smells, sounds, and the very feel of Key West.

Two days before, very early in the morning, he'd bought a one-way ticket at the main bus terminal near the confluence of the Allegheny and Monongahela Rivers. When Grabowski boarded the southbound bus out of Pittsburgh, he never looked back. With good reason.

The pickup jerked and belched smoke, chugging its way across Duval as Grabowski stepped off the curb to cross Caroline Street. He was nearly hit by two lime-green scooters, jumping back just in time as the riders turned off Duval and onto Caroline, racing and yelling at one another, the scooters belching more smoke. The riders were obviously already drunk and it wasn't even noon. *Or maybe their Friday night just hasn't ended yet,* Grabowski thought.

At only five seven and a hundred and fifty pounds, Grabowski often thought himself to be invisible. It wasn't the first time he'd nearly been run over. He didn't have any distinguishing marks, scars, or tattoos, and wore his blond hair short, just over his ears. His unremarkable face now bristled with a two-day stubble. Back home, he looked like a thousand other guys. Here, he stuck out like a sore thumb among the cast of oddball characters that make up Key West. Crossing the street, he stopped to let his feet cool in the shade of an awning covering the entrance to a T-shirt shop.

Looking across the street at a travel agent's storefront, Grabowski noticed a map of the state that they had taped to the inside of the front window. It was hanging loose from the top right corner, the employees either not noticing or not caring to fix the tape, which had lost its adhesiveness in the humid air.

Tilting his head slightly to the right, Grabowski looked at the map at a whole new angle. Ninety degrees from its usual angle, the long East Coast highway called US-1 now wound its way from left to right, ending right here.

Key West has got to be the reservoir tip of the Florida condom, Grabowski thought. Glancing up and down Duval Street, he could actually see the dense air as the midday sun seemed to melt the asphalt, heat waves shimmering up from everything. Grabowski watched the other people on the sidewalks as they shuffled through the oppressive heat of the day. *All the little swimmers moving around in a daze, bumping into one another, then moving on,* he mused.

Michal Grabowski had an unusual way of looking at things. He'd learned to just take each moment in time and everything that was going on in it on its own merit. He didn't have good or bad days, just moments that he accepted for what they were and used for what he could. A practical young man, who acknowledged what fate handed him and enjoyed what he could.

Continuing up Duval Street, weaving in and out of pedestrian traffic on the narrow sidewalk, he hurried through the areas exposed to the brutal sun and slowed under the awnings of the businesses and bars that afforded shade.

Like many, Grabowski had come to Key West on the run. Three days ago, he'd ripped off a coke dealer. He'd been planning it for weeks, building up his courage as he sold off his meager belongings. Finally, when he was down to just a few changes of clothes, with nothing else in his furnished apartment that he could sell, he decided it was time to get out of the Three Rivers area. Grabowski knew he could get away with it, because he knew the dealer and his habits. The two were occasional drinking buddies. Sometimes, they smoked weed together and Michal never turned down the offered line on a mirror. The dealer was small-time, moving grams at street level. An acquaintance, not really a friend.

The fact that the guy would get into serious trouble with the dealer who fronted him a kilo every other week never even occurred to Grabowski. Lenny snorted and partied away all his profits during a three-day binge party after scoring the coke. Grabowski figured there'd just be no way for Lenny to even consider trying to find him, unaware that the dealer who supplied Lenny did so on credit and moved thousands of pounds in the Pittsburgh area. That guy had a bit longer reach, another notion that had escaped Grabowski's attention.

So, Michal planned the theft as carefully as he could. He knew Lenny's routine as well as Lenny did. The guy didn't seem concerned with taking any precautions. Michal knew that Lenny scored a kilo every other Wednesday, late at night, in preparation for the three-day party. Michal had attended a number of the nonstop affairs himself, where coke and weed were passed around freely. So he just happened to be there on delivery night, when Lenny was breaking the brick up into several hundred single-gram packets. He waited, even offered to help by making coffee for the guy.

When Lenny went to the john, Grabowski made his move. He quickly gathered up all the little packets, wrapped the rest of the unbroken brick tightly in its foil cover and stuffed everything in his oversized pants pockets. Driving quickly, he was three blocks away at the Greyhound station, boarding the first bus headed south, before Lenny even noticed that he and the party supplies were gone.

Selling a few grams here and there on the trip south, Michal quickly doubled his meager stash of running cash. He was careful, though. Being small made a person careful. Being invisible helped a lot, as well.

Michal had only bought a ticket to the next stop and kept only two or three grams in his pocket for a possible sale. The rest was stashed in his backpack. He made sure to conduct the actual sale when the bus stopped. And that seemed like it happened in every little town they came to.

If he didn't make a sale, he bought another ticket to the next stop heading south and reboarded the same bus. If he did make a sale, he let the bus and buyer continue on and he caught the next one. Always headed south.

Wanting to avoid any kind of confrontation, he had to take what precautions he could. Having speed and agility on his side meant that being in the open, where he could move around, was safer. That way, he was certain that, if anything happened, he could outrun the cokeheads he targeted. If that didn't work, he was capable of defending himself, but not in the confines of a rolling bus.

Michal had always been small. Growing up in a tough neighborhood, being small meant being picked on and beaten up on a weekly basis. Sometimes more often than that. His dad had spent a year in Japan and learned a few judo moves, which he'd taught to his son. At the age of nine, Michal had learned all that his dad could teach him and was enrolled in a judo school across town.

The small boy grew into a small man. He worked hard and learned fast, eventually becoming a part-time instructor at the school. Judo seemed to meld with the way he looked at life. Watch everything going on around you, step out of the way of things that can hurt you and take advantage of the things that can't.

Standing in the bus's lavatory halfway between Uniontown, Pennsylvania, and Morgantown, West Virginia, Michal caught a look at himself in the stainless steel mirror, as he held a tiny spoon to his nose and sniffed. *I still don't see the attraction*, Michal thought, wiping his nose.

It'd been seven years since Michal had quit the Bushido dojo to work full-time at the foundry. He tooted when the opportunity presented itself, but had never actually bought coke before. Union strikes and layoffs were part of everyday life and he found himself drinking and partying more. He hadn't worked out, or practiced judo, in several years now. *A new location and a new life,* he thought. *Maybe I'll open my own dojo in Florida.*

Checking his nose again, he capped the small vial and put it in his pocket, always careful to leave a tiny grain or two of the fine white powder on his mustache to attract customers. It worked better than a sign hung around his neck.

The farther south he went and the more of the stolen drugs he sold, the farther south his ultimate destination became. Soon, that destination had a name. When someone asked where he was headed, he'd picked the destination at random because it was the furthest south you could go. As far from the steel mills as he could get. He was through with the gray slushy winters. Key West.

Sales of the little packets increased the further south he rode on the busses. Upon reaching the terminal in Miami, he had a dinner stop and a one-hour wait for the next bus that would take him all the way to Key West. Altogether, he'd sold twelve grams of the white powder and another half a gram went up his nose, one little spoonful at a time. He kept his personal stash in a tiny glass vial, the spoon on a chain attached to the cap. Cokeheads had sharp eyes and could spot the telltale white flakes under his nose from the other end of the bus. He kept the little jar half-full, to entice prospective buyers.

When he finally got to the end of the line in Key West, he had a little over five thousand dollars in his backpack, but at some point his wallet had been picked from his

pocket. He figured it had to be while standing in the crowded departure area in Miami, remembering that he'd had it at the restaurant and found it missing after boarding the bus. It didn't have any cash in it—he had that stashed in his backpack. But it did have his driver's license and three credit cards, of which two were maxed out. Just another event that he accepted and moved on.

Figuring to start a new life, Michal considered the loss of the cards and license to be part of doing business. With more than a pound of the key unbroken and almost four hundred little packets ready to sell, he thought his prospects were pretty good. Those packets alone represented two years' worth of wages to him. He'd need to find a place he could buy a lot more of those little Ziploc packets. He'd looked around the bus, wondering if the pickpocket was aboard, but hadn't seen him.

Thinking back, Michal knew it had to have been in the crowded line, where people were pushing and shoving to get on the bus. Only one person stood out in his mind and that was because he stood out less than Michal himself. There'd been a guy near him in the line, shorter than Michal's five seven. An ugly little guy with greasy hair, acne, and a crooked, hooked nose. Michal remembered him because he stunk. He'd also sold him an eight ball when they stopped in Belle Glade on the south side of Lake Okeechobee.

Michal had broken his own rule on reboarding a bus after a sale. The next one out of Belle Glade wasn't until morning. He tried to avoid the nasty little cokehead on the trip to Miami. The guy tried offering him a hit from his crack pipe, but Michal didn't want anything to do with that.

The crackhead wasn't on the bus from Miami to Key Largo. He'd looked for him after realizing his wallet was missing. Arriving in Key West late last night, Michal rented a room at the cheapest place he could find, but it was still a hundred bucks a night. In his mind he calculated he could afford that for over a year if he was careful. Being optimistic, he only paid for a week in advance. It was four blocks off the main drag on Fleming Street. Michal envisioned moving up to better digs in the very near future.

Having decided to not drink very much and leaving the bulk of his cash hidden under the mattress in his room, Grabowski went from one bar to another, getting a feel for the bustling little tourist town. With enough cash, it was easy, tipping bartenders and waitresses and buying shots for the people they tended to talk with more than others. Locals hang with locals.

So Michal ingratiated himself with the locals, the big spender looking for some fun. He made a couple of quick contacts and before last call, he'd managed to buy four more little packets, adding them to his stockpile to resell. He planned to limit his own use, but wanted to quickly gain a reputation as a user so he could meet the sellers. To him, that seemed like the easiest way to map out the ground rules and territories and stay out of the dealers' way.

Now, under cover of daylight, he needed to find a few distributors for himself to get his fledgling operation off the ground. He also needed to find a job of some kind, knowing the quarter million dollars' worth of coke in his room wouldn't last long down here. With a part-time

cover job, though, he could easily stretch it out much longer.

Hurrying past yet another bar with no awning, this one having roll-up doors beneath big arched windows, one of Michal's brand-new flip-flops broke and he stepped right out of it, the concrete suddenly very hot on the bottom of his foot. Picking it up, a cold blast of conditioned air from inside got his attention. He hopped on one foot into *Irish Kevin's* bar, examining the broken strap. One of the little rubber buttons on the bottom had actually melted and pulled through the rubber sole, which was now frayed and sticky around the edges.

"Leather," Grabowski heard a voice behind him say. He turned around. Behind the bar, a woman with a Boston Bruins cap looked at him and smiled. A tangled mess of short, knotted hair stuck out from under the cap, but it was her belly that caught his eye. A cutoff T-shirt revealed her flat, deeply tanned abdomen, as she reached up on a shelf above the bar for a glass. The woman had abs a gymnast would kill for.

She tilted the glass under one of the many taps. "You need good Kino sandals, not that cheap rubber crap."

Grabowski recognized the very familiar red-and-white bull's-eye logo on top of the tap. He'd drank more than his share of Iron City Beer.

CHAPTER TWO

Rounding the little island, I started swimming against the current of the falling tide, pulling harder with every stroke. Changing my breathing to the right side, away from the light chop, I pulled and kicked harder, feeling the pull of the current. I'd only increased the frequency of my three-mile swims a few months earlier. Since then, I was swimming three miles every other day and it felt good.

A few months ago, I'd taken to wearing a small pair of goggles to allow me to see underwater. After swimming the same three miles, every other day for over four months, I knew the bottom terrain like a New Yorker knows the sidewalk in front of his brownstone.

Getting back in shape wasn't easy. I'd let myself go these past few years, both physically and psychologically. I'd gotten soft. After the first month of swimming every other day, it got easier, and I added a five-mile kayak paddle through the shallow backcountry west of my island.

Paddling early in the morning at sunrise allowed my mind to wander, even more so than when swimming. Afternoons were just too hot for any exertion above water.

On my off days, Carl and I worked our little vegetable patch, trimming, weeding, and harvesting in the hot sun. It was backbreaking work, but the results were worth it. Carl and his family live on my little island in the Content Keys and take care of the place. Without their help, I never could have pulled this off.

The Content Keys are a small bunch of mangrove islands north of Big Pine Key, out on the edge of the Gulf of Mexico. It'd been eight years since I'd bought it and four since I built my home here. Now the island sported four small structures, my house, Carl and Charlie's little house, and two bunkhouses. Carl built his pretty much by himself and I'd built the other three. My house was nice, but Carl and Charlie's was a whole lot nicer.

After a hard forty-five minute swim, I reached the shallows on the north side of my island by the pier and waded out of the water. The swim left me breathing heavy, but feeling better than I had in a long time. Island time can be harmful if you're not careful. Drinking too much, especially over the last two years, I'd put on nearly fifteen extra pounds. Swimming to me is the ultimate exercise, using every muscle group to its maximum. Some guys go to the gym, but I'd always found weight-lifting to be very boring.

Since I started working out more, I'd shed the excess weight, replacing it with toned muscle. It took months, but I was back down to what I called my combat weight of two twenty-five.

Whenever I went down to Marathon, I tried to squeeze in a three-mile run as well. At least once a week, anyway. Every Friday, I picked up my girlfriend in Marathon and she stayed with me on the island over the weekend. We always ran the loop around Sombrero Beach before coming back here.

Linda Rosales is an agent for the Florida Department of Law Enforcement and we'd been seeing each other for nearly a year now. Just as friends and running partners at first, but we'd taken it up a notch last winter. She works out of the Miami office, but went to Tallahassee last month on an assignment and would be gone most of the summer.

Since fall, my youngest daughter Kim had been living here full-time, but she'd left the same week Linda had, to get a jump on her studies through a summer program at University of Florida.

Walking out to the end of the pier, I rinsed the saltwater off before going to see how Carl was doing on our boat. Carl's wife Charlie and their two kids, Carl Junior and Patty, met me halfway to the foot of the pier, each carrying a towel. My big dog Pescador was leading the procession.

Charlie smiled as they approached. "Looking pretty good there, Jesse."

Her comment surprised me. Charlie wasn't usually the joking around type and flirting just wasn't in her nature. "I'm feeling a whole lot better lately, thanks."

"How much have you lost?"

"Not sure, probably a few pounds." Then as they walked by, I gave Pescador a scratch on the ear and said, "Y'all enjoy the water."

The saltwater I rinsed off was replaced with salty per-spiration before I even made it to the little temporary shack we'd built next to Carl and Charlie's house. Mid-summer in the Keys can be brutal. But it sure beats a lot of other places around the world where I've been.

I called out to Carl as I approached the little shack. "How's it coming, compadre?"

He had the canvas sides of the temporary structure rolled up to take advantage of whatever breeze there might be. There wasn't much today, just the sweltering tropical heat. Carl was on his back in the forward cockpit of the little runabout, only his legs visible up on the seat.

"I think I got it," he replied, reaching an empty hand up. "Hand me that multimeter."

Carl is sort of a jack-of-all-trades. We'd been building this boat since fall and it was nearly ready for a sea tri-al, except for a problem in the electrical we found after installing the engines. I handed him the device and it disappeared under the dash. A second later, I heard a beeping sound.

"Yes!" he exclaimed. "We had the wires crossed on the ignition. Everything looks good now." Twisting and turn-ing, Carl extricated himself from the small storage space under the foredeck of the wood boat, his hair plastered to his head with sweat.

Grinning, he nodded toward the console. "You want to do the honors?"

"You do it, you're the electrical expert."

He slid under the wheel and turned the ignition key to the on position. A whirring sound from the two large blowers indicated they were working. The air intakes are in the front face of the seat bottom in the rear cockpit, blowing tons of cool air across the twin air-cooled engines.

When he pushed one of the starter buttons, the port engine immediately sprang to life, the unmistakable sound of the powerful V-twin silencing the noise of the small waves lapping the shoreline just twenty feet away. He pressed the other button and the starboard engine added its own rumble as it fired up.

Stepping back from the boat, I yelled, "Holy crap! Those things are really loud." We'd pretty much finished construction of the boat a month ago and had to wait two weeks for the engines to arrive. We'd decided several months earlier to go with an idea a friend had given us and ordered a pair of big motorcycle engines, each producing over a hundred and sixty horsepower, yet weighing less than the single V8 Carl had wanted, or the single diesel I'd wanted.

Carl revved the engines using the foot throttle, the noise reaching ear-splitting level. The exhaust ports were just below the waterline and would act as the only muffler.

Shutting off the engines, Carl climbed out and stood beside me, admiring the little boat. "It'll be a little quieter in the water and when it's up on plane the sound will fall behind it. I think we're ready for that sea trial now."

"Now?" I asked.

"Tide's still high enough. We just gotta get it to the water."

Carl had scrounged around Skeeter's boatyard on Big Pine and found a couple of small four-wheeled trolleys, originally designed to pull jet skis up on the beach. He modified them to fit the contour of the hull and the boat now rested on them, ready to be moved to the water.

While we were waiting for the engines to be delivered, we'd cut a narrow path to the water through the dense undergrowth that surrounds my island. Beyond the arching mangrove and banyan tunnel is a natural cut close to shore, created by the twice-daily rush of water around the island during the tide changes. It's just wide enough to float the boat to the pier at the south side of the island, but it's very shallow just beyond this cut. We'd scraped the shallow bottom a little deeper on the far side to allow us to get the bow of the boat turned in the channel.

What we'd designed and had now built was a throwback to early years, an all-wood boat, with seating for three in the forward cockpit and a separate rear cockpit for three more. It had a shorter foredeck than modern speedboats and a long rear deck, which covered the spacious engine compartment before sloping downward to the swim platform at the stern.

At twenty-four feet in length, with a narrow six-foot beam, it looked fast just sitting there. The gunwales flared inward toward the stern, rounding out the aft section in what's called a barrel-back design. The small swim platform was barely above what we hoped would be the waterline. Between the two cockpits, nearly centered fore and aft, was a narrow two-foot deck, with built-in storage. The teak, cherry, and mahogany, overlaid with clear epoxy, gleamed with a rich, glossy shine.

I nodded at my friend. "Let's do this."

Climbing out of the boat, Carl went to the bow and crawled under the hull to secure a line to the front trolley. Tying the other end off to the boat's bow cleat, he threw the loop around one shoulder and across his chest to pull both the trolley and boat at the same time.

I went to the stern and leaned back across the sloped transom, gripping the swim platform.

"On three," Carl called out. "One, two, three!"

I pushed hard, digging my bare heels into the sand, but it wasn't really necessary. The fat tires of the two trolleys rolled easily on the packed sand. Once in the water, Carl waded across the narrow cut, keeping the bow centered in the area we'd scraped out, until the stern was clear of the mangroves. Careful to avoid the two trolleys, which had fallen into the deeper water of the cut, we slowly turned the boat so that the bow was facing south, into the current. Floating there like that, with the water moving along the hull, I could tell already that we'd nailed the design. The boat looked just like one of the early racing boats I remember seeing as a kid and the sporty swim platform barely touched the water.

I moved up along the port side, motioning Carl around to starboard. "You take the helm first."

While I held the boat steady, Carl slid over the low gunwale and started the engines. The sound from the exhaust ports burbled up through the water and as he revved the engines, the boat actually surged forward slightly, just from the force of the exhaust.

He nodded to me, and I climbed over the starboard side and settled into the passenger seat, as Carl put the heavy-duty Velvet Drive transmissions into forward.

When both transmissions were in either forward or reverse, the throttles for both engines were controlled by the foot pedal. They could also be operated independently with the shift knob to allow the boat to maneuver better at low speed by simply shifting one engine to reverse and the other forward.

Beyond the narrow cut, the water is less than knee-deep at high tide. As we idled slowly along the shoreline, I had to stand to lift a couple of low-hanging branches over the swept-back windshield.

To the north and west of my island, the shallows extend all the way past the Contents, before dropping off to the deeper waters of the Gulf. To the southwest is a maze of small islands and shallows all the way to Key West, a jumble of unmarked cuts and channels. There are ways through, but if you didn't know where to look, you'd end up beached on a sandbar, as evidenced by the many gouges around the fringe of shallow water.

We idled south toward the other pier I'd built on the spoils of the deeper channel that provides access to my house from Harbor Channel about fifty yards away. Going as far as the end of the south pier, Carl reversed and backed up to the other side where we could tie off. Leaving the engines rumbling at idle to warm up, we checked the bilges. Opening the access in the rear cockpit deck, I noted a little water. In the bottom of the engine compartment we found about the same. Both Carl and I checked thoroughly for any water leaks.

Satisfied that the only water we found was from where we'd splashed aboard, we untied the lines and idled out to Harbor Channel. Carl made the tight left turn into it using only the transmissions, first spinning the boat to the right almost completely around before shifting both transmissions and spinning the opposite way until we faced the long channel. Everything worked perfectly and he shifted both engines to forward.

We slowly idled in Harbor Channel, which runs almost straight for four miles to Turtlecrawl Bank. There, it turns north into the deep water of the Gulf.

Carl grinned. "Ready?"

I nodded. "Mash it!"

Carl floored the pedal and the two big motorcycle engines roared simultaneously, launching us forward and accelerating faster than any boat I'd ever been on. She lifted up on plane in a second, seeming to just leap up out of the water. On plane, we continued to gather speed. I started the stopwatch function on my dive watch to measure the time to the lobster traps we had set up exactly two miles from the entrance to my channel.

Responding like a rocket sled on rails, we negotiated the two sweeping curves in the channel. It only took a few seconds to again reach top speed. Looking back, there wasn't much of a wake off the stern at all, but the twin propellers created two distinct bulges in the water, culminating fifty feet astern with a pair of small rooster tails. Very little of the hull was in contact with the water, just enough to create drag and let the thrust of the props keep the rest of boat up out of the water.

As we roared past the trap's floats, I stopped the watch and looked at it as Carl slowly brought the speed down. "A hundred and eight seconds!"

"That's almost seventy miles an hour!" Carl shouted. "From an idle, no less!"

"We need to mount a GPS. We must've been going close to eighty-five there at the end."

"Let's keep that to ourselves, if Charlie asks."

He looked at me and I grinned, arching an eyebrow. "A lie of omission?"

We both laughed, knowing that he never kept anything from his wife. "Maybe she won't ask," he said, as we idled in the wide part of the channel, just before the curve north to the open Gulf.

Switching seats, I piloted the boat back the way we came at a more sedate speed, planing and weaving back and forth across the channel. Even at half throttle it seemed like we were going as fast as my charter boat, *Gaspar's Revenge*.

Charlie, the kids, and Pescador met us at the south pier. "We heard you all the way to the end of Harbor Channel," Charlie said as she took the line Carl tossed her. "How fast is it?"

"Not sure exactly," he replied, being somewhat truthful. "We'll have to put a speedometer in the dash. It's pretty fast, though."

"Well, keep it at a slower speed when the kids and I go out with you."

Once tied off, Carl and I checked the bilge and engines again. Putting on a scuba mask, I got in the water and checked the underside of the hull for any visible stress fractures in the clear-coat finish. We'd added two short stabilizing fins extending two feet back to the prop shafts, with small rudders aft the props. The stabilizers were an afterthought, once we'd calculated that the high speed the powerful engines might produce would be too much for the nearly flat-bottomed hull to allow it to turn at high speed. Declaring the boat to be sound, we decided to go to Marathon for lunch.

Twenty minutes later, after we'd all rinsed off again and put on clean clothes, we idled away from the pier. I let Charlie sit up front with Carl Junior and Carl at the helm and I sat in back with Patty and Pescador.

As Carl started down the channel, I said, "Know what we forgot? To measure the draft."

Carl turned east into Harbor Channel. "We'll take the deeper route until we're sure it can navigate the cuts at idle." When Carl gassed the engines to get up on plane, little Carl and Patty both covered their ears.

We hadn't had any kind of wind in days and the water lay as calm and still as the heavy air. Carl followed the cut south of Turtlecrawl Bank, then turned due south into Big Spanish Channel. Cruising along at what I guessed to be forty knots, the boat performed really well as Carl slalomed a few crab traps, the boat barely heeling at all. With the Seven Mile Bridge in sight to the southeast, Carl put his son on his lap and let him pilot the boat for a while. Carl Junior was no stranger to running a boat, even at eight years old. Carl had earned a living from the sea all his life, as had his father and his grandfather before him.

Leaning back and looking over the engine compartment and sloped transom, I could nearly see the waterline, the swim platform now about three inches above the water streaming out from under the hull. I sat back and stretched my legs out. The feeling was incredible. We'd dreamed this up nearly a year ago, sketching and drawing for months. Some parts had had to be built off island, but every single rib, spar, plank, and dowel we'd installed ourselves.

Reaching Bahia Honda Channel, Carl continued south and turned left just before the bridge crossing from Scout Key to Bahia Honda. We followed deep water around the north side of the island, Carl keeping the boat about fifty yards off the Seven Mile Bridge.

Charlie pointed up to the cars on the bridge and shouted, "They have a speed limit. We don't."

Carl looked back and I nodded. Bringing the speed up until we were passing the cars in the northbound lane, I could tell by the tone of the engines that we weren't quite up to top speed, but I guessed we were going at least sixty.

CHAPTER THREE

W hat do you mean you lost it?" the voice on the phone shouted.

Lenny Walcza had put off the call as long as he could. The man on the other end of the phone he was now holding away from his ear was former Steelers linebacker GT Bradley, known for his quick temper and vicious punishment of anyone he considered to have crossed him, both on and off the field.

"I only turned my back for a second, GT," Lenny confessed. The fact was, when he went to the john, he was so high he'd tripped over the dirty laundry strewn about the floor and hit his head on the toilet bowl, passed out and pissed himself.

It wasn't until after he came to and cleaned himself up that he noticed Grabowski and the key of coke were gone. Thinking Grabowski was just pranking him, Lenny tried calling, but the call went straight to voicemail.

Lenny had left Grabowski a message, telling him the joke wasn't funny.

Lenny had considered taking off after Grabowski himself. However, Lenny lacked the funds and didn't know where to start. He'd already gone to the guy's place and the landlord had told him that Grabowski had turned in his keys the night before, leaving with nothing more than a backpack as far as the old man could tell.

"What's his name? Where's he live?" GT growled over the phone.

"I already checked there, GT. Landlord said he skipped out last night with nothing but a backpack and driving his beat-up old Corolla. He's not answering his phone, either. Name's Michal Grabowski."

"Grabowski?" GT muttered, with obvious distaste. "He's a damned worm. You stay put, shithead. I'll be there in ten minutes."

Lenny stared at the phone, the call now disconnected. It was nearly nine o'clock and Grabowski had at least a six-hour head start. Knowing the old Corolla was near the end of its life and had four bald tires, Lenny doubted he could have made it very far. Especially if he was driving fast.

GT had a network that covered the whole Three Rivers area and contacts throughout southwestern Pennsylvania. If anyone could find Grabowski, it'd be GT.

Minutes later, Lenny heard the sound of tires squealing as a car suddenly stopped in front of his house. Looking out through the front window, he immediately recognized GT's white Escalade, with the dark-tinted windows. A large black man with a shaved head climbed out of the driver's seat, as GT himself came around the hood in a hurry. Lenny knew the other man from his deliveries. Erik something or other. Looking like book-ends, the two men hurried toward the front door, each wearing a gray sports coat.

Lenny met them at the door, motioning them inside and then put on a show of looking up and down the street before closing and locking the door. GT stopped in the foyer, as the other man went on into the house. Lenny could hear him going room to room opening and closing doors.

"We went by the bus station," GT said, turning and walking into Lenny's living room. "Grabowski's piece-a-shit car was there, keys still in the ignition. Even in this neighborhood, nobody stole it. You're telling me he was here when Erik dropped the stuff off last night?"

"Yeah, he dropped by with a case of beer and we watched the Pirates game, then he just kinda hung around."

"What'd I tell you about having anyone over when a delivery was made?" GT shouted. "You owe me thirty-five large, asshole. Where is it?"

In the back of the house, Lenny heard something break and something large being turned over. "I don't have it, GT. Ya gotta believe me. Why would I try to rip you off, man?"

"Because you're an idiot!" GT barked, getting worked up as the sound of more crashing and things breaking could be heard from the back of the house. "Tell me everything you know about Grabowski."

With his house being ransacked, Lenny told him all he knew, which wasn't much. Grabowski's mom had died years ago and he'd been raised by his dad, a steelworker who'd died last year. Grabowski had a girlfriend that he brought around from time to time, but Lenny hadn't seen her in several months. When he finished, the other man came out of the back of the house and started jerking open drawers in the kitchen, dumping the contents on the floor, tearing open every box and container of food and drink, dumping that on the floor as well.

Finally, Erik came back into the living room and handed GT a wad of cash and shrugged. "Only thing I found, GT. Just shy of five grand."

Looking at the wad of cash, GT slowly brought his face up and glared at Lenny. "This all you got?"

"A few hundred in the bank," Lenny stammered, growing more afraid. GT had a habit of killing people who let him down. "I can probably sell some stuff and get you a couple grand more by the weekend."

GT's right hand snaked under his jacket in a flash, causing Lenny to cringe. Pulling out a pack of Pall Mall cigarettes, GT shook one loose and put it in his mouth. Erik produced a lighter, flicking it under his boss's smoke. GT grinned and puffed to get it lit. Lenny relaxed a little.

Putting the pack of smokes back in his shirt pocket, GT grabbed the grip of his stainless steel Colt 1911 and pulled it out, placing the barrel just inches from Lenny's forehead in a blur.

The report of the big handgun was deafening in the small living room. Blood and brain tissue plastered the wall and window, then began to ooze down the glass, as Lenny fell backward, crashing through the glass insert of a coffee table.

"By the weekend, huh?" GT asked the corpse, with its arms and legs spread-eagle, slumped in the heavy wooden frame of the table. "Yeah, you get back to me on that, dickweed."

Turning to Erik, GT said, "C'mon, let's go talk to the ticket agent."

CHAPTER FOUR

W e idled slowly up the canal to my favorite watering hole, the *Rusty Anchor Bar and Grill*, owned by my longtime friend, Rusty Thurman. Rusty and I met in boot camp in '79 and stayed close ever since.

The burbling of the twin motorcycle engines caused more than a few heads to pop up out of the hatches of the liveaboards, and a few locals streamed out of the bar to see if a biker had ridden into the canal.

Rusty met us at the end of the canal, where his big barge is tied at the end of the large turning basin. Approaching the barge at the end of the docks, Carl threw the starboard engine into reverse and gunned it for a second, nearly stopping the boat and sending it into a slow spin to the right. We barely bumped the fenders on the barge.

Charlie quickly stepped up to the deck of the barge and tied us off, as Carl shut down the engines. He opened the bilge compartments for another look and I raised the cover on the engine compartment. Both were dry and the float-switch-activated bilge pump was off.

"Now that's a mighty fine-looking boat," Rusty commented as he approached. At just under three hundred pounds and barely five feet six inches tall, Rusty had a personality that matched his girth.

Jimmy Saunders, a friend and my former first mate, strode over to the side of the boat and looked down into the engine bay. "What the hell kinda engines you got in that, man?"

"Big air-cooled V-twins," Charlie said, grinning and taking Patty as I handed her up. She herded the kids across the barge and, satisfied that we had no leaks, Carl and I followed, with everyone asking questions. I let Carl field most of them and stopped on the dock for a moment to look around.

Looking around was a habit, something I'd once done constantly when I was in the Corps, especially when exiting a vehicle. I had a platoon sergeant on Okinawa that double-timed up and down our lines as we moved along a trail, constantly reminding us, "Head on a swivel!" At times, he'd jump up in someone's face and ask what color the rock was that another of the Marines ahead had slipped on, or which way the mongoose was going in the underbrush. Staff Sergeant Russ Livingston saw everything and missed nothing.

At the same time I realized my body wasn't in the shape it used to be, I came to the conclusion that neither were my habits. Looking around can clue you in to possible hidden danger and I'd lost that edge.

This look around, while almost immediately dismissing any prospect of danger, took in the familiar surroundings. In the eight years that I'd lived here, I'd been lulled by the small town atmosphere on this little island chain.

Locals call it island time and sooner or later it catches up with everyone. The trouble with being on island time, you tend to lose focus. I'm fortunate, I can turn it on and off. I've found that compartmentalizing things in my mind has allowed me to perform better at the things I've done, by keeping outside influences away from the task at hand. Another of Russ Livingston's sayings was, "Not my circus, not my monkeys," meaning that anything that didn't have a direct bearing on the mission at hand was to be ignored.

Right now, island time was on. By the standards of most people, it was a miserably hot day. Several of the liveaboards were connected to shore power and I heard a number of small air conditioners humming. Down the dock and around behind the bar, there were a few people lounging on the deck, all of them at tables shaded by palm thatch umbrellas.

Far beyond the dock, a set of ruts followed the canal. Out at the end sat my airplane, *Island Hopper*. She's a deHavilland Beaver, built more than fifty years ago and equipped with pontoons for landing on water and wheels, which retracted into the pontoons, for landing on a runway. The son of the friend who I bought the plane from died in a fiery explosion just beyond there at the boat ramp.

Dressed in lightweight khaki pants and a long-sleeved shirt, I enjoyed the heat. However, getting burned by the sun's rays wasn't a good idea when you're outside as much as I am. Sweating has a purpose. Cooling by evaporation. I kept hydrated and sweated heavily. So I stayed cool, even in this tropical heat.

Inside, Charlie took the kids out the back door to see if Rufus needed any help in the kitchen. Rusty had just added the closed-in cooking area to the backyard, replacing a series of tarps. His old Jamaican chef loved cooking outdoors, so the whole kitchen area had big roll-up doors. Watching Rufus cook had become sort of an attraction for some of the locals.

The *Anchor* was pretty much a local's hangout. Rusty didn't advertise and the place was hidden deep on the property, invisible from US-1. Dense overhanging foliage nearly hid the crushed-shell drive and there wasn't any sign out there for "Cold Beer." Open whenever Rusty was awake, it was a gathering spot for local watermen, and the liveaboards that now lined his docks. It had been this way for three generations of Thurmans.

Every morning, before the sun rose, Rufus would fire up his grills and burners and then roll up the shutters over the long countertop surrounding the kitchen. Big exhaust fans soon spread the scent of grilling onions, lobster, fish, Jamaican sausage and eggs for probably five square miles on a still day like this. Within minutes, people would climb out of their boats and start pulling up in skiffs. The parking lot might only have a car or two, but every stool around the kitchen would be full, people anticipating a great breakfast. For the liveaboards, this was included in their slip lease.

Rufus had once been a gourmet chef at a very popular five-star restaurant in Jamaica. He'd retired here after the death of his wife and lived in a tiny shack that had once been Rusty's grandfather's rum distillery. Nobody really knew for sure how old the wiry little Jamaican man was. My guess was mid-sixties or early seventies, but it didn't show and most strangers would guess much younger.

Carl and I sat at the bar, where Rusty produced two bottles of water. Not long ago, it would have been water for Carl, who rarely drank, and a beer for me. Or coffee, if it was early. Even late coffee on many days. And before noon with the beer on many days, as well. Island time isn't measured by clocks.

"You're looking damned near a hundred percent, Jesse," my old friend said. "Still swimming?"

"Every other day. How's Julie? Heard from her this week?"

Julie is Rusty's daughter. He'd raised her himself, after her mother died giving Julie life. She'd recently moved to Washington DC with her husband, Deuce Livingston. He'd been promoted to commander in the Navy and reassigned to take over the Caribbean Counterterrorism Command of Homeland Security, or CCC. He was also the son of my former platoon sergeant and the two of us had become quick friends a couple years ago.

"Talked to her for an hour last night," Rusty replied. "They're still getting adjusted. Said she'll be down in September for some training with the new team in Largo."

The CCC consisted of two teams of highly skilled operators that came from all branches of the military and several law enforcement agencies. Julie is a petty officer in the Coast Guard Reserves and trained for their elite Maritime Enforcement. She was attached as a reserve element to Deuce's teams, helping to teach small-boat boarding tactics to the others.

"Be good to see her again," I said as I turned on my stool and looked out the windows, shaded from the sun by awnings. Rusty could afford to air condition the place, but chose not to. I knew this, because I was a silent partner in his business. To most of the clientele he served, air conditioning was achieved at twenty-five knots over open water. The *Anchor* was built to take advantage of the prevailing wind and had long overhangs on the roof and awnings over the windows. There were a number of ceiling fans that constantly moved the air around inside and there was almost always a cooling breeze off the water.

No breeze today, though. Not much anyway. Every now and then a slight movement of air could be felt through the large open windows that surrounded the bar area. Out beyond the side yard, I could see the little boat sitting there and marveled again at the gleaming lines.

"How fast is she?" Jimmy asked, sitting on the stool next to me and following my gaze.

"Not sure," I replied. "No GPS or speedometer, but she covered a two-mile stretch, from idling speed, in just over a hundred seconds this morning."

Jimmy whistled softly. "Most of them antique replica boats are all show, man. But that's seriously fast."

A familiar voice from the other end of the bar said, "Boat like that can get up and grow legs."

I glanced over and recognized Bill Woodson, Wood to his friends. He was a gruff and cantankerous man and a longtime resident of the Keys. A bridge builder and engineer, he'd probably had a hand in either building or repairing half the bridges in the Keys. Semiretired now, he lived on an island not far from mine.

I nodded to the older man. "Long time, no see, Wood."

"Way I like it," he replied gruffly. "See you coming and going from time to time. Ya oughta keep a close eye on that boat."

"I will," I replied.

Without another word, Wood got up and walked out the back door with his beer, heading toward the dock. Looking out the window again, I watched as a small center-console came idling up the canal and I recognized the two men on board. One was a guy about my age, Mac Travis, who lived on one of the canals off Boot Key Harbor. Mac had been Wood's diver for the better part of twenty years and was now a commercial lobsterman. His sidekick and crewman was easily recognizable even from a distance. Taller than me, with a set of polished teeth that probably glowed in the dark, Alan Trufante was known to be close by whenever there was trouble, usually right in the middle of it. Wood met Mac's boat at the dock and stepped down into it. Mac turned in the canal and they headed back out the way they came.

"He's right, ya know," Rusty said, polishing a beer mug. "A sharp-looking boat like that could disappear in a heartbeat."

"What's on the menu for lunch?" I asked, turning back to my old friend.

"Leftover janga soup from last night and fish," Rusty replied. "Or a burger," he added with a grin.

What Rufus called janga were the crawfish that Carl and I raised in our aquaculture garden. The waste from the crawfish and catfish tanks nourished the plants, which in turn kept the water clean and filtered. Janga are a distant Caribbean cousin to the crawfish, and ac-

cording to Rufus, the hill people in Jamaica consider them to have an aphrodisiac quality.

"Janga soup for me," Carl said with a grin.

Getting up from my stool, I said, "Think I'll go out and have a word with Rufus."

Out on the deck, I strode over to the kitchen door. Charlie was inside, helping Rufus serve customers. That was just her way. If something looked like it needed doing, she just pitched in and did it. Her kids were out in the backyard, running and playing with Pescador.

"You got a minute, Rufus?" I called into the kitchen.

The old Jamaican man turned and smiled. "Sure ting, mon." He came to the door and we sat down at an empty table nearby. "Ah see dat you been taking bettah care of yourself," he said.

"That's what I wanted to talk to you about. Think you can give me some ideas about eating? What to stay away from?"

"Ya, mon, I can do bettah dan dat. I and I wrote a cooking book. Yuh wanna copy?"

I told him I'd love to borrow it and he left, trotting across the yard to his little shack, as Charlie came out of the kitchen carrying a tray. The smell of Carl's soup reminded me how hungry I was.

A moment later Rufus returned with a thin, professionally published paperback cookbook and handed it to me. I don't know why, but I was expecting a handwritten notebook. The old Jamaican never ceased to amaze me. On the cover was a picture of him, shirtless and standing on one foot in knee-deep cobalt-blue water, the setting sun highlighting the white chest hair and beard against his ebony skin. His back was arched, arms raised over his head, grasping his other foot in a vertical split. I'd seen him go through his sunset routine a few times.

"Dis book have some of my favorite recipes, Cap'n. Not tings I and I make here at di restaurant. But tings Rufus make fuh his own self." He grinned broadly. "Tings dat keep di old feeling young."

Looking at the guy, his eyes still sparkled with life and though he was small, I knew he was in excellent shape, having watched his evening routine. He'd stretch for a few minutes then go through a series of slow-motion karate-style moves, flexing every muscle.

"When you said a book, I assumed a notebook," I said. "This is really cool and I promise I'll get it back to you after I try a few."

He laughed. "Yuh keep dat, mon. I and I have many. Dere comes a time in a man's life when he must also use di cosmic forces in di battle wit time."

"Thanks, Rufus. I think." I raised the book and said, "None of the ingredients in here are illegal, are they?"

"No, mon," he replied with his wide, gap-toothed grin. "All of Rufus's recipes come directly from di gods to man. Nuts, berries, herbs, and di fish and crawlers from Mudah Ocean. I and I used to dabble in di other tings, but dat was many appearances of di Suhdurn Cross ago."

I grinned back at his reference to the annual winter event in the Caribbean, including here in the Keys. Contrary to popular belief the Southern Cross constellation can be seen here, but only for a short time late at night and for only a few nights in winter.

"Well, thanks," I said again. Rufus was rarely so talkative, preferring his seclusion at the back of the property. "I'll try some of these out."

"Yuh do dat, Cap'n. Time be a vengeful demon." He went back inside the kitchen and I headed back to the bar, flipping through the book. Each page held a different recipe, probably a hundred in all, each one with a professional-looking color picture of the finished dish. *Must have cost a small fortune to have them printed*, I thought.

Reentering the bar, I saw Charlie by the door, yelling at some guy. "Take that crap on back to Key Weird!"

I tucked the book into the back pocket of my pants and took my stool at the end of the bar. "What's going on?"

"Some crack monster was trying to sell his shit to Charlie," Carl replied, calmly eating his soup.

Charlie isn't a very big woman, shorter than Rusty and about a third his weight. However, she at least matched the big man in heart and grit.

"What the hell makes those idiots think I smoke crack?" Charlie mumbled as she came back to sit beside her husband.

"Who was he?" I asked Rusty.

"Never seen him before," he replied. With him having grown up here, as had his family for many generations, that meant the drug dealer wasn't from anywhere around here. There weren't many people in the Keys he didn't either know or know about. "He came in about a half hour ago for lunch and a beer. Ugly little guy. I made him for a crackhead as soon as he sat down. Rotten teeth, pimples, and you can smell it on 'em."

I walked to the door and watched as the little man scurried along the driveway. He was dressed like he'd slept in his clothes for at least a couple of days and his black hair was stringy and greasy looking.

When I sat back down, Rusty pulled a credit card receipt from the box under the bar. "Name's Michal Grabowski. Ain't never heard of him, neither."

CHAPTER FIVE

Ripping off the coke dealer on the bus was easy, but didn't produce much gain. There wasn't any cash in the guy's wallet, and two of the three credit cards he found in it were maxed out. No telling what he could do with the third card. It had already been two days since Will Byers had pinched the guy's wallet while standing in the crowded queue at the bus station in Miami. Byers had boarded the bus in Orlando, nearly broke and recently evicted from yet another roach-infested furnished apartment. He had spotted the dealer right away. The telltale white flakes clinging to his mustache hairs were a dead giveaway.

The guy's coke was good, but not exactly Byers's drug of choice. Though he was down to less than four hundred bucks, he sprang for an eight ball anyway, not wanting to dip into his own stash of crack. The price was right and the shit was primo. Byers knew he could always lift another wallet. He was good at it.

Byers had assumed the dealer kept his cash in his wallet and was disappointed he didn't. The guy was careful. Byers had persuaded the dealer to give him a sample on the bus, but when he offered to buy an eighth of an ounce, the guy said he'd have to wait until the bus stopped again. He'd finally made the buy at the last stop before Miami. Both men got off the bus and walked into the parking lot, making the deal between two parked cars.

Aside from the bus they came in on, the next one out of the little redneck town on the shore of Lake Okeechobee wasn't until the next day. Byers tried to get close to the guy at the ticket counter there, but some fat lady with two kids managed to beat him to the next spot in line.

On the trip out of Belle Glade, Byers offered the dealer a hit from his stash, as repayment for the sample the dealer had given him earlier. The guy didn't want anything to do with the crack, so Byers went back to the bus's lavatory and lit up a small rock.

Finally, after wolfing down a greasy cheeseburger and fries at the downtown Miami bus station, Will Byers saw another opportunity as the coke dealer was waiting to board another bus. In the jostling crowd, Byers managed to get close enough to lift the dealer's wallet. He disappeared into the crowd and, after the bus left, used the guy's card to buy a ticket to the end of the line in Key West.

Byers got into an argument with the bus driver as they entered the town of Marathon. The driver smelled the crack Byers was smoking in the bus's lavatory and pulled over to the shoulder, waiting outside the lavatory when Byers came out. Byers was ejected from the bus in front of a small strip mall on the north side of the highway.

Seeing a couple of sports bars, he started that way. Suddenly, he caught a whiff of something on the breeze coming off the ocean to the south. It smelled good. Looking up and down the highway, he didn't see any restaurants, only a crushed-shell driveway that disappeared through the trees.

Sweating heavily only minutes after getting off the bus, Byers crossed the busy highway. He figured that if someone was grilling, he might be able to sneak through the woods to the backyard and grab something off the grill when the homeowner went inside for something. Barring that, he could always go to one of the sports bars and use the dealer's credit card.

Staying close to the edge of the brush that lined the driveway, just in case he was spotted, Byers quickly reached the end and realized it wasn't someone's home. There was a parking lot with a few old pickups ahead. To the right was a long canal where nearly a dozen boats were tied up. Byers shrugged and walked toward the door of what looked like a hole-in-the-wall type bar. The smell was surely coming from there and he was hungry.

Byers sat near an open window, wondering why they didn't have them closed and the air conditioning cranked up. The heat and humidity was stifling. A big fat man with a bald head and reddish beard asked what he wanted and he ordered his usual cheeseburger, fries, and two cold beers.

Byers was low on cash, but he had a pretty good stash of crack and half the eight ball of coke left. He could probably sell a rock or two, just to have a little more walking around cash. He started watching the other patrons as he ate. There weren't many people in the place. One old

man at the end of the bar was nursing a beer, and a couple of stools down, a long-haired guy was talking to the fat bartender while drinking water.

Neither looked like a crack smoker. The old guy was obviously not into anything other than his beer and the long-haired guy looked like one of those health types. Byers had met a few of them before. They drank nothing but water and smoked nothing but weed.

About to leave, Byers heard a sound outside the window. The throaty exhaust from an old wooden boat burbled as it approached. He watched as several people went outside to meet the boat. There were two men and a woman with two kids on it, along with a shaggy brown dog. One guy he dismissed immediately, an obvious jock type, tall with broad shoulders and hair barely over his ears. The other guy was a possible customer, but he felt pretty sure about the woman. With two kids, she probably needed something to calm her down and he had just the thing.

CHAPTER SIX

GT Bradley leaned menacingly on the ticket counter in the Miami Greyhound station. The guy on the other side hadn't touched the twenty-dollar bill he'd placed on the fake wood between them.

One of GT's employees in Pittsburgh was a computer gamer that had some serious hacking skills. Give the guy a name and address and within an hour he'd give you all the guy's credit card activity. Staying in touch with his guy for the last two days, GT had followed Michal Grabowski's card all the way to the Florida Keys.

Grabowski had used it mostly to buy bus tickets, always headed south, but only to the next stop. *The kid's careful,* GT thought. Erik had driven fast from one Greyhound station to another, all the way from Pittsburgh. Now he was out of road.

The ticket agents were usually eager to pull up the ticket sale on their computer after GT passed them a folded twenty. He fully intended to take the additional

expense money out of Grabowski's hide when he caught up to him.

GT growled in a low and menacing voice, "Pick up the bill, numbnuts. Then give me the destination and what time the bus left. Your options here are limited, man. A free lunch or a trip to the ER and eat through a straw for a few months."

The ticket agent glanced around and quickly palmed the twenty. "I'm really not supposed to do this."

"Just give me the information."

The man typed in the card number GT had given him on a piece of paper and then punched a few keys. "The card number you gave me was used to buy a one-way ticket, Miami to Key West, left yesterday evening and arrived at midnight. That's really all I can tell ya, mister."

GT turned away from the counter and strode quickly to the exit. Erik Lowery waited in the idling Escalade next to the curb in front of the station. Climbing in the passenger side, GT said, "He bought a ticket to Key West last night. Arrived at midnight."

"Key West? What's after that?" Erik asked, pulling the big SUV away from the curb and joining the traffic headed south on Highway 953, then merging onto US-1.

"Ain't nothing after that but the ocean. We'll find him in Key West. It ain't that big a town."

An hour later, GT's cell phone rang as they were leaving Tavernier on the Overseas Highway. He answered it and listened for a minute, jotting something on a small notepad. "We're less'n an hour from there now," he said before ending the call. Riding in silence for the next forty miles, GT thought about all the ways he was going to hurt Grabowski.

Finally, as they entered the town of Marathon, GT read Erik the address and said, "It should be coming up pretty quick now. That last sign said this is the town." The Escalade slowed as the numbers got smaller, nearing the destination GT had jotted on the notepad.

"You passed it!" GT shouted at Erik. "It's on the other side of the road, back there."

Erik turned the Escalade into the next storefront parking lot, a marine electronics store called Sea Wiz. "Sorry, boss. I didn't see no sign for a bar."

Going slower now, GT pointed to a leaning mailbox next to a crushed-shell driveway. "There. That's the address."

"Don't look like no bar to me, boss." The big tires crunched on the driveway as Erik turned off the main road and they were enveloped by the tropical foliage.

Parking the big Escalade next to a couple of rusty pickups, the two men strode toward what looked like a rundown old bar from some past era. There were no signs saying it was a bar, but the hacker had called GT just an hour earlier, saying that Grabowski had bought lunch and a couple beers at a place called the *Rusty Anchor Bar and Grill* twenty minutes before that and giving GT this address. Even though there weren't any signs, not even beer signs in the windows, GT recognized a dive when he saw one.

As the two approached, GT noted very little activity outside. The quiet hum of a few air conditioners drift-

ed up from several boats tied up in the canal. A small, sporty brown one at the end of the canal caught GT's eye. It was different from the other small boats. It was wood and looked faster.

Opening the door, GT let his eyes adjust for a moment before entering the dimly lit bar.

CHAPTER SEVEN

After lunch, Rusty and I sat at a table and caught up on what was going on around the islands. Lately, I didn't even come into town on Friday, as I had before Linda went up north, preferring to stay on the island. It'd been over two weeks since I was last here.

Sometimes, I'd take the *Revenge* out and anchor in a secluded cove for a day or two. Just swim in the gin-clear water, fish and explore the shallows in the kayak. I hadn't had a charter in over a month, preferring to just enjoy life and the solitude for a while.

Two fishing guides came in from the deck, one of them taking the second man's empty bottle, along with his own, and going behind the bar. The second man nodded at me and said to Rusty, "Add a coupla more and two fish sandwich baskets to my tab, Rusty?"

My old friend nodded. "Sure, Dink. How's the fishin'?"

Brian "Dink" Wilcox had been a fishing guide in Marathon since arriving here ten years ago as a high school dropout. Tall, gangly, and stumbling, he was accident-prone most of the time. He seemed to have perpetual sea legs. On a boat, he was fine. More than fine, in fact. Able to pole his skiff and maneuver into and out of some of the skinniest patches in the backcountry, Dink was well known for his ability to find fish.

"Tarpon migration was great, but they're about gone. Just gettin' by till snook season opens, now."

The other guide, a man I'd seen around a few times but had never met, brought two beers from the cooler and joined Dink two tables down from Rusty and me. The *Rusty Anchor* is that kind of place. Off the beaten path, not in any tourist brochures, a place that still had an old Florida style, like a few places I remembered visiting down here as a kid. Pap may even have brought me here way back when. Rusty pulled a small notepad from his shirt pocket and noted the men's orders, without bothering to ask if they'd told Rufus.

"I'm telling ya," Rusty said, putting the pad and pencil back in his pocket and turning to me, "there's no way Deuce would be involved in that kind of thing."

Rusty's son-in-law had pulled a fast one, just before taking his new position in DC. At least it looked that way to me. One of his team members was Charity Styles, a young woman that had been through a lot in her short life. She could fly a chopper like nobody's business, but a few years back, while she'd been an Army medivac pilot in Afghanistan, she'd been shot down and captured, then tortured, raped and sodomized repeatedly at the hands of the Taliban.

Charity had accompanied me on a manhunt last year. The former head of the CCC turned out to be dirty. Real dirty. Jason Smith had murdered his wife for her inheritance years before and tried to kill both Deuce and myself when we got too close. The bomb he'd meant for us had killed a young Marine we'd been trying to help. He and Charity had formed some kind of connection, or bond. When we finally found Smith down in the Turks and Caicos Islands, Charity killed him with her bare hands.

During the trip, which covered half the western Caribbean, she opened up to me a little, especially on the return trip. Killing Smith seemed to give her some closure, but left her feeling cold and empty. She told me that Jared was the only one she'd felt close to since her days in Afghanistan. I never did think she was all there emotionally, but I never would have thought she'd do what everyone believed she did.

"At worst he let it happen," I said. "I don't buy for one minute that she stole the chopper and disappeared."

Leaning in closer, Rusty dropped his voice to a conspiratorial whisper. "And what do you base that on? Running all over the Caribbean with Charity stashed in the cabin, till you caught Smith last year?"

"Neither story rings true, Rusty. Think about it. If I'm right, then Deuce is covering for her and she's on some sort of secret assignment for the DHS. If I'm wrong, why hasn't he found her? Stealing a government chopper isn't something the DHS secretary would allow to happen without a full investigation. He knows and he's keeping it under his hat."

Just then, the door opened. A big, bald black man was silhouetted by the blinding light from outside. He stepped in and another large black man followed him through the door. The second man let the door close and the two stood there waiting for their eyes to adjust to the darkness inside the bar. After a moment, the two men, both wearing sports jackets, headed toward the bar.

Definitely not from around here, I thought as Rusty got up from the table and went around behind the bar. Not because of their skin color, but nobody in their right mind wears a jacket when both the temperature and humidity are near triple digits. Unless they're hiding something under the jacket.

The back door opened and Rufus casually walked in, carrying two plates of food for the guides, sitting by an open window. I watched the two men carefully, some sixth sense alerting me to trouble. They looked close enough alike to be twins, but one was maybe an inch taller and ten pounds lighter than the other. The shorter, heavier guy seemed to be the leader. He looked vaguely familiar, but I couldn't put my finger on it.

As I watched, I saw him push something across the bar to Rusty, saying something in a tone so low I couldn't hear his words. From the look on Rusty's face, whatever the guy said definitely meant trouble. I slowly and quietly stood up from the table and nonchalantly made my way to the far end of the bar.

Jimmy was sitting two stools over from the leader, who was now leaning across the bar. The second guy was standing behind his boss. From the look on Jimmy's face, I knew there was about to be an altercation. Jimmy was as laid-back as any islander, but always seemed to be able to sense trouble.

Rufus stepped up beside the big black man and looked at him, with a quizzical expression. Kind of like a snake might look at a third mouse after eating the first two and having his appetite sated.

"Di cosmic grouper told I and I just last week dat you be here very soon," Rufus said to the man leaning on the bar. "But yuh won't find what yuh seek in dis place."

The big man glared sideways at Rufus, slowly straightening to his full height and turning toward him. "I ain't talking to you," he said through clenched teeth.

Standing at the end of the bar I was shielded from the two men's sight and slowly reached back and put my right hand on the grip of the Sig under my shirt. I naturally assumed what they were hiding under their jackets were guns. Hopefully not guns and badges.

"You're not in the big city anymore, friend," I said, pulling the Sig from the holster and holding it just below the bar top.

The first man stepped back from the bar, his partner retreating a step to give him room. The leader of the two turned so he could see me, Rufus, and Rusty together.

Behind him, chair legs scraped the floor as Dink and the other guide stood up. The feeling in the air was electric and the two guides had picked up on it. Islanders are a tight-knit bunch. If you step on one of our toes we'll all say, "Ouch."

"What the fuck's that supposed to mean, tough guy?" the leader asked me.

I slowly pulled the Sig up and rested it on the bar. I didn't have to check to see if there was a round chambered. I heard the distinct sound of two hammers being thumbed, cocking pistols, one coming from the guides by the window and the other from under the bar in front of Jimmy. These sounds hadn't escaped the attention of the two men, either.

The sound of a shotgun chambering a shell got the first man's full attention. I kept my eyes on his as Rusty slowly drew his twelve-gauge sawed-off deck sweeper from its holster beneath the bar and brought it up across his chest.

"What he means is," Rusty began in an even tone, "everyone down here has guns. Now, real slowly, using just your left hands, pull those pistols out from under those coats and slide 'em down to the end of bar."

The first man looked slowly around the bar, noting that there were now at least four guns already drawn and both he and his partner still had their jackets buttoned.

"Do what he says, Erik," the first man said as he slowly unbuttoned his coat with his left hand and lifted his stainless .45 from its holster.

The two men slid their guns down the bar past where Jimmy sat. Jimmy studied the leader's face a moment and said, "I know you, man. Pittsburgh Steelers linebacker, late nineties, right? Gerald Tremont Bradley. You blew your knee out in a game against Miami in ninety-nine."

"GT," the man corrected Jimmy. Looking back at Rusty, he said, "We don't want no trouble, mister, just looking for someone that owes me money. He bought lunch here about an hour and a half ago."

"He was charged with trafficking a couple times, Rusty," Jimmy continued, ignoring GT Bradley's comment. "A few years back, man. Up in Pittsburgh."

Rufus stepped in front of the two much larger men. "Like I and I say, yuh won't find what yuh seek here. Di stars aren't aligned for you yet." Looking back over his shoulder at Rusty and me, Rufus said, "Put away di guns, mon. Dere will be no trouble from dese two men."

Rusty nodded to me and slowly lowered the shotgun, putting it back into its hiding spot below the bar, and I holstered my Sig.

Rufus turned back to the two men and spoke evenly, but very quietly. "Mistuh GT, yuh must leave now."

GT Bradley lowered his head and stared at the small old man in front of him. It was obvious he was unused to being told what to do and much more accustomed to others cowering in front of him.

"Old man, if these others didn't have me outgunned, I'd break you in half for just thinking you could order me around."

Rufus's eyes never left the much bigger man's. He spoke again with the same calm and quiet voice, but more firmly this time. "No suh, Mistuh GT. Di spirits have left you. Your aura is low, flat and dull blue. Impotent. The guiding light burns bright over my head. It say dat you cannot do dis ting."

GT's eyes flashed with the ferocity of a jungle cat, and as quick as a lightning bolt, his right hand shot out at Rufus, his speed surprising me. But it never connected. Rufus was suddenly beside the much larger man and in a blur of movement, he spun and caught GT in the middle of his back with an open hand. The impact and GT's forward momentum sent him crashing into the bar with a solid thunk as his chest impacted the heavy mahogany armrest of the bar.

Before the second man could move a muscle, old Rufus was on him, literally climbing the man's tree trunk of a body like a monkey, stabbing him from groin to head with short, soundless punches, then vaulting over the man's shoulder and landing lightly on the ground behind him.

As GT turned around to face the old island man, Rufus pulled a chair from a table and placed it behind the one called Erik, whose eyes were already closed. Rufus slowly lowered the bigger man into the chair, where he slumped forward.

Rufus stepped around the unconscious man in the chair and faced Bradley, calmly, his shoulders and arms hanging loosely. I'd seen this posture before, when Rufus would begin his stretching exercise. "Like I and I done told you," he barely whispered, but was clearly heard all over the room. "Di spirits say you cannot do dese tings. What you seek is not here. Go, Mistuh GT, while you are still able to do so."

Bradley was holding a hand to one of his ribs and looked in astonishment at the little Jamaican man, meanness evident on the bigger man's face.

Bradley snarled, "I'm gonna kill you!" as he started to take a step forward, blinded by fury.

Again, Rufus moved faster than my eyes could follow. In less than an eye blink, he was standing two feet in front of the larger man and placed a fingertip to Bradley's forehead, freezing the charging rhino of a man dead in his tracks.

Rufus stood there for a few seconds, his fingertip barely making contact with the big ex-linebacker's forehead. Suddenly, Bradley collapsed to the ground at Rufus's feet, like a marionette with its strings cut.

Rufus smiled at Rusty. His voice taking on the more singsong tone of his heritage, he said, "See, mon. No trubba heah. Everting is irie."

Turning to an empty table, Rufus scooped up two plates and two glasses and headed out the back door toward his kitchen.

I shook my head, trying to make sense of what I'd just witnessed. "What the hell just happened?"

"Dude!" Jimmy exclaimed with an astonished expression. "That was intense!"

"I'm not sure I can even comprehend what I think my eyes just told me," Rusty agreed, coming quickly around the bar.

Both GT and Erik were out cold, but there wasn't a mark on either man. I checked for a pulse and found both strong and steady. They just seemed to be sleeping. I glanced toward the door that Rufus had disappeared through, then Rusty and I dragged GT, lifting him into a chair next to the other man. I checked their pockets and did a quick pat down, finding a small .38-caliber Smith and Wesson in an ankle holster on Erik's left leg and handed it to Jimmy.

Suddenly, both men simply woke up and lifted their big bald heads, looking around very confused. Finally, GT's eyes settled on me. "What happened?"

"My guess is you got your stars realigned a little," I replied, still not fully understanding what I'd witnessed. "What do you want here?"

GT blinked, confusion still showing on his face. "A guy was here about an hour ago. Bought something with a credit card. He owes me a lot of money and I been following him all the way from Pittsburgh."

"This is my bar," Rusty said, a bit of anger rising in his voice. "A lot of people eat and drink here."

"Paid with a credit card. Name's Michal Grabowski."

"Figures," Rusty said and turned toward the bar. "Another damned smug druggler."

"You see what I mean?" I said to my old friend. "This isn't what I came down here for. And it's getting worse."

"Yeah," Rusty said and then turned back to Bradley. "Your *friend* was here a while ago, ordered lunch. Short guy, long, greasy hair, rotten teeth, and a really ugly mug? He tried to sell drugs to one of my friends. Now the two of you can do the same as he did. Get your asses outta my bar and don't even think of coming back."

Both men still looked confused as they slowly stood up. "What about our guns?" Bradley asked.

"What guns?" Rusty snarled. "Come back again and I'll blow your heads off with them."

CHAPTER EIGHT

Michal Grabowski hurried along Duval Street in the sweltering late-afternoon heat. Today, he sported a new pair of Kino sandals and his feet were tinged pink from the previous day's hot sun. The girl last night had given him a lot of advice about how to dress under the tropical heat, but he was determined to at least get some sun on his legs and feet before taking her advice. She was spot-on about the sandals, though. The leather didn't seem to transfer the heat as bad as the rubber flip-flops he'd bought his first day here.

Michal had spent the prior afternoon and most of the evening at *Irish Kevin's*, talking with the bartender. She'd said her name was Coral and she was from Boston, but had now been living in Key West for three years. Michal had lost all track of time and purpose, enchanted by the girl's ready smile and sharp wit.

Forgetting his mission to unload the coke he'd stolen, he'd nursed a brace of beers while watching the girl work, occasionally talking with her about Key West and how to dress so as not to be marked as a tourist. Then she'd asked if he liked hockey. She was a huge Bruins fan.

Being a Pittsburgh native, Michal was a Penguins fan. In fact, hockey was his favorite sport, being one of the few physical team sports where size took a backseat to agility and speed on the ice. It was obvious that she had more than a bartender's passing knowledge of the sport.

Watching Coral work the tourists and locals alike was similar to watching a play, he'd decided. She was friendly, smiling and even a little flirtatious with the guys that visited her bar. Dressed in cutoff denim shorts and a short *Irish Kevin's* T-shirt, she moved around behind the bar like a dancer. Her tip jar quickly filled.

During a lull, he'd asked about her hair. What he'd at first perceived as a short, tangled mess were actually dreadlocks, like they wore in Jamaica.

"Baby dreads," Coral had explained with a bright smile, shaking her head, causing the braids to bounce around beneath her Bruins cap. Leaning close on the cooler, she smiled, fiddled with one of her blond locks and added, "Like in the Kenny Chesney song. I like everything to be in a no fuss, no muss kind of way."

While Michal couldn't be certain, he thought she was paying him slightly more attention than the other men at the bar. When she finished her shift at seven, he mustered his courage up to ask her out.

New place, new life, new person, he'd thought at the time. Overcoming his awkward shyness, he'd asked her to have dinner with him.

Coral had touched his hand then and smiled very warmly. "I never go out with someone I just met." Then, with a teasing grin, she asked, "Will you be back here tomorrow?"

He'd promised he would and stood at the door watching as she'd climbed into the front seat of a big black taxi, driven by a silver-haired black man.

All morning, he'd been anticipating returning. She'd finished her shift before sunset last night and disappeared in the taxi, so he was pretty sure she didn't live nearby. If she worked a later shift today, he'd been planning to just nurse a couple of beers until then.

Feeling the cold blast of air as he opened the door, Michal stepped inside, letting his eyes adjust to the dimmer light inside *Irish Kevin's.*

Coral was behind the bar, her back to him, as she stocked a cooler with beer bottles at the far end. She was wearing the now familiar Boston Bruins ball cap, loosely covering her baby dreads.

Michal walked around to the end of the bar, stealing a glance at Coral's firm ass and legs as he passed the bar's length and took the stool in the corner. She was wearing a bright neon-green T-shirt this time. Again it was cut off and exposed a couple of inches of fit, tanned belly. Below that, she wore high-waisted spandex shorts, with no sign of a panty line. The bright red shorts were very revealing, barely covering her ass cheeks, and so tight that there was very little left to a man's imagination. But imagine he did.

When Michal sat down at the bar, Coral looked up, surprised. Bending over the cooler as she was, her T-shirt hung loosely from her shoulders, the V-neck offering a substantial view of the cleavage between her small, firm breasts. On the front of the shirt was a little bearded man, wearing a green top hat. Below that, in big dark green letters, it proclaimed, "I'm A Fucking Leprechaun." But the U was replaced with a shamrock, covering one pert nipple.

Coral smiled brightly. "I'm glad you came back, Michal. Wasn't sure if you would after I saw that the cruise ship that was at the docks yesterday had left some time last night."

"Not on a cruise," he said with a grin. "I'm here for a while. Maybe permanently if everyone's as friendly as you, Coral."

She spun around and pulled a frosted mug from the cooler below the long row of beer taps, tilting it under the Iron City Beer one. She filled it with a nice foamy head, which she deftly swiped with the blade of a long knife, and placed it on a coaster in front of him.

"I'm off in two hours, if that invitation to dinner is still on," Coral said, a coy smile lighting her face as she twirled one of her dreads.

Michal couldn't believe his luck. Back home, women mostly ignored him, which he sometimes attributed to his invisibility. But here, it was different. His plain, normal features were a novelty.

He grinned from ear to ear. "Absolutely!" Emboldened by her forwardness, he added, "But you'll have to pick where we go. I only got into town three nights ago."

"Edith raw?" Coral said, her smile becoming brighter still. At first, Michal misunderstood her words and blushed. She winked and enunciated more clearly, "Edith, like Archie's wife in *All in the Family*? The *Half Shell Raw Bar* is a couple blocks away, over on Key West Bight. Edith raw is kinda their slogan."

"Raw bar?"

"Oysters are great for the libido," she said, twirling her dreads once more, amused at his misunderstanding, though she'd done it intentionally.

She turned away to wait on other customers, giving Michal a better view of her perfect little body as she stretched high on bare feet for a wine glass from the overhead rack. She disappeared down the bar, Michal grinning like the Cheshire cat.

Earlier in the day, he'd been able to sell quite a few of the small packets and had several hundred bucks in his pocket. More importantly, the guy he'd sold them to was a local he'd met the night before, and he'd said he knew a guy that might be able to buy quantity. He explained that things were kinda dry at the moment. Michal had planned to sell it off a little at a time, but the longer he had it, the more chance there was of selling to the wrong person and being caught by the law.

Looking out the front window, Michal thought this was something he'd have to consider. He could probably unload all he had left to one person, but then he'd only make a tenth of the money. *Selling ounces could go faster,* he thought while watching the throngs of people walk by on the sidewalk. *Feed the guy an ounce at a time.* He'd try to find the guy again tomorrow.

"Penny for your thoughts?" Coral asked, surprising him as he nursed his beer.

"Oh, I was just thinking how nice it must be to live here. I'm considering making it permanent."

"You said last night you worked in a steel mill. I doubt you'll find that kind of work here. Can you weld?"

What's she know from welding? he wondered. "Yeah, I'm a welder. Arc, mig, tig, steel, aluminum, just about anything."

"Cool," she said, leaning over and opening the cooler in front of him again, giving him another look down the neck of her loose T-shirt. Coral slid the cover back in place and made a note on a pad next to it. "I do a little welding on the side. At a bike shop."

"You're a welder?"

"What? Girls can't do tough guy jobs?"

"No," he replied quickly, not wanting to insult her or anything. "Nothing like that. Some of the best welders I've ever met were women. It's just that none of 'em looked like you."

"Well, there's a lot of welding work around here," Coral said. "The whole island is practically a boatyard, and good welders are hard to find. You should check around some of the bigger marinas. I helped out on a job a year ago, but on account of my size, I'm more comfortable working on something not quite so big, like a custom chopper."

He thought about that a moment. He had a pretty good stake. If he could unload a bit more, he could easily make a go of it, living legally. The young woman in front of him was being more helpful than anyone he'd ever met. Before he could check himself, he blurted out, "Why are you so nice to me?"

"You're cute and you don't smell like fish," she replied with a wink, picking up her notepad and whirling to the cooler on the other side of the bar to check the stock.

When she bent over, she bounced her hips to the music from the jukebox, shifting from one leg to the other.

Michal had a magnificent view of her perfect little butt in those tight spandex shorts and was staring. He nearly fell off his stool when Coral looked back suddenly and caught him, winking and giving her backside another bump before moving off down the bar to wait on other customers.

Michal was nearly finished with his second beer, nursing them slowly, when a new waitress went behind the bar and Coral started to cash out her drawer, stuffing the money from the full tip jar into a small purse under the bar.

"Care for another beer?" the new waitress asked him, a tall brunette with long straight hair and bangs to just above her eyes. She was just as beautiful as Coral and dressed the same way. But she was a lot taller, at least four inches taller than Michal.

"No, thanks," he said, as Coral slid his tab in front of him. The brunette went down to the other end of the bar.

He looked at the bar bill, took a twenty from his pocket and placed it on top of the tab, smiling at Coral. "Keep the change."

Coral gathered both the tab and the bill and went back to her cash drawer. A few minutes later, she closed it and took a fresh, chilled mug from the cooler and held it under the Iron City tap. She placed the frosted mug in front of him and winked. "This one's on me. Take your time, while I go get changed."

Ten minutes later, Coral sat down next to him at the bar. She was wearing a lightweight and loose-fitting yellow sundress, with thin straps over her tan and slender shoulders. If possible, the bright yellow dress made her tan look deeper and richer and her bright blue eyes and blond hair lighter. It was obvious that she wasn't wearing a bra under it and when she sat down on the stool, the short dress exposed nearly as much of her tanned thighs as her shorts had earlier.

Gone was the Bruins cap, though, and for the first time Michal could see all of her dreads. *On anyone else*, he thought, *that would look just plain ridiculous.* She made it look ridiculously fun and cute.

"Hurry up with that brewski, Michal. I'm starving."

"Then let's rock," he said, standing up and draining the mug. When she stood next to him, he felt like a giant, despite his size. Looking down, he saw that she now wore flat sandals that laced halfway up her calves. Lifting his eyes to take her all in, he found the top of her head barely reached his nose.

"How tall are you?" he asked.

"You mean how short? I'm just under five feet, handsome." Coral waved goodbye to the new bartender and turned back to Michal. "I do have some six-inch stilettoes if you prefer women tall like her."

Michal blushed slightly, which caused Coral to giggle for a moment. As they left the bar and headed down Duval Street toward the docks, he felt like he was walking on air. She quickened her pace and grabbed his hand, nearly dragging him along.

"We have to hurry, or we'll miss it," Coral said.

"Miss what?"

"Sunset! When it goes down here, it's a reason to party."

They quickly made their way across Duval at the next corner and walked hurriedly down Greene Street a block, then cut through a couple more side streets, before arriving at Mallory Square.

Michal had never seen anything like it. The dock area was about five hundred feet long and a hundred feet deep, with all kinds of temporary vendor carts and displays set up. Everywhere he looked, street performers crowded the space, playing music, juggling cats, selling cookies, and just a whole lot of weirdness all in one little place. It was sensory overload.

It's like a circus, he thought. People were crammed into nearly every spot, watching the street performers and gazing out over the water as the sun sank toward the horizon.

Coral led him by the hand to the edge of the docks, near where a man was walking a tight rope, which wasn't very tight, and juggling bowling pins at the same time.

To his left, a huge cruise ship was docked about a hundred yards further down. Aside from the craziness all around, the dock in front of him was empty.

Michal looked around in wonder. "This happen often?"

"Every evening! Crazy, huh?" Coral leaned against the rail, her short dress riding up the back of her shapely, tanned legs. Michal stepped up beside her and looked toward the setting sun. Coral turned and considered the side of his face. "They say that when the last of the sun disappears below the sea, if you make a wish and see a green flash, it'll come true."

"A green flash?" Michal asked.

"It's rare, but it does happen. At the very moment the last of the sun disappears."

They stood at the large concrete barrier and looked out over the water. The sun was barely above the horizon now and as they watched, a stately old schooner sailed by, the deck crowded with people. There were a number of other boats on the water, mostly sailboats, but the schooner dwarfed most of them.

Looking down, Michal saw a number of brightly colored fish of various sizes swimming just below the surface, attracted to some kind of food that kids were tossing in the water. The breeze blowing off the sea was cooler and seemed to suck the heat of the day away from this spot. Looking back out over the water, he was mesmerized by the sheer beauty. Low clouds near the far horizon looked as though they were ablaze as the sun sank lower, the clouds tinged bright orange at the end nearest the sun and fading to red and pink to the north.

Coral reached down and took his hand. "Watch closely, or you'll miss it. The ocean is about to reach up and grab the sun."

She'd no more than said the words, when it seemed as though the water actually did rise up and take the sun in its grasp, pulling it lower and lower. Coral felt his hand tighten in hers and heard his sharp intake of breath, as she watched him watch the sea.

Stepping closer to Michal then, she pulled his hand around her narrow waist before releasing it and leaning against him, slipping her arm around him.

Just as the last of the sun was about to disappear, he closed his eyes for just a second, his lips moving with a silent wish. When he reopened them, the sun quietly slipped below the sea and disappeared, but he didn't see any green flash.

All around him, people started clapping their hands, cheering and whistling. "Did I miss it?" he asked, looking down at Coral's upturned face.

"Like I said, it's rare. They're just cheering Mother Ocean's show. Make the same wish tomorrow and it might come true." Then she reached a hand up and twirled one of her dreads, cocking her head and smiling seductively. "Who knows? You might get your wish anyway. But not before you feed me. Come on."

CHAPTER NINE

When we got back to the island, Carl and I pulled the boat up onto the trolleys and then, with a lot of grunting, swearing, and tugging, we pulled it back into the little cover to give it a good inspection in the morning.

"Sure was a lot easier going in than coming out," Carl gasped, dropping to the sand.

I knelt on one knee next to him, breathing hard from the exertion. "Always the case, bro. I used to know a guy who always said, 'Sometimes the easiest way out is go straight through.'"

"I think maybe you should start drinking again," Carl said. "That makes no sense at all."

"No, but what you said reminded me of him. Maybe you're right, though. I haven't had a beer all week."

"Humph, more like a month. Unwind, man. There's not a bad guy with an Uzi at the wheel of every boat."

Once we'd caught our breath, we went out to the north pier, where Charlie and the kids were rinsing under the freshwater shower after cleaning up in the lagoon. Pescador was jumping back and forth with the kids, biting at the steam of water, and they were trying to mimic him.

As Charlie hurried the kids toward shore, Pescador stopped for a quick ear scratch and Charlie said, "I'll get dinner started while you two get cleaned up." She smiled at her husband and added, "I brought home a big pot of Rufus's janga soup."

Carl and I each grabbed a bar of soap from a box mounted at the end of the pier and dove into the warm, clear water. Minutes later, we were toweling off while walking toward the shoreward end of the pier.

"What'd you make of that today?" I asked Carl. "I mean the two dope pushers arriving at the *Anchor* about the same time?"

We sat down at the table nearest the big stone grill. Carl opened the cooler and took out two Red Stripes and a bottle of water, offering me either. I took the beer and opened it with a bottle opener laying on the table. The first pull on the beer was delicious and cold, with just a bit of the grainy texture I like.

"Wish I'd been inside to see old Rufus in action," Carl said. "There's a lot of rumors about him, nothing substantiated. All kinds of mystical stuff he was supposed to be involved in here, a long time ago. The two pushers? I don't know, man. It seems to just get worse and worse around here."

"Mysticism, huh? If I believed in any of that, it'd make sense of what I saw. You're right about it getting worse, though. But I don't think we have any kind of drug problem here on the island."

Carl laughed. "No, definitely not here. Charlie'd kick my ass if I even smoked pot."

"You ever tried it?"

Carl looked at me, questioningly. "Yeah, I used to smoke quite a bit. That was before I met Charlie, though. You?"

"Nope, never had the occasion or desire to try it. Wonder how that big guy was able to track the other guy all the way from Pittsburgh?"

"I dunno, maybe he's part bloodhound. What exactly did he say after Rufus cleaned their clocks?"

I thought it over a minute. "Credit card! The big guy said that the guy's name was something Grabowski and he paid with a credit card. He was specific about that, but how would he know?"

"Wouldn't be hard for a computer hacker to get that information," Carl said. "Why's it important?"

I just shrugged. "I don't know, just curious, I guess. I wouldn't think an ex-jock-turned-dealer would be all that great at computer hacking."

"Maybe he has help. Like Chyrel does for you guys."

Chyrel Koshinski is a part of Deuce's CCC team. A former CIA computer analyst, she's able to hack just about any security system in the world, including the CIA's.

"I'm gonna go make a call before supper," I said as I got up and headed toward my little stilt-house on the other side of the island. It wasn't a long walk. The clearing in the middle of my little island is barely more than an acre, with the two houses and two bunkhouses nestled into the tree line along the shore. The whole island is hardly two acres at high tide.

In the house, I checked the table in the corner of the small galley before looking around the tiny living room. Going back to the bedroom, I searched the nightstand and dresser.

The boat! I thought. I'd called Linda the night before last, while anchored in Jewfish Basin about fifteen miles southwest of here. I made my way outside and down to the south pier, opening the door to the dockage area under the house. Vaulting over the gunwale, I found my phone in the drink-holder of the fighting chair. The battery was dead.

I plopped down in the chair to think. I've lost quite a few chargers and more than one cell phone over the last seven years since moving to the Keys. I just never make a lot of phone calls.

I jumped up from the chair, remembering that when I called Linda, the battery had been dead that time also, and I'd called her from the bridge, where I could plug it in.

Finding the charger where I'd left it at the console, I connected it to my phone again. It'd take a few minutes to charge enough for a short call, and the only place it gets a signal is on the deck directly above where I was sitting. *Not far above*, I thought, powering the phone on and standing up.

With the phone at head level a few inches below the overhead, and it having a clearance to the deck beams of two feet, that meant the only spot I'd ever gotten a signal on the whole island was only about nine feet above where I was now holding the phone. The signal meter showed one bar for a second and then it disappeared. I dropped the phone into a drink-holder on the console.

I could use the satellite phone Deuce had given me. It was fully charged and turned off down in my cabin. After learning from Deuce's predecessor that the sat-phones the team used could be tracked by the DHS, since they technically owned them, I left it off all the time.

"What the hell?" I said to nobody. "Where else would they expect me to be?"

Retrieving the sat-phone from its spot under my bunk in the forward stateroom, I powered it up as I left the boat and returned to the deck above the docks.

Linda answered on the first ring. "I miss you. I miss the island. And I miss the water."

"I miss you too, babe," I said. "But is that how you always answer the phone?"

"You're calling from your satellite phone. The number's stored on mine, but it's always turned off when I call it. Where are you?"

I sat back in one of the four rockers Carl had built so we could watch the sunsets. Sometimes the mosquitoes were too bad on the pier or the beach in front of Carl's house. "I'm at home."

"Battery's dead in your regular phone, right?"

It was a statement, not a question. The woman knew me too well. Linda and I had met almost a year ago on an island in the Bahamas. She had been working undercover as a professional call girl and helped put together the pieces when some bad guys were trying to kill us. *Us* being a group that had gone over there to locate the treasure of the *Nuestra Señora de Magdalena y las Angustias*, a seventeenth-century carrack that had been driven onto the reef by a hurricane. Another former first mate, Doc Talbot and his wife Nikki had found a clue to its location and brought in a few people to help find it, mostly from Deuce's team. Doc had been a Navy Corpsman many years ago and more recently a member of Deuce's team.

"Yeah, left it in the fighting chair when I called you a couple nights ago. Why all the missing?"

"Sorry, I'm just venting. I hate it up here. It's a frigging college town and even the government is run like a damned fraternity."

"Ahh," I said. "The big brick wall of chauvinism didn't fall with your first kick, huh? Know what Pap used to tell me?"

She laughed, knowing I liked to quote Papisms. I liked her laugh. "That's pretty much it. A bunch of good ole boys here in Tallahassee, and they consider it their own little boys' club, no girls allowed unless you're serving drinks or blowjobs. So, what sage words of wisdom would your Pap have given me?"

I'd become accustomed to her occasional cop talk. I guess being a woman who excels in a job held mostly by men would tend to make one a little jaded.

"He applied this to all facets of life," I replied with a smile, remembering the many different ways I'd used this one little piece of advice. Russ's comment about the easiest way out of something being to go through it meant pretty much the same thing, and I'd employed the advice of both men a few times. "He'd say, 'If that don't work, get a bigger hammer.'"

Linda laughed again. The kind of laugh that made me feel good hearing it, no matter the circumstances. "You should run for the Florida senate, Jesse. You'd sure shake these fools up here in the capitol."

I laughed with her. "No, sometimes I think using a sledge on delicate balsa wouldn't work out in anyone's favor."

We talked for twenty minutes as I watched the sun slowly sink toward Water Key half a mile away. The sky was clear and bright, just a string of low clouds far to the west. The southern tip of the line of clouds seemed to glow like the end of a cigar. I did my best to describe it to her, knowing that she missed watching it with me.

The truth was, I missed her. We'd become very close these last few months. Every Friday afternoon, I'd pick her up at the *Anchor* and she'd stay until early on Monday morning. Sometimes, not so early.

After ending the call, I joined Carl and his family for supper and then turned in early. I wanted to spend a few hours going over every inch of the new boat. Until Carl and I could work something out down below, we'd have to tie it up to one of the piers, or haul it out and put it under the temporary shed.

I didn't much like either option, but the dock area under the house was full. Besides the forty-five-foot *Revenge*, there was a Cigarette boat, two center-consoles and two skiffs down there.

I had an idea about relocating the boat hoist I'd built long ago to lift my skiff out of the water before a storm. Since then, I'd enlarged and enclosed the whole area below the house and hadn't used it. I could winch Kim's skiff up, since she'd be gone most of the year, secure it up high, and dock my skiff below it. That'd free up enough room for the new runabout.

I drifted off to sleep about twenty-two hundred and dreamed about sawing and nailing.

CHAPTER TEN

S o, you've seen it before?" Michal asked after he and
Coral had eaten two dozen oysters and chased them
down with two bottles of beer. "The green flash?"

Coral smiled. "A few times. I try to watch the sunset
every evening, but in winter it's already over before I get
off work."

Michal was curious about why the setting sun seemed
to be so important here. "What's the big deal about the
sun going down? It does it every day."

Looking out over the water outside, a deep peace came
over Coral's face. "It's more than just something that happens every day, Michal. And there's no guarantee that you
will see another. It's the symbolism that marks the end of
the day, a time to reflect on what you've accomplished."
She turned back and looked deeply into Michal's eyes.
"Too often, I watch it and can't mentally jot down anything I did that was worthy of the day I was given."

"What did you wish for, when you saw it?"

"Always the same thing. To live one more day in paradise. And here I am, so one of those wishes must have worked."

"Maybe just wishing at sunset works for you."

Coral smiled. "Could be."

Michal looked out over the now-dark water of the bight. Several long docks extended out toward the break-water and beyond that, the seemingly endless ocean. Halfway down the sky, a half-moon glowed, creating sparkles on the surface as far as his eyes could see. "I can sure see why you wished that."

"I do believe the bug has bitten you, Michal. I can tell when you looked out over the water at the dock and again just now."

"I do like it here. Is it always so hot?"

"For a few months in summer. Most of the year it's very comfortable, especially winter. There's no better way to celebrate the beginning of a new year than taking a midnight swim in the ocean. Why are you here, Michal? I mean here in Key West."

Michal thought for a moment, wondering how much he could or should tell her. "Just tired of the cold winters up north, I guess. New place, new start. You?"

"My aunt lives here. She's a palmist and tarot card reader. Aside from that, pretty much the same reason." She stared into his eyes as if trying to come to a decision. "Are you running from something or someone, Michal?"

"Why do you ask?"

"A lot of people come here to escape their old life." She sighed, just a tinge of melancholy in her voice.

"Yeah, I guess so," he replied, acknowledging both the question and the statement, but not really saying which. Changing the subject, he asked, "What's your last name?"

Coral sat up straight and smiled. "La Roc, capital *L*, *a*, capital *R*, *o*, *c*. Coral La Roc." She extended her hand across the small table.

"Michal Grabowski," he said, taking her hand in his and feeling a rush of warmth from the contact. "Wait! That's a palindrome."

Coral beamed. "You have a quick mind. I like that in a man."

"And it seems your folks must have had a really great sense of humor."

"They didn't come up with it. I did."

"It's not your real name?" Michal asked.

"The first name, I was born with. I had my last name changed legally when I moved here."

Michal lifted his beer mug in a toast. "Well here's to *your* sense of humor, then."

Coral raised her own mug to his. "And to *your* quick mind."

Over Coral's shoulder, a passing figure caught Michal's eye. It was the pickpocket from the bus station, walking through the parking lot just outside the far window. The guy he'd sold an eight ball to up in Belle Glade.

Keep the credit cards and just keep walking, asshole, Michal thought. He didn't need the ugly, stinky little man ruining things. Coral turned in her chair and followed his gaze out the open front window, but the pickpocket was out of sight and she turned back to Michal.

"What was it?" she asked, hesitantly.

"Oh, nothing," he lied. "Just someone who looked like a guy I used to know."

Coral looked out over the water and took a deep breath of the salty air, listening to the gentle sound of the rigging, clanking on the masts of the few sailboats tied off to the docks. "Know what would be really great right now?"

Michal was admiring the side of her face. Her small chin and tiny mouth lifted to the breeze, elongating her slender neck. "I sure do. Probably not the same thing you're thinking, though."

Coral giggled and reached up to touch her hair again. Michal suddenly realized he hadn't seen her do this with any of the other guys at the bar. "All things in their time," she whispered. "What I was thinking is, I'd love to smoke some weed right now."

"You get high?" he asked incredulously.

"Sometimes. When I really want to relax and unwind."

"Wish I had some."

She stood quickly and came around beside him, tugging on his arm. "Let's go to my place. I have some."

With no further urging needed, Michal rose from his seat and dropped two twenties on the table. They left the restaurant and walked south on Margaret Street, arm in arm. A block later, they were swallowed by the tall, stately trees of Key West's charming and historical Old Town.

Half a block further, Coral steered him into an alley between two white picket fences, and they emerged in a tiny but well-kept yard by a small cottage. It was no more than twenty feet wide and not much more than that deep. The little house sat on brick pilings and was painted pale blue with bright yellow trim. Two windows, one on either side of the front door, had long louvered shades that would block the sun, but you could still see through.

Stepping up onto the little porch, Coral took a single key from her small purse and opened the screen door. She inserted the key in what looked like a centuries-old lock and turned it, with a heavy click. Turning the doorknob, the heavy-looking wood door opened on silent hinges. "I'm guessing Michal Grabowski is your real name, huh?"

"Yeah," he replied, a little confused and holding the screen door open for her.

"If someone's looking for you, you should change it. Wait here, while I light a lantern."

Coral disappeared into the dark house, leaving Michal wondering who it was that might be looking for her. A moment later he heard the scratch of a wooden match and stepped inside slightly, still holding the screen door open. Coral was standing on the far side of the small room, next to a wood-burning fireplace. She held the glass globe from an antique oil lamp in one hand and a lit match in the other, lighting a lamp on the mantel.

"You don't have electricity?"

The flickering light from the match strengthened as it touched the wick. The dim yellow light dancing across Coral's face created a very stunning and erotic image in Michal's mind.

"No, they never ran wires to this cottage. It used to be an icehouse. At least the main room was. The rest was added on. I bought it as is, at a ridiculously low price, and have come to love not having power. No phone or cable either. But, I do have plumbing."

"But no hot water?"

"There's a gas water heater, but I turned it off since it's rarely needed. Out back is a huge rain barrel up on stilts where the sun heats the water. In winter, it's barely lukewarm and I have to heat a couple of gallons on the gas stove to take a hot bath. Cheaper than heating thirty gallons."

She replaced the globe, and the light spread across the tiny room, revealing the furnishings. The exterior walls were all covered with a dense, heavy-looking wood, having light and dark swirls of grain. It appeared the same as on the outside, Michal noted, but the inside was unpainted. Not paneling, but rough-sawn planks, probably original. On the walls hung a few brightly colored tropical paintings. There was a recliner next to the front window, turned at a slight angle so a person sitting in it could see the front porch. Another oil lamp sat on a small table next to it for reading.

Opposite the door, the whole wall surrounding the fireplace was filled with bookshelves. They ran floor to ceiling, and there was even one of those ladders on wheels like in some old libraries. All of the shelves were nearly full.

A small love seat was against the interior wall to the right, with a tiny wooden coffee table in front of it. Next to the love seat was the opening to what looked like a small alcove-type kitchen. Beyond that, a short hallway extended to the rear of the little house, a door on each side and another at the end, presumably the bedroom, bathroom, and linen closet.

To his left, the other exterior wall was empty, just a window with the shade pulled completely down. Coral walked slowly toward Michal and closed the screen door behind him, leaving the heavy wooden door open to let the heat out of the room.

"Welcome to my home."

"But you got in a cab after you got off work last night," Michal said, somewhat confused. "We can't be more than a few blocks from there."

Coral laughed. "A friend of my aunt. He's an old Bahamian man, sort of a mother hen to a lot of us that he sees as vulnerable. He insists that he pick me up when my shift ends. Then we stop and pick up a few other girls at different places where they work and he circles the island before dropping us off. He's really nice. You'll probably meet him sooner or later."

"Smart idea in a party town like this."

She crossed over to the coffee table and, bending over it, she opened a small drawer, hidden from sight on the other side. Michal stood, staring. The back of her little dress rode up her thighs and he gasped slightly when he saw that she had nothing on under it.

"Let's relax," she said as she took out a small plastic bag, a lighter and some rolling papers. "Can you roll?"

"Sure," Michal replied.

Coral shoved him down onto the small couch and said, "Good. Get to work and roll us up a nice fatty and I'll be right back."

When Coral disappeared down the hall, Michal opened the bag and held it to his nose, breathing deeply of the pungent aroma. Working quickly, he rolled two nice-sized joints, judging from the smell that her stash wasn't the greatest weed in the world. He liked weed better than coke. It seemed to work directly with his natural tendency to take things as they came, where coke did the opposite.

He heard a toilet flush and water running into a basin. A moment later Coral came back into the room. He noticed that she'd removed her sandals. She smiled when she saw he'd rolled two instead of one.

Without a word, Coral picked up one of the joints. Straightening, she lit it and inhaled deeply, arching her back, her small breasts straining at the light fabric as she tossed the lighter in Michal's lap.

Picking it up, Michal lit the other joint and took a long drag. As he leaned back on the love seat, closing his eyes, he could feel the effects of the herb spread quickly through his body and decided he had been premature in his assumption. The heat began in his face, spreading around to the back of his head, the way really good weed does. The sensation passed throughout his body to his fingers and toes, then settled in his groin.

When he opened his eyes again, Coral stood before him. She bent over and placed her joint in a big porcelain ashtray resembling a sea turtle. When she stood back up, the lamp over her shoulder highlighted the short locks of hair from behind, causing them to look like flickering yellow flames. It also made her body completely visible under the thin, lightweight dress.

He'd felt how narrow her waist was when he had an arm around her earlier. Backlit as she was now, he could see the swell and curve of her hips, tapering upwards to the tiniest waist he'd ever seen on a grown woman.

With both hands, Coral reached up and hooked the straps of the little yellow dress with her thumbs, pulling them slowly down and over her tanned shoulders. When she released them, the dress fell gently, exposing her breasts before stopping at her waist, the straps hanging on her elbows.

Michal exhaled, his mouth hanging open. Her firm little breasts were as tan as the rest of her body. The warming effect in his groin turned up a notch as Michal blinked in disbelief.

Coral smiled at him and lowered her arms slowly until finally the dress flowed across her hips, falling into a pile around her feet. She slowly stepped out of it and came around the table. She took his smoldering joint and placed it with hers in the ashtray.

Michal's brain seemed to quit functioning at that point. When Coral took his hand, he felt the same electric rush in her touch as he'd felt earlier, and the heat in his groin grew instantly to an inferno. Rising, he stared in amazement at her perfect little body. Her dark, luxurious tan was all over and she had a tiny triangle of light blond pubic hair.

Coral lowered her head slightly to the left and did the thing with her hair again. Lifting her head a little, she looked at Michal from the corners of her hooded eyes.

"Now we can unwind. Get your clothes off."

CHAPTER ELEVEN

The old bus slowly pulled to the curb in the sweltering heat, kicking up dust and belching smoke, as
Will Byers stood on the side of the road with his thumb
out. He'd chosen this spot wisely. There was a small spot
on the shoulder that the bus pulled into. He was far
enough from the start of what looked like a really long
bridge for someone to pull over and give him a ride. He
hadn't figured on a city bus.

As Byers approached it, he smelled the distinct odor
of weed, the aroma mixed with the fumes from the bus's
exhaust. Along the side of the bus were the words Lower
Keys Bus Service.

The smell of the weed got stronger as he approached
the bus's door, which suddenly opened. The sound of
rock music blared from inside and a hazy cloud of blue-
gray smoke drifted up from the open door, stark against
the cerulean sky.

Byers looked up at the bus driver. "How much to Key West?"

"Four bucks, man," the driver responded. "From anywhere, to anywhere, between Marathon and Key West."

Byers climbed onto the bus and was hit fully by the overpowering tang of the heavy smoke as the driver started the bus moving forward. Byers pulled a ten from his wallet and offered it to the driver, who pointed to a cash box and a sign on it. *No change made. Ever.*

Cramming the ten in the box, Byers figured it was still a good price, ten bucks for a forty-mile ride. He moved back along the rows of seats as the bus bounced back onto the highway, an air horn from a big motorhome blasting behind them. At least three people were openly smoking joints on the bus. One was a long-haired guy in a black T-shirt sitting on the wide seat in the very back. Byers plopped down in the seat next to the lavatory, leaving an empty spot between him and the dude smoking the joint. His T-shirt had a *Hog's Breath Saloon* logo stenciled on the shirt pocket.

Not an iron-on, Byers thought and made him to be a bar worker, and the T-shirt was his uniform. The guy took a long hit from his joint and held it for a few seconds before blowing it out slowly and offering the joint to Byers.

"Welcome aboard the Magic Bus, man."

Taking the joint, Byers nodded to the stranger beside him. "Thanks, man. It's really okay to smoke weed on the bus down here?"

"This is the afternoon run and everyone's headed to work. It's cool. So long as we do it while crossing the Seven Mile, Brad don't give a shit, man. Brad's the driver. I'm Keith."

Taking a toke on the guy's joint, Byers inhaled deeply. It was good, but weed didn't do much for him anymore. He handed the joint back and exhaled the smoke toward the ceiling, where it mingled with that of several other smokers. Byers noted that quite a few more people had lit up, now that they were on the long bridge.

"Byers," he said by way of introduction.

"Like the rum, man. Cool."

Sharing the joint back and forth until there was just a tiny roach left, Keith put it out on his tongue, placed it in a small tin with several others and lit a second joint.

When it was gone, they still had a couple of miles of bridge left. Byers offered the guy a hit from the little coke vial. The dude nodded enthusiastically, tapping his knees with his hands in time to the music blasting on the bus's stereo.

Using the little spoon attached to the cap, Byers offered it to his new friend. Keith took it, holding it just below one nostril with a practiced hand. Pressing the other nostril with his index finger, Keith snorted the fine white powder and handed the spoon back.

Byers did the same, finishing it just as they came off the bridge onto Big Pine Key and he screwed the little cap back on.

The driver turned the radio off and shouted over his shoulder, "Put 'em out, gang." Without waiting for a response, he turned the stereo back on, but at a much lower level. Half the people on the bus lowered their windows and the haze quickly disappeared.

The bus slowed, the driver very familiar with the laws on Big Pine Key, and though his passengers might be stoned to the gills, he wasn't. The little window beside him, directed right at his face, let just enough air in, so even a contact buzz was unlikely.

An hour later, the bus came across the bridge from Bahia Honda onto Stock Island. Keith had told Byers about the only motel in the Lower Keys that charged less than a hundred a night, and this was the stop for Byers to get off.

"Stop by *Hog's Breath* for a drink once you get settled in, man. Plenty more weed where that came from, but not much else on the island lately." That information piqued Byers interest. "That motel's right down that road." Keith pointed across the highway from where the bus had stopped as Byers got up from his seat.

The road was hot and dusty as Byers shuffled along the crushed-shell shoulder, the only sound coming from an occasional passing car on the highway and the near-constant buzzing of cicadas. Finally Byers walked into the lobby of the cut-rate motel to check in. The clerk didn't even ask for his ID. Byers held his breath as the old dude swiped the stolen credit card.

A moment later, the clerk shoved a pen and a little slip of paper under the glass. Byers made a scribble that looked like the name on the card and slid it back under the glass.

Pointing out the lobby to the left, the old guy said, "Room eight." Then he slid a key under the glass and turned back to his TV.

Entering the room, Byers looked around and turned the A/C on high. It sputtered and coughed to life, belching out slightly cooler air. Pulling a small baggie from his pocket, he stashed his crack under the mattress, noting he was down to less than a quarter ounce. Reaching down into the front of his pants, he removed a tightly sealed plastic bag and stashed it with the crack.

Reassessing what Keith had said on the bus, Byers pulled the little vial from his pocket and retrieved both bags from under the mattress. Sitting on the edge of the bed, he placed the two small bags on the nightstand and opened them. He took a pack of cigarettes from his shirt pocket and lit one, then removed the cellophane from the pack.

For later tonight, Byers thought, putting four small rocks of the crack into the cellophane and rolling it up. Scooping the little vial into the other baggie, he filled it with coke. Though he rarely used it, he felt that he might be able to score big-time, from what Keith had said, and was definitely going to go to this *Hog's Breath* place later.

The coke in the baggie wasn't the eight ball he'd bought from the coke dealer on the bus. He'd scored a half pound in Orlando just the week before. For over a year now, he'd been able to buy big in a town with plenty and sell small in a town with little, living off the profits, always moving around from town to town.

He'd had to leave Mouse-town in a hurry, though. Not that he owned much, but he couldn't even get back in his apartment there. The manager had changed the lock and said he could get in to get his stuff when the back rent was paid. The month of back rent was more than he owned, so he'd simply shrugged and left.

Byers hid the two baggies back under the mattress. He'd sold Keith about a gram for a hundred bucks. Keith had had to borrow part of it from several friends on the bus. Byers knew exactly what he wanted to spend the hundred bucks on.

Knowing he smelled pretty bad, but not realizing how bad until now, he emptied his pockets on the small dresser and removed his belt. Turning on the water in the shower, he stepped into it fully clothed.

It wasn't the first time Byers had washed the smell from his clothes and body at the same time. Once he'd lathered his shirt and jeans, then rinsed the soap out really well, he pulled his clothes off and wrung the water out, hanging them on the towel rack. He then paid special attention to cleaning his threadbare shorts. They were dirty and stained, but he could get the smell out, at least.

The rubbing caused him to become aroused and he felt himself getting harder. Looking down, he cursed himself for the millionth time, knowing that even though his dick was fully erect, it barely made a bump in his shorts.

Oh well, he thought. *Hookers don't get paid by the inch.*

The clothes were still wet when he put them back on, but he didn't care, knowing they'd be dry from the sun before he got back to the bus stop. Keith had told him the county had a number of busses that ran back and forth from Marathon to Key West, and one would stop there again in about an hour. It was only Brad's bus that you could smoke on, he'd cautioned. And then only when crossing that long bridge.

It hadn't been quite an hour, Byers guessed, since he'd gotten off the bus, so he walked back up the street toward the main road. The old man from the office was standing outside smoking a cigarette and Byers angled toward him.

"Hey, man, know where a guy can find a little female company for a price?"

"I look like a fucking pimp to you?" the old man hissed, a scowl on his creased and leathery face. "You'll find just about anything on Duval Street."

The heat hit Byers from all sides, even coming up from the blacktop, as he walked the short distance to US-1, then dashed across between cars. Taking a seat on a bench with no shade, he noted that his clothes were nearly dry, except around his crotch, which was starting to chafe a little. The overbearing heat lay heavy and still on the little island, except when an occasional car sped by, stirring the thick, humid air.

Twenty minutes later, Byers grabbed a bus schedule from the rack by the door and stepped off when the bus stopped in downtown Key West at the corner of Caroline and Duval Streets. From here it would circle the south side of the island and head back up the Keys.

Walking down Duval Street, it didn't take Byers long to know he was in the right place. He'd already spotted two hookers, one dragging a john down a narrow side street and another climbing into the passenger side of a rental car.

Finding a spot in the shade where he could lean on a light post, Byers waited. He didn't have long to wait. After a few minutes, the guy he'd spotted disappearing down the side street with the hooker stepped out of the shadows and started south on the sidewalk. Another minute passed before the hooker emerged. Adjusting her short skirt, she quickly crossed the street toward Byers.

"Wanna make it two?" Byers asked when she stepped up onto the curb.

The hooker stopped short on seeing him and looked him up and down in a flash. "Not right now, sugar. I need something a little more filling." She forced a smile, showing stained teeth. "Buy a girl a burger first?"

"Twenty bucks and a burger for a blowjob?" Byers offered.

"Follow me," she replied. "The Half Shell makes a killer cheeseburger."

Byers fell in beside her and the two walked back up Duval toward Caroline Street. He pointed to a burger joint across the street. "What about that place?"

"They won't let me in there," the hooker replied, grabbing his arm and pulling him along like an errant child. Coming out of a bar next to the burger joint, Byers saw the coke dealer whose wallet he'd lifted. A woman in a yellow dress was nearly dragging him, pretty much the way this hooker was doing him.

Byers frowned and thought he'd gotten a shitty deal. The hooker with the coke dealer was a lot better looking than the one he was with. *I'll need to keep an eye out for him*, Byers said to himself. *Maybe I'll get another chance to get to his stash, or maybe sell him mine at least.*

Byers watched as the coke dealer hurried after the hooker in the skimpy yellow dress. His hooker turned, pulling him across Duval and down Caroline Street. Several blocks later, they arrived at a seafood place and took a table in the corner. They each ordered a burger and ate impatiently as the sun slipped below the horizon.

"They call me Tiffany," the hooker said, her hunger sated.

"Byers. Say, maybe we can do a little bartering?"

"Pay for the burgers any way you want, Byers. The blowjob will be twenty bucks cash, as we agreed."

"Trade a boulder?" he whispered and watched as some of the dullness left Tiffany's eyes.

Her lips peeled back, exposing her brown and rotting teeth. "I know just the place."

Byers paid the tab, leaving a measly tip before they left the deck area of the restaurant, Tiffany leading the way. Turning toward the water, they walked out onto the long dock, a little past the restaurant.

Tiffany led him out onto the end pier, which extended nearly a hundred feet, with shorter docks at right angles, several stacked high with lobster traps and a few boats tied up between them. They didn't look like pleasure boats, Byers noted. *Fishing boats or work boats,* he thought.

Tiffany found a spot fairly well hidden by the traps and Byers pulled his little glass pipe from his pocket. He then took a decent-sized ten-dollar rock from the small cellophane-wrapped stash and held it up in the moonlight.

Tiffany eyed it with the fervor of an obvious addict. "Payment up front," she nearly pleaded, one hand on her cocked hip in a pitiful attempt to look sultry.

Byers put the flame from his lighter to the small bowl at the end of the tube, heating it quickly and handing it to her. She put the pipe to her lips and Byers dropped the little rock in. It immediately vaporized, filling the bowl and stem with bluish-white smoke, as she gently rolled the glass tube back and forth between her finger and thumb. In one long drag she'd spent the whole rock and handed the pipe back to Byers. She leaned her head back, holding her breath and stroking her heavy breasts.

Byers watched her hungrily as he deftly reheated the bowl and dropped another rock in the pipe for himself. The cellophane-wrapped rocks and glass stem quickly went back into his pocket as he unbuckled his jeans and hastily pulled them down.

A few minutes later, Tiffany staggered along the dock, laughing uncontrollably and wiping her mouth with the back of her hand. Byers hurriedly pulled up his jeans and went after her.

He caught her arm and said angrily, "I didn't get my money's worth!"

"Sure ya did," Tiffany replied, jerking her arm away and producing a switchblade out of nowhere. The blade flicked open with a snap, the steel glinting in the moonlight.

"You paid, I did my thing and you did yours. End of transaction." She laughed again at the ugly little man, attracting the attention of several people on the main dock. Loud enough for them to hear, she added, "I guess a dick that little just can't last very long. That's gotta be the tiniest one I've ever seen." With a wary eye over her shoulder, Tiffany hurried back to the parking lot, laughing all the way.

Embarrassed and dejected, several people on the docks whispering and pointing at him, Byers tried to go after her. But she'd disappeared and he again cursed himself. Angry now, he stalked off through the parking lot in front of the Half Shell Raw Bar, unaware of the large black man that had been standing in a darkened part of the dock when the hooker had ridiculed him. The black man stayed to the shadows as he followed Byers discreetly.

CHAPTER TWELVE

As they drove slowly through Big Pine Key, Erik glanced over at GT. "Aside from being short, the description the fat guy gave doesn't match Grabowski at all, boss."

Sitting in the passenger seat, GT was still pissed about those people getting the best of him. And worst of all, he and Erik were now unarmed. GT felt naked without a gun in his shoulder holster.

"One of three things," GT surmised. "Grabowski either dumped his wallet and somebody found it, or he got robbed. If it's one of those, we're on a wild-goose chase. Third thing, Grabowski has a partner and the partner has his plastic. We find him, maybe we find Grabowski."

Just then, the phone in his pocket played a Beyoncé song. When he pulled it out and saw who it was, he hit the accept button and said, "Give me some good news, Stewie."

After a moment, he said, "Hang on. Let me write that down." Fishing his notepad and pen from his inside jacket pocket, he told his computer hacker to go ahead. He wrote the information down and, without another word, ended the call.

"Step on it, Erik. The ugly dude with Grabowski's card just checked in to a cheap motel on Stock Island." Digging around in the detritus from three days on the road, he pulled out a map of the Florida Keys. "Stock Island's the last one before Key West."

Erik accelerated, but kept it just a little above the ridiculously low speed limit. Within a mile, they saw blue flashing lights ahead. A cop had a car pulled over and was pointing to a sign right in front of the car, ranting at the driver.

The sign read, *Endangered Key Deer Next Three Miles.*

"Keep it at the speed limit. That's the third cop I've seen since coming off that long-ass bridge. These guys take shit to another level with them deers."

Erik nodded, slowing the big SUV to forty-five as they passed the cop car. Once off Big Pine Key, he accelerated to sixty, slowing only when the various city speed limits required him to.

Less than an hour later, they rolled onto Stock Island, the GPS on the dash telling Erik to take the next left. A bus pulled up onto the road, belching blue-gray smoke, as Erik slowed to make the turn. A block later, they stopped in front of a seedy-looking motel wedged between two dilapidated boatyards.

"Wait here," GT said and climbed out of the car, looking around the nearly empty parking lot. There was only one car, a beat-up and rusted old Chevy.

The lobby was small, with fake plants in the corners and a thick glass window between it and the clerk behind the counter. When the man sitting there looked up, GT gave his best smile.

"Looking for a friend. Name's Grabowski. Checked in sometime today? Michal Grabowski?"

"Room eight," the man said without glancing at his computer.

"You sure?" GT asked. "You know the room numbers and names of all your guests without looking?"

"It's summer and lobster season ain't open yet, so we don't get many. He's the only one checked in today."

GT muttered a thanks and went back out to the idling Escalade. Climbing in, he said, "Number eight. But park a couple spots down from it."

With the quiet interrupted only by the ticking of the engine as it cooled, the two men climbed out of the SUV. It was late afternoon, but the heat and humidity were still unbearable, especially in the jackets they were wearing.

"Lose the jacket and holster," GT instructed, quickly shrugging out of his own and using the door to shield anyone watching as he removed his empty shoulder holster and tossed both in the backseat.

Approaching the door to room eight, GT noticed the peephole. His back to the wall, he reached a long left arm out and knocked three times, then twice more, before pressing himself close to the wall and listening. Erik hugged the wall beside him.

Waiting only a moment, he knocked again. No answer. The guy was either not inside or cagey and not making any noise. "Wait here," he ordered Erik and turned to go back to the office.

Stepping into the dusty lobby, GT stepped up to the glass again. "Are you sure he's in room eight?"

"Never said he was," the old man behind the glass replied, looking up from a little TV on the desk. "You didn't ask if he was here, just if he'd checked in. Left not twenty minutes ago. Asked where he might find a hooker! Like I'm some kinda pimp."

"Look, mister, I need to find him," GT said, knowing that even if he had his gun, the thick glass between them meant he couldn't intimidate the man. He pulled a twenty from the roll in his pocket and slipped it into the tray under the glass. "If he was successful in finding what he was looking for, where do you think I might find him?"

The old man snatched the twenty. "Duval Street, where you can find anything." He grinned and added, "One end swings one way, the other end swings the other, families in the middle." Then he turned back to the TV and turned it up, the familiar sound of a porn movie coming through the little holes drilled in the glass.

"Duval Street," GT said as he climbed into the car. "It's the main drag in downtown Key West, just across the next bridge."

With the air conditioner turned on high, the big Escalade maneuvered through the traffic on Truman and then went up and down Duval Street for the next two hours, which was exactly three trips. Not that Duval Street is long—it's barely over a mile end to end, but traffic was very slow moving. After the first trip to the south end, they both realized that they wouldn't find the guy there. It was mostly a quiet residential area, not a hooker in sight.

The narrow pavement north of Truman Street, coupled with the high volume of tourists, in cars, on mopeds and bicycles, and on foot, made for very limited space to maneuver the enormous SUV. GT noted a few girls who looked like hookers, even a couple of girls, who looked like guys, who looked like hookers. So he knew they were in the right area.

"We might as well park somewhere," GT said. "We can move just as fast on foot and split up, covering twice as much ground."

Erik was forced to park two blocks off Duval on Truman Street. "Remember," GT instructed, as the two walked back to Duval. "The guy's short and ugly. The guy that said he was short and ugly was short and ugly himself. That means we're looking for a really short, really ugly guy, with scraggly hair and a nasty smell."

When they got to Duval Street, they split up. Erik took the right side and GT the left, as they moved north. Before splitting up, the two men agreed that with all the noise, they'd be better off sending a text message if either of them saw a guy fitting the description.

Within a block, GT realized the guy had definitely exaggerated about end-to-end fun. Everywhere he looked on this part of the street he saw mostly guys, some walking hand in hand and some even making out. Then it dawned on him what the old guy said about one end swinging one way.

Gradually, the gay bars thinned out and there were more restaurants, some of them pretty nice. *Must be the family part in the middle,* GT thought. He and Erik agreed that they'd just walk the street first and then start checking the numerous bars on the way back.

It seemed that most of the traffic, particularly people on foot, were heading north. Crossing Southard Street, GT looked to the left and noticed that the sun would be going down very soon.

The two men continued walking, catching sight of one another from time to time in the crowd. GT quickened his pace. Not because he was in a hurry, but because there were very few people walking toward him, and the only way he could see those going in the same direction was to overtake them.

Nearing the north end of Duval, most of the foot traffic was now on the same side that GT was walking, everyone seeming to have an urgent destination. Erik stuck out like a sore thumb on the other side, half a block behind him. At the next crossing, nearly the whole crowd of people turned left on Greene Street.

GT stopped on the corner and looked over at Erik, waiting to catch his eye. When Erik looked his way, GT motioned for him to continue up Duval, then come back down his side and follow him. Erik nodded and continued northward, as GT followed the crowd.

He soon arrived at a large open area. To his left, a giant cruise ship was docked, looming over the island and casting a long shadow over the buildings. All around the dock area ahead of him, some kind of circus or celebration was going on, the blazing sun getting closer to the horizon.

Must be a thousand people here, GT thought.

He moved toward the dock about a hundred feet ahead, figuring that he could drift down the center of the throngs of people from this end to the other, scanning both sides.

A flash of bright yellow caught his eye. A woman stood by the rail, leaning over it. She wore a very short yellow dress which the setting sun had no problem shining through. GT could clearly see the bottoms of her ass cheeks as the dress rode up. But then she turned to a guy next to her and took his hand.

Guy's not much to look at, GT thought. *How's a guy like that score a cute little hard-body like her?*

GT turned and started down the middle of the square. There were all kinds of street vendors, magicians, performers, and musicians, even a fortuneteller. They were set up all over the whole dock area, each with a hat or coffee can for people to put money in.

The phone in his pocket vibrated against GT's leg. Taking it out, he read a message from Erik, saying he was in the square now, but didn't see GT or the guy.

Looking over the crowd in general, he decided most of these people weren't the type to visit hookers. A lot of them had families. As he stood in the center of the large crowd, suddenly everyone started cheering.

GT looked around, but saw nothing worth cheering about. The sun had just gone down and it was getting dark fast, but he hadn't seen a hooker anywhere in the square. *Dude wouldn't be here, then,* GT thought.

Pecking a message back to Erik, instructing him to head back to Duval Street and they'd start checking the bars, GT made his way back the way he came. Nearing the spot where he entered the square, he saw the little hard-body in the yellow dress again. She was hurrying ahead of the dissipating crowd, dragging the guy she was with by the hand. GT noticed her hair for the first time. She wore short dreadlocks.

CHAPTER THIRTEEN

The smell of coffee woke me. Rather than an alarm clock, I use a twelve-volt coffeemaker with a timer. I'd had my fill of alarm clocks and preferred to wake up with my coffee ready for me.

I rose and padded naked to the dresser, where I put on clean boxers and shorts. I looked out the large south-facing window. The only light on in the house was a little red one on the coffeemaker, so my eyes were well adjusted to the darkness.

The rest of my island is connected to an electric grid, powered by a huge bank of deep-cycle twelve-volt batteries, kept charged by a large generator. My house is still connected to the original system I installed six years ago, four marine batteries kept charged by a solar panel and wind turbine on the roof.

Nearly all electric on the island is twelve volt and the things that run constantly, like the refrigerators and freezers, run off of propane. My house has a small alcohol stove I'd salvaged from a boat many years ago. Charlie has two propane oven-and-stove combinations in her kitchen, for when we have visitors.

The half-moon was near the western horizon. It lit the water's surface and the islands to either side of Harbor Channel like an old black-and-white TV show, casting long, dark shadows. A light glow emanated from the south, several miles away in Big Pine.

The wind looked calm, barely a ripple on the water. Above the horizon, stars lit the inky blackness of the night sky by the millions, unabated by the glow from town. You really can't enjoy looking at the stars from shore, unless you're in the middle of a desert. Other light sources wash them out and reduce your night vision. Out on the blue, they stretch across the heavens to the far horizon in all directions with equal intensity, each winking out as it slid below the western horizon, only to be replaced by another to the east.

I went outside to where I keep my kayak and gear on the south deck. The kayak rests on brackets just below the roof overhang and above the window, where everything's handy. Ten minutes later, with a thermos of coffee, a cooler of bottled water, and my favorite rod and reel, I paddled away from the house. At best, I'd drink half the coffee and one bottle of water, but it's always a good idea to carry more than you need when you go out on the water.

My kayak is a 4.7-meter Trident Ultra made by Ocean Kayaks. Unlike a traditional kayak that you sit inside of, this kind you actually sit on top of. It's made of hard molded plastic and the top deck is depressed in the hull for sitting and storage.

Mine's set up for fishing, with several rod holders, storage wells, even a small tilt-up console for a fish finder and GPS. The console snaps shut between my legs, out of the way for heavy surf.

It was still full dark as I paddled silently south along Upper Water Key toward the shallow gap between it and Lower Water Key. The setting moon and stars cast more than enough light for me to see.

Turning west, I left the channel and crossed the shallow sandbar separating the two islands. Very little of the area around my home is navigable for any kind of powerboat. Some areas are deep enough, but surrounded by very shallow sandbars and cuts like I'd just crossed. Way too shallow even for my skiff to pole across, but the kayak glides easily in just a few inches of water.

Knowing the tide was almost full, I raised the console and switched on the GPS, striking out at a fast pace and easily getting into the rhythm. I was very familiar with the area and knew I'd have at least two feet under the keel for several miles. I only used the GPS to monitor my speed. At a brisk five knots, I settled into a smooth constant reach and pull with the paddle, using my whole body with every stroke.

Having no need for it in the calm shallows, I had the rudder raised out of the water. The Ultra has a rudder for ocean paddling, so you can steer it with two pedals by the footrests. Just forward of the rudder is a deep recess behind the seat, large enough to store a scuba tank and dive gear. I was hoping to use it for something different this morning. It's the perfect kayak for my needs.

After ten minutes, I eased the pace, catching my breath, already sweating in the hot, still air. After a few

more minutes, I stopped stroking altogether, resting the paddle across my thighs as the kayak continued to glide silently across the still and shallow water. I took a bottle of water from the cooler and drank half of it before replacing it and pouring a mug of coffee.

Leaning back in the seat, I enjoyed my coffee and looked up at the indifferent night sky. After only a minute, I saw the first of several shooting stars. *A good omen,* I thought.

The moon was slowly sinking toward the horizon beyond Raccoon Key, which lay just ahead and to the south. Most of the stars to the west were lost in the brightness of the moon, but to the north and south they sparkled like tiny diamonds under a bright light.

Out here in the dark, away from everything and everyone, you could imagine being in a completely different time. A time where everything around you was calm, beautiful, and innocent. A far cry from the events of the day before.

Carl was right, it is getting worse. Anywhere man could go easily soon became trashed. The more people, the more trash and crime. Build a bridge to an island and it too soon became trashed. I don't mean just litter, but the human trash, like the three guys at the *Anchor.*

My island is my escape from all the trash that society brings with it. Out here in the backcountry, I feel more alive. Finishing my coffee, I began paddling, slower now. I'd come about two miles and my destination was just ahead, Cudjoe Channel.

The shallows all across this flat were just one or two feet deep before dropping into Cudjoe Channel and then back to just a couple feet on the other side. It's a very narrow and natural channel, cut by the constant changing of the tides. Twenty feet deep in some places, it was deeper than it was wide in most. That deep trench has always been a great spot for big grouper, particularly this early in the morning. I approached the edge of the channel at the north end, where the waters from the Gulf entered.

I paddled slower, making no sound whatsoever, like a tiger would move through the grass after unsuspecting prey. With the sun just starting to purple the eastern sky, I dropped my bait into the water at the north end of the channel and let the current carry me south. I had a half dozen finger mullet, a favorite of game fish. After drifting like a ghost for the whole length of the channel, down to where it spilled out into the flats surrounding the Tarpon Belly Keys, I lifted the paddle once more.

I left the bait in the water and slowly paddled against the current to the north end of the channel once more. This time, as I drifted south past Riding Key, I got a bite. Reaching back, I released the bungee holding the rudder out of the water and pulled back on the rod, setting the hook. The rod bent, bouncing a little, as I held it tightly with one hand and secured the paddle in its holder with the other. The fight was on.

The big grouper instinctively headed north against the current, toward the Gulf and open water. I could just make out the shallow edges of the channel and used the rudder controls to muscle the big fish away from one side and then the other, using his own pull to allow me steerage and angle away when he'd run, pulling the kayak sideways at times.

The fight only lasted ten minutes before the big fish tired and rolled near the surface. As I approached, he flipped his giant tail, smacking the surface and sounding, pulling out line against the drag. The effort only lasted a few seconds and I reeled him back to the surface next to the kayak.

It was a big black grouper. So big I had no need to measure, it was obvious the fish was a good foot longer than the twenty-two-inch legal limit and probably weighed forty pounds. That'd make for a few good meals. Strapping the big fish in place behind my seat, I stowed the rod and began paddling toward home.

We don't usually catch large fish, simply because there is an abundance of smaller ones, and catching larger fish means refrigerating it. But my daughter Eve and her husband were coming down the next day, with my grandson, little Jesse. His full name is Alfredo Jesiah Maggio. Eve and Nick call him Alfie, but I think he prefers what his pappy calls him. The big black would be perfect to feed everyone and save a little for the next day.

Pushing harder than I had on the way out, I maintained a fast pace all the way back to the house. Arriving, I was sweating hard and could feel the burn in the muscles along my sides and back. Swimming exercises a lot of muscle groups, but paddling really isolates the long, thin muscles from the low back to the groin. Let go, these form "love handles."

The sun was just peeking above the eastern horizon, when I reached the house. Carl was already up, the east door open, and I could hear the quiet burble of the big outboard on the Grady-White. I'd given him and Charlie the twenty-foot center-console, so they'd have a means of getting the kids to the bus stop on Big Pine.

Carl was standing on the dock as I paddled up. "Whoa, man! That's some big black."

"Caught him in Cudjoe Channel," I replied as Charlie and the kids walked out onto the pier, with Pescador trotting alongside the kids. Though he was my dog, he spent a lot more time with little Carl and Patty, playing tag in the clearing or swimming in the lagoon.

We exchanged good mornings, then Charlie had to hustle off to get the kids to the bus stop on time. As always, Pescador went along with them. She was planning to do some grocery shopping while in town and Pescador would wait for her at the marina.

Carrying the big fish by the gills with both hands, Carl ducked into the dock area under the house while I took my gear up and rinsed everything at the shower under the cistern before putting it away. By the time I got down to the cleaning station, Carl had already filleted the big fish and cut the fillets into portion-sized steaks.

"This'll make a fine meal when Eve comes tomorrow," Carl said. "You're sure her husband will be here this time?"

Eve had come down from Miami with little Jesse twice in the last few months, always with the intent of bringing her husband for me to meet. Each time, he'd gotten wrapped up in a legal case in the city and couldn't make it.

What Eve didn't know, nor Carl, for that matter, was that I'd already met Nicholas Maggio. Last winter, he and his father had sent some local muscle to Elbow Cay to try to steal the treasure when we found it. They'd failed, and Deuce had made arrangements with his boss for Nick and his father, Alfredo, to avoid prosecution. He'd said it was mostly due to the fact that Nick was married to my daughter.

However, I knew that they were both well-connected attorneys and it's always good to have a lawyer in your pocket. In exchange, the Maggios had to cut ties with the crime scene and start taking pro bono cases for the poor Cubans in Little Havana. They quickly gained a much better reputation for championing those without a voice and actually gained more paying clients because of it.

"I sure hope so," I replied to Carl. "But you know how busy those hotshot lawyers are."

"Yeah, you mean a tee time at Fisher Island."

"You got room in your fridge?" I asked, nodding to the grouper steaks. "Mine's about full of lobster and crab claws, left over from last season."

"Yeah, Charlie cleared a spot when she heard you paddling out," Carl replied with a grin. "The woman has a sixth sense."

When he left with the fish, I told him I'd be down in a few minutes, I needed to make a call. Remembering that I'd left my cell phone on the bridge, I boarded the *Revenge* and climbed up to get it. A moment later, I sat down in one of the rockers on the south part of the deck and pulled up Kim's number.

She answered on the first ring. "Hey, Daddy, what's up?"

"A chicken's butt when he eats," I replied, which never failed to get a chuckle out of my youngest.

"You get me with that every time. Hey, I was just leaving to meet a friend for coffee before chemistry class, so I only have a few minutes. How's things on the island?"

I told her about the new boat and how it handled, then we chatted for a few minutes about Eve and Nick's visit tomorrow and how her summer classes were going. She planned to do the same thing next year and get her bachelor's degree in just three years. I didn't mention the drug dealers at the *Anchor*. She had to go, so we said our goodbyes and she promised to come down for a week before Labor Day.

Shoving the phone in my pocket, I caught up with Carl at the temporary shack where the runabout rested. I told him about my idea of hoisting Kim's skiff and parking mine under it to make room for the new boat.

"Yeah, I think we can do that. Probably won't take more than a couple of hours."

"We'll go take a look at what we might need," I said. "Once we're done inspecting the wood boat."

"It needs a name," Carl said. "Bad juju to go around in a boat without a name, man. We can't just keep calling it the wood boat, or the runabout."

"What do you suggest?"

"I don't know. Something that goes with the old barrel-back racing design."

"Most of those racing boats back in the day had numbers for names, like fighter planes," I said.

Carl grinned. "Not late."

"Knot like the speed?"

"Yeah, and a capital-ell-dash-eight for late. Not late."

I had to admit, it certainly fit the boat's character. "Okay, from now on, she's called *Knot L-8*."

We spent the rest of the morning, crawling over every inch of *Knot L-8*, using bright flashlights to search for any cracks or stress points in her gelcoat finish, above and below the waterline, inside and out.

I raised the engine cover and leaned over the backseat, crawling head first between the engines and down both sides, examining every joint in the sturdy oak ribs, spars, beams, and hull strips.

Carl did the same under the foredeck, which was too small for my frame. He spent nearly an hour under there, examining all the electrical connections and running a new power cable to a spot in the dash where we decided to install a touch screen GPS.

Finishing the engine bay, I pulled up the deck hatch in the aft cockpit to check the bilges while Carl cursed and groaned, squirming around in the confines of the small storage area under the foredeck. Charlie brought out sandwiches a little before noon, just as we were finishing up and climbing out of *Knot L-8*.

"I didn't see a problem anywhere," Carl said, wiping his hands on a towel before sitting down at one of the large picnic tables.

"Me neither," I said, stuffing a huge bite of lobster salad sandwich in my mouth. After swallowing it and washing it down with a gulp from a water bottle, I added, "Not a drop of water in the bilges."

After lunch, we spent an hour in the hot sun, checking the irrigation system and tanks for the aquaculture system. There were now four tanks to the system, doubling what we had originally built.

The two growing tanks are barely tanks at all. Long and wide, but only eighteen inches deep, they're more like ponds, resting on a raised bed of sand inside a cinder block base. Each plant grows in its own square basket, made of a strong synthetic mesh, filled with crushed coral and partially submerged in the flowing water.

The baskets are supported by stands made of PVC pipe wider at the bottom, and equally spaced in perfect unison, with the bottoms all touching. We have six rows of plants and twenty plants in each row. A lot of the plants have root tendrils trailing out of the baskets in the gentle current to soak up the nutrients in the warm water.

The other two tanks hold crawfish and catfish separately, with dividers to keep the mature from preying on the young. These tanks are deeper and don't have as much surface area. They sit a few feet from the ends of the vegetable tanks, water feeding from them to the fish tanks by gravity through large pipes connecting them.

From the fish tanks, the water cascades from the end over six stacked beds of broken coral, where bacteria flourish in the wet environment and break the dissolved fish waste down into nutrients which the plants thrive on. The racks are inside large collection tanks, the bottom half submerged in the ground. Each of these tanks is connected to a pair of pumps that push the water back up to the vegetable tanks through a series of sand filters to further clean the water. The pumps are activated periodically by float switches in the bottom of the collection tank, coming on when they get full and shutting off after pumping most of the water out.

Although everything is partially in the shade of the surrounding mangroves, gumbo limbos, banyan, and lignum vitae trees, we lose a lot of water to evaporation and irrigating the many fruit trees surrounding the edge of the clearing. The evaporated water is replaced by a reverse-osmosis unit on the east side of the island, turning sea water into nonpotable fresh water for the garden, the drip irrigators around the fruit trees, and the showers in both houses and the end of the north pier. Drinking water comes from two rain cisterns, one mounted above the back of my deck and the other at the end of Carl and Charlie's house.

And they said you couldn't grow food on a mangrove-covered coral rock with an elevation only two feet above sea level.

Carl was right, it only took two hours to remove and rehang all the hardware at the far end of the dock area. Originally, it was used to lift my skiff out of the water and up into an enclosure that could be covered on the bottom. I'd only used it once, during Hurricane Wilma, and it had worked perfectly. Now it was above the center pier and pretty much useless.

After moving the hardware to the east side of the dock area, I stood on the center pier and looked up into the recess. "Hey, Carl, you know what's right above this spot?"

Carl looked up, then looked around the underside of my house, seeing where the light spilled through from the surrounding deck. "Looks like it's near the back living room wall."

"Right about where my workbench is, between the bedroom and head hatches."

Carl looked at me quizzically. "You just did it. Switched straight from island time to tactical mode."

I just shrugged. "Old habits, man. If this is where I think it is, maybe I can use it."

"Lemme guess. A storage spot for some kinda high-tech weapons?"

"You misjudge me. I was thinking it could be used for the frame around a ladder well. When Rusty and I first visited here, he said how cool it'd be to come down to where the boat was docked through the floor."

Carl looked back up into the heavy oak-framed recess. "It's way bigger than a stairwell, but yeah, we could use that big oak to build a strong frame. You're thinking spring-loaded steps and a pop-up trap door?"

I laughed. "Let's take some measurements. But no, I was thinking more like a regular ladder, with a rail around it up above."

"Okay, maybe you're not switching gears."

By late afternoon, the kids were back from school, playing with Pescador in the lagoon, while Carl and I enjoyed a beer on the deck, relaxing in the rockers after a hard day's work.

We'd completely removed the heavy oak planks and cut what we needed from the two smaller ones. Storing the twenty-foot planks for something else, we built an enclosure where I wanted it, using it to reinforce the floor we were going to cut away. I'd get the pipe and fittings later to build a simple ladder, descending from the back living room wall to the center pier.

A sudden vibration against my leg startled me before I realized it was my cell phone. I'd left it in my pocket all day and was surprised I hadn't lost it somewhere.

The number on the display was local, in Key West, but not one I recognized. Feeling relaxed, I answered it anyway. "McDermitt."

"Hi, Mister McDermitt," a woman's cheery voice said. "We met a year ago. My name's Dawn. Dawn McKenna."

It took a moment for me to remember. "Oh, yeah. Dawn McKenna, Nikki's friend." Carl glanced over quickly. "Um, hold on a second, will ya?"

Without waiting for an answer, I muted the call and looked over at Carl. "You know her?"

"For quite a few years. Nice lady. Makes a living as a fortuneteller and actually does have a gift for it."

I don't believe much in fortunetellers. Each of us makes our own destiny and can change it over and over. I'd only met the woman once, very briefly. A friend of Doc's wife, Nikki, she'd said she was a tarot card reader, or palm reader or something. A small and quiet woman, with light brown hair.

I clicked the mute button again. "I'm sorry, Dawn. You were saying?"

"That's right, Nikki's friend. I asked around to some people down here and your name kept coming up. Nikki mentioned you as well, and gave me your number. Hope you don't mind."

Nikki should have known better, I thought. Privacy had become more and more important to me lately and I didn't like it being interrupted or intruded upon.

But I was polite. "My name kept coming up?"

"Yeah. A friend of my niece is having a problem and asked me if I knew anyone that might be able to help him."

"Maybe he should go to the police?" I suggested.

"Well, it's kind of a sensitive matter," Dawn replied.

"Can you sum it up in a few short sentences?"

Apparently she couldn't and began to explain how her niece's boyfriend had gotten himself involved with a drug dealer from up north and now the guy was in

Key West looking for him. I was just about to tell her that people had given her the wrong impression about me and hang up, when she mentioned the drug dealer's name, GT Bradley.

CHAPTER FOURTEEN

Michal wasn't able to get much sleep. After being ordered to remove his clothes, Coral informed him that she only had one rule in life and that one rule was that she made all the rules and could change them at any time.

Standing and facing one another, naked, she explained that she never had sex on the first date, but he was welcome to stay the night as long as he remained naked.

He thought it a weird request, but if it meant he could even see her perfect little body, he'd play along. They got high on her weed and Michal asked if she'd ever tried coke. He loved the way her eyes sparkled when he mentioned it. They'd snorted a couple of lines and smoked some more weed, and then Coral suggested they play a game.

"I don't think I can concentrate on a game with you naked," Michal said.

"It's how I live. If you want to hang out, it's without clothes."

Coral went to a closet and brought out a heavy padded blanket and spread it on the floor in front of the fireplace, while Michal rolled two more joints.

Sitting with her legs tucked under her on the blanket, Coral smiled and patted the spot in front of her. "Sit here, Michal. I think you're gonna like this game." Awkward and embarrassed, Michal stood up, unable to hide his obvious excitement.

Michal's face was beet red when he sat down. "Where's the game?"

She did that thing with her hair and smiled. "We're the game, Michal. Are you embarrassed, being naked? You shouldn't be. You have a nice body. Don't worry, you'll relax after a while. I'm serious, though, about no sex. Sit on your knees like I am."

Michal knelt on the blanket and passed her one of the joints. His hands shook while lighting it for her. He then lit the other one and placed the ashtray on the blanket between them.

The dim yellow glow from the single lantern lit one side of Coral's face and body, and Michal reveled in the sight as she took a deep hit, her lungs expanding as she arched her back, lifting her small breasts.

Not gonna be any relaxing tonight, Michal thought.

Blowing the smoke toward the ceiling, Coral said, "Okay, here's the rules. We try to get as close together as possible, but not touch anywhere."

Facing each other, they'd taken turns trying to get as much of their body as close as possible to the other without making contact. They both failed miserably, ending up rolling on the floor, tickling and kissing.

"New rule," Coral said, rolling over and giggling. "Touching and kissing anywhere is okay, except the groin area."

A rule I can live with, Michal thought.

They lay on their sides facing one another and Coral traced a line down Michal's arm, while rubbing the outside of his thigh with the inside of hers. Then she reached over him for the ashtray and lighter, pushing him flat on his back.

Curling up under his arm, her head on his shoulder, Coral placed the ashtray on her flat belly. She relit both joints at once and passed one to Michal.

"Well, I guess we both lost that game," Coral said. "But hey, you got a lot further than most guys do. Very few guys like to take orders or follow my rules."

After finishing the joints, they tried the game again in the shower, but Coral's rule of no sex remained in place. She promised that the next time would be different.

After showering, they spread towels on Coral's bed and lay facedown, enjoying the tingling feeling of water droplets evaporating into the sultry night air.

Coral pulled a small framed mirror from the nightstand. "You know, there's not much coke in town right now. I'd been thinking of quitting, anyway. But since you brought it up...." She pushed the little mirror toward Michal.

Michal went to the living room and fished the vial from his pants pocket. Coral was right, he was starting to relax. *Whatever games she wants to play,* he thought, *I'm in.*

Returning to the bedroom, he found Coral lying on her side in the soft light of the full moon shining through the open window behind her. She had one knee pulled up slightly, accentuating the curve from her narrow waist, up and over her hips and thigh.

He gently lay down beside her and tapped a small amount of the white powder onto the mirror. Using a playing card that was on it, he separated the coke into two lines.

"I was thinking of quitting myself. It's fun, but very expensive. I really prefer weed. It makes me feel invisible."

"Invisible?"

"Well, it did back home, anyway. An average-looking guy, a little on the short side, no tats or scars. You know, invisible in a crowd."

She brushed his hair back off his forehead. "But here in Key Weird, you're not invisible?"

Michal laughed. "Maybe when a cruise ship ties up and discharges half of New York."

He pushed the mirror toward her and Coral rolled over to reach into the nightstand. The sight of her perfect little ass made Michal wince.

"How much of that do you have left?"

"Enough," Michal replied and left it at that.

"Okay, well, when it's gone, how about we both quit together?"

"Together?"

"Yeah, if you want to hang out for a while. I like you."

When she rolled back over, she extended her hand and gave Michal a one-hundred-dollar bill. "You first."

"Yes, ma'am," Michal replied, rolling the bill into a small tube.

"They say that every hundred-dollar bill in Florida has trace elements of coke on it."

Michal leaned over the mirror and noticed the painting on it for the first time. It was a nude of Coral, herself. The painting was on the reverse side of the glass and perfectly done. She was lying on her side, pretty much as she was now.

"Yeah, I'd like to hang out with you. But it might take a while till all this is gone." He moved the tip of the bill along one of the lines, inhaling through the other end.

"We can hang out anytime you want, Michal. I like to have fun, but very few men have been so tolerant of my rules."

Michal handed her the bill and Coral bent over the mirror, her dreads rolling forward as she did so. In a flash, the second line was gone.

"To be honest, I really don't have any direction right now, so having someone to direct me is perfect."

"You like my mirror?" she asked.

"I like it very much. Must have cost a lot to have made."

Coral put the bill on the mirror and placed it on the nightstand, then lay flat on her back, shivering and sniffing. "No, it didn't cost anything. A girl I know painted it."

"A girl?"

Coral scooted her body over toward him. Pulling his arm around her neck and draping it over her shoulder, she placed his palm on her right breast and snuggled even closer.

"Yeah, a girl. Does that bother you?"

Michal laughed. "No, not even a little bit."

Coral reached out and pulled him toward her, kissing him passionately. While her hand explored his body, he gently massaged her breast. But her hand never strayed beyond his belly, so Michal kept his above the waist as well.

He returned the kiss, arching his back and pressing himself against her thigh, his excitement once again undeniable. Pushing him away a moment, she said, "You're making it hard for me to follow my own rules."

So Michal went to the living room and got Coral's stash and rolled another joint, sharing it this time, while slowly caressing one another's bodies. Rolling back onto the soft fluffy pillows, Michal asked her about her past.

Coral then told him her story about having been what she called a trophy wife to an older man. A sadistic man, who enjoyed inflicting pain, both physically and mentally. When she'd finally had enough, she contacted her only living relative, an aunt living in Key West.

Her aunt told her to get her ass down here any way she could and not leave a trail. Coral drugged her husband that night and while he slept, she went online and transferred half the amount held in their joint checking and savings accounts to a new account she'd set up in her name only. Her aunt had given her the number to an offshore account she owned in the Cayman Islands, and Coral then moved all the money from the new account into her aunt's offshore one.

Within an hour of doing that, Coral received two emails, one from her aunt and the other from the Cayman bank, thanking her for opening her new account. Her aunt said she'd created the account for her, and then moved all of Coral's money into it.

Before her husband woke the next morning, Coral had taken one suitcase with just a few clothes and disappeared. Arriving in Key West, later that evening, her aunt took her to a lawyer friend and Coral changed her name, having the record of it sealed.

"So, that's why I make the rules. Anyone who doesn't want to follow my rules doesn't have to, but they also don't get anything else from me. I'll never go back to that kind of life."

The combination of drugs had heightened and dulled Michal's senses and level of excitement. But with a beautiful, naked woman within arm's reach the whole night, he was always at a higher-than-usual level. His senses were heightened by the coke, and with the calming effect the weed had, he felt very relaxed, almost harmonic. His earlier assessment of the weed seemed off, or maybe it was Coral herself.

Without thinking, Michal then told her his own story about growing up in a tough neighborhood, losing his mom at a young age and recently losing his dad. He ended the story by telling her how he stole the pound of coke, and about the long bus ride to Key West.

He wasn't sure why, but he just kept talking, telling Coral how he needed to unload the coke in a hurry, but still make enough money on it so he could survive for a while.

Coral had listened patiently, and when he'd finished and turned to look at her, he was sure she'd kick him out. Instead, she said she had an idea.

"We'll go see my aunt. She's a mystic."

"I don't need a mystic. I need a buyer."

"Oh, that part's easy. Like I said, the island's dry. I'm sure I know at least a few people who would pay top dollar. That's some really good toot."

"So, why do we need to see a mystic?"

"Just trust me," Coral said, rolling into his embrace and smiling seductively in the soft moonlight. "She reads for me every week. Just last weekend, she told me you'd be arriving. Maybe after we see Aunt Dawn, we can go out on that second date. Tomorrow's my day off."

CHAPTER FIFTEEN

H e's still here," GT told Erik after ending another phone call from Stewie. "At a place called the *Half Shell Raw Bar*, about twenty minutes ago."

They'd spent the last hour ducking into one bar after another and hadn't gone but about three blocks on Duval Street. GT saw more than a few women who looked like hookers. But no sign of the ugly little man. The call from Stewie was their first solid lead in hours.

"A lot of bars and restaurants here," Erik said. "I don't remember seeing one by that name."

Grabbing a guy that was walking by, GT said, "Where's the Half Shell Raw Bar, man?"

The guy looked like a local. However, just like half the women in this town seemed to look like prostitutes, it was hard to tell.

"Relax, man," the guy said. "This is Key West, no need to get all weirded out. The Half Shell is a couple blocks north on Caroline Street."

"This way, boss," Erik said, pointing up Duval to the end where the crowd had been at sunset.

GT shoved the guy away and proceeded up the sidewalk at a quickened pace. They were close and he knew it. A few minutes later, having turned north on Caroline, GT saw the girl in the yellow dress again, crossing the street two blocks ahead.

A waitress at the restaurant remembered the guy with Grabowski's card, her memory being jogged with yet another twenty from GT's pocket.

"Lousy tipper and uglier than homemade sin."

"Know where he went from here?" GT asked the girl.

"How would I know? I'm not a travel agent. But the chick he was with, I've seen her around. A prostitute. They probably went to her place."

Erik stole a quick glance at the waitress's name tag and gave her his most sincere smile. "I bet there's not much chance a girl like you would know where that might be, is there, Karly?"

Though they looked enough alike to be brothers, their personalities were polar opposite. Where GT was edgy and hyped nearly all the time, Erik was smooth and mellow.

Karly couldn't help but smile back at the big man, "Not exactly, no. Stock Island is the best I can tell you. I know she's from up island a ways, Key Largo or Islamorada. Started smoking crack a year ago and now she sells her body for the stuff."

"Thanks, Karly."

"They went out the back door, if that helps. Nothing there but the boat docks."

Both men glanced out the long row of windows. Erik looked back at Karly and said, "Yeah, it does." He slipped ten dollars from his own pocket and handed it to the girl. "To make up for the lousy tipper."

"Thanks," she said, then nervously added, "I get off at midnight if you wanna get a drink or something."

Erik smiled. "Yeah, I might be thirsty around midnight."

"You didn't have to give her more money," GT said when they stepped out the back door and looked up and down the dock area. "She'd already told us what she knew."

Erik grinned. "I might wanna come back here later. You know, if we end up spending the night."

"They left here half an hour ago. Let's split up again." GT pointed to the right end of the long dock, with even longer piers sticking out into the little harbor. "You go that way and I'll go the other. Circle around the block and we'll meet in the parking lot out front. Text or call if you see him."

Without waiting for an answer, GT turned and started down the long dock. The first two piers he came to had gates in front of them with signs saying they were off limits to anyone but residents. Beyond the gates, a number of boats were lit up and he could hear music coming from a couple.

Residents only? GT thought. *They're boats, not houses.*

Moving on to the next pier, it looked more like a gas dock. He went out on it anyway. There was a small shack at the end where two people could hide behind.

The girl with the ugly guy being a prostitute told GT that they'd go to a secluded place, not her house. Street whores were cheap and drugs were expensive. They had to make up for in volume, what the call girls GT paid got for a single date. So, they'd go someplace close. Someplace quick.

Finding nobody behind the dockmaster's shack, GT moved quickly back to the main dock. The next pier only had a handful of boats tied up and he didn't see any place on the pier where a person could hide, but he walked out just the same. Any one of the boats, all of which were dark, could be used for a quickie.

One by one GT searched the piers, catching an occasional glimpse of Erik doing the same, working the north end. Reaching the end, where the marina office was located and still open, he marveled at the size of the huge sailboats taking up two entire piers, their masts soaring far above the other smaller sailboats.

Turning inland, GT walked the nearly empty block toward Caroline Street, angling through a large parking lot on the corner. He scanned the shadowy places between the parked cars, knowing that street whores liked parking lots. When his phone vibrated in his pocket, he pulled it out and read the text from Erik, then immediately called him.

"I'm headed your way. Follow the guy."

Walking at a brisk pace with the phone to his ear, he followed Erik's running dialogue. This wasn't the first time they'd had to chase someone down in a busy city. *Hell*, GT thought, *this is easy compared to Pittsburgh.*

Out of nowhere, a guy stumbled onto the sidewalk and nearly collided with GT. The big black man stopped in his tracks. The guy in front of him couldn't be more than five three, with stringy dark hair, a crooked nose and old acne scars all over his face and neck.

"You!" GT roared, nearly taking the guy's head off with a sharp right cross. Erik came up behind the little man and managed to grab him from behind before the guy hit the ground, then stood holding him up under the shoulders.

"Take him down that alley and then go get the car," GT ordered.

Dragging the limp little man into the alley, Erik deposited him next to a dumpster, then bent to check his pulse. "Out cold, boss. The car's a coupla blocks away. It'll take me a few minutes."

"Go, I'll stay here with him."

"He won't be able to tell us anything if you hurt him more, boss."

GT turned and glowered at his employee, the rage barely contained behind his dark eyes. "You just go get the fucking car and get back here."

Erik took off at a jog, not wanting to anger his boss any further. GT paced the alley entrance for a few minutes. When he was sure nobody was around, he entered the alley and looked down at the little man on the ground. Drawing his foot back, GT kicked him hard in the meaty part of the thigh with the toe of his shoe.

The pain shot through Byers's body, waking him with a muffled groan. As he reached down to his injured thigh. GT knelt beside him. "Good, you're awake."

Looking into the big man's eyes, Byers realized he was in really big trouble. "Why'd you punch me, man? I didn't do nothing to you."

"You know something I want to know, you little turd fondler. And you're gonna tell me what it is. If you lie, you're gonna get hurt real bad."

A revolting smell drifted up and GT realized it wasn't the putrid garbage in the dumpster. The guy had just shit his pants.

"I'll tell you anything you want to know, man. Just don't hurt me anymore."

"You've been using a credit card that belongs to a guy by the name of Grabowski."

"In my pocket, man. Take it. I'm sorry." Byers thought for sure that this hulking black guy must work for the coke dealer.

"I ain't reaching in your nasty pants, asshole! Don't want the card, anyway. Keep it. I want Grabowski. Where'd you get his card?"

"At the Miami bus station, man," Byers replied, somewhat confused. "I lifted his wallet in a crowd."

"You picked Grabowski's pocket in Miami?" GT roared, realizing that he and Erik had not only been following the wrong guy, but were over a hundred miles from where Grabowski and the card had gotten separated. To make matters worse, the city where the split had happened was one of the biggest in all of Florida.

GT stood up as the big Escalade stopped at the alley corner. He was very tempted to just stomp the man's head until it cracked open like a ripe watermelon.

Byers lay trembling on the ground at the big man's feet. He realized suddenly that the guy didn't work for the coke dealer he'd robbed at all. He was looking for him.

Byers often traded information for drugs, money, or food. He remembered things and traded little scraps of information to the cops, to dealers, to pimps, anybody who didn't have that one particular scrap of information which he held. Information was valuable. Whether it was true or not didn't matter. A lot of times lies were much easier to sell.

Byers knew he had an ace in the hole and played it. "Yeah, but he's here, man. He's right here in Key West."

CHAPTER SIXTEEN

*W*hy do I let shit like this bother me? I thought, lying awake in the forward stateroom of the *Revenge*. The dock area has shore power, and the boats were connected to the island's main power source. I'd just never felt the need to connect the house. Until this summer. And tonight was one of those nights. The disappearance of the sun did nothing to squelch the heat and humidity.

The wind here is nearly always from the eastern quadrant, and there are few completely calm days. They're so predictable and constant that early mariners called them "trade winds." They learned that sailing south out of Spain to lower latitudes, then turning due west was usually faster than sailing a direct route to the southwest. These huge ships carried trade goods to and from the islands of the Caribbean, and the size of a captain's purse was measured by his ship's speed.

Now and then, we get a night like this, the air completely still and miserably hot. Sitting high above the water, my house remained a little cooler most of the time, even on nights like this. But the Trents' house sits lower and on the lee side of the island. While the slightest shift in the atmosphere brings fresh air over the banyans and mangroves and through the windows of my house, the Trents' house is blocked by the rest of the island and the tree canopy that keeps it cool during the day. Charlie insisted that the view of the setting sun from their front porch was worth it. Until last night, and tonight was hotter.

Simple enough to remedy, when you live like we do here on the island. The Trents crash in my house and I come down to the boat and switch on the air conditioning. Unable to sleep, I got up and went to the salon, the low hum of the air conditioner sounding strange to my ears, but a necessary distraction. When the boat's closed up, it gets really hot inside.

My boat is the second to carry the name *Gaspar's Revenge*. Nearly identical to the first, this one has a dark blue hull all the way up to the gunwale and quite a few improvements over the original, which had a number of non-factory upgrades itself.

Unable to sleep, I padded into the salon, wearing only my boxers. Between Jimmy and Chyrel, my boat was a floating data center. I'd been secretly learning my way around the Internet, always surprised at the amount of information that was available. Jimmy had set up the hardware, turning my boat into what he called a "hotspot." When the modem is turned on, my laptop and even my phone connect to it without any wires. The modem is connected to the Internet through a satellite link. A small dome on the roof picks up a signal from a communications satellite in space and my charter business has an account with a satellite Internet service provider.

Knowing from experience how easily these things can be tracked, I leave most electronic devices turned off unless I'm underway. When I want to know something, it's simply a matter of opening my laptop, which automatically turns on the modem. Powering up the laptop, it took only a few seconds before my cell phone, which I'd forgotten to power off and was sitting on the settee, vibrated after connecting to the modem and the screen on the laptop came to life.

For nearly an hour, I dug into Mister Gerald Tremont "GT" Bradley's background. He actually had a page on Wikipedia, but I'd learned not to put too much stock in that. The websites I visited spoke of a troubled childhood and adolescence. Yet he'd managed to get a full-ride athletic scholarship at Pennsylvania State University. His off-the-field antics had gotten him in trouble with the law more than once, but that hadn't stopped the Pittsburgh Steelers from drafting him in the first round as a linebacker in '96.

He'd suffered a career-ending knee fracture in a game against the Miami Dolphins eight years ago. Everything since then was mostly arrest records and newspaper headlines about the arrests. It looked like he'd quickly replaced his exorbitant NFL income with a pretty good illegal drug profit, building a small empire among the middle class in the Pittsburgh area. Not one of the charges stuck, but he'd been investigated nine ways to Sunday on everything from extortion to trafficking, even murder.

Opening another, very recent, news website, I thought, *Okay, so he's a shit-bird. None of my business.* Or as Sergeant Russ Livingston used to say, "Not my circus. Not my monkeys."

But it was my circus. My friend and her family had been exposed to a world far from the idyllic one she and Carl wanted their kids to grow up in when the ugly guy had tried to sell her crack cocaine. Then the near-violent altercation when GT had arrived and asked about the pusher.

My monkeys, too, I thought, looking at a close-up picture of GT Bradley and his chauffeur, Erik Lowery. They were coming out of a federal courthouse in Pittsburgh with his accountant, who had gotten Bradley off of a tax-dodging charge on a technicality.

An icon on the bottom of my laptop screen flashed. I had an incoming instant message. When I clicked on it, a small window opened, a picture of Chyrel above a message that read, "Not a good guy."

Below the message was an icon for a camera and I clicked on it. The window expanded, Chyrel's picture being replaced with a live video feed.

The background was different, though. She wasn't in her office in Homestead. It looked more like a house or an apartment. The background in her office is a bare white wall that doesn't give anything away as to time or location. Behind her now was a window and through the drapes, streetlights shone.

"The DHS snooping on me again?" I asked.

"Nope," Chyrel replied, unperturbed. "I'm on my home computer, my own connection. With some people, I keep an instant message box open, and it tells me when they're online. What's the interest in the Pittsburgh coke dealer?"

"Deuce tell you to monitor my Internet activity?"

"No, Jesse. In fact he told everyone on the team that, until you and he iron out the problem you're having, we're not supposed to have any professional contact with you."

"So why are you snooping on what I'm looking at?"

"You're my friend, Jesse. I look out for my friends. And I wasn't actually snooping. Well, yeah, I guess I was, but only if you used certain search words that might get you in trouble."

Exasperated, I realized that it was well past midnight. "What are you doing up this late, anyway?"

"Late? It's not even one o'clock. I never go to bed before three. So, is this Bradley guy a threat to national security? I can't help you if he is. That'd be breaking Deuce's rules."

"Purely PerSec," I replied, meaning it had to do with personal security, which it did. In a way.

"In that case, I wouldn't be violating Deuce's rules. Can I help you with something? This poor football player ruffle someone's feathers in the Keys?"

"What do you mean *poor* football player?"

"He's on your radar, right? That can't be good for his health."

A plan started formulating in my mind. Chyrel could run circles around most computer hackers and was leaps and bounds ahead of me. "Maybe there is something you can help me with."

"Just name it," Chyrel eagerly responded, hunching forward over the keyboard.

"Can you create a fake background for me?" Chyrel cocked her head and lifted an eyebrow. "Never mind, of course you can."

"Who do you want to be?" she asked.

"Stretch Buchannan. Make me a big-time cocaine importer, with ties to a Cuban cartel. Throw in a few arrests, trafficking, attempted murder, that kind of stuff."

Her fingers were already flying on the keyboard. "I'll have it in a couple of hours. It won't withstand scrutiny by the CIA or FBI, but I can make it deep enough to fool local LEOs and any bad guys that look you up on the web—some postdated news reports, stuff like that."

"That'll be a big help. Thanks."

"I'll email you the dossier. You'll have it before sunrise." She stopped typing for a minute and looked at the screen. "Deuce isn't involved, Jesse."

Trying to look unconcerned, I asked, "Involved in what?"

Chyrel grinned. "You and I need to play poker someday. I'd like living on that big, fancy boat of yours."

I was starting to feel tired and sighed. "Where's he at with the investigation into Charity's disappearance?"

"I'd be breaking the rules if I could answer that question. But, since there is no ongoing investigation, I can't."

"That doesn't strike you as odd?"

She stopped typing again and leaned in closer to the screen, as if worried someone would hear. "Deuce is the *acting* deputy director, remember?"

"Yeah, so?"

"His name hasn't been submitted to Congress for approval to take over as the formal deputy director, nor has anyone else's."

"You mean…"

"I don't mean anything. We're not even having this discussion. But I'll tell you this. There are things only a deputy director can do, and some of those things, an *acting* deputy director can't do. As far as no ongoing investigation striking me as odd goes, keep in mind who I used to work for. I'm very good at ignoring stuff that's above my paygrade."

I sat back in my seat, searching her face for a clue. *Damn, I hate this spy-versus-spy crap*, I thought. Then it hit me. "Stockwell's still in control?"

"I'll send you the file shortly, Jesse. Oh, and I already located Bradley. He just used an Amex card and checked into the Hyatt in Key West. It was good talking to you. Bye."

The screen went blank and I was left staring at the image of Bradley, his driver and his accountant. I'd recognized the face of the accountant instantly. With so many government alphabet agencies looking for him, I thought it was odd that Chase Conner had let his picture be taken by a reporter.

Sitting back once more, I closed the laptop and ran this new revelation around in my head. Stockwell had retired just a few days after Charity disappeared this past spring. He'd come to work for me soon after that and it'd worked out pretty good for the most part. We didn't charter very much, but with neither of us needing the money, we didn't need to.

It occurred to me that he hadn't talked much about leaving the job with Charity's disappearance hanging over him. I know that after a lifetime of service, with all his accomplishments, something like that had to be bothersome. There's no way I could just up and walk away from it.

Then there's the fact that Deuce wasn't even pursuing an investigation. That, coupled with what Chyrel had intimated about Deuce not actually being in control, meant that he had been ordered to look the other way. Deuce is the kind of guy that follows orders. Especially those with national security implications. He'd put the mission above all else, even friendship.

Was Chyrel really reaching out to me on her own? I wondered. *Or is this Deuce's way of extending an olive branch?*

I switched off the lights in the salon and made my way down to my stateroom, just as the generator kicked on. Lying on my bunk, I thought about the more immediate concern. I'd told the psychic lady that I'd meet with her at noon tomorrow. She'd given me an address just off the middle of Duval Street in Key West.

If Bradley was at the Hyatt, I could dock there, or if they were full, Key West Bight had plenty of dock space. I decided I'd leave at the first rays of dawn and maybe do some recon around the Hyatt. I had to figure out a way to get Bradley to think I might be his ticket to a big import contract and hopefully get him to bring his accountant down here.

Chase Conner used to work for Florida Department of Revenue. He had been on hand, representing the state in the sale of a bunch of gold bars recovered from a Confederate blockade runner. The bars were being sold to the Florida History Museum, and Conner was to ensure a proper accounting for taxes. The sale went off without a hitch, but he'd planted a bug on my boat in the hopes of getting a tip on other treasures.

I'm not a treasure hunter. Deuce's dad, Russ was and Rusty's a licensed salvor. A few opportunities had presented themselves over the years and we'd found treasure. It's out there. Conner had learned about the most recent find and enlisted the help of a Croatian crime boss in Miami. My son-in-law and his father handled legal matters for the Croat and they'd become involved, sending mercenaries to take the treasure. Several people had died and Doc had taken a bullet meant for me. Then there was the matter of my boat being blown out of the water. Yeah, I needed to talk to Chase Conner.

Stretching out across my bunk, I reached over and switched off the bedside light, when the generator shut down. With only the A/C running, the batteries would hold a charge for about three hours before it came back on. I stored that information in my mind so it wouldn't wake me when it did, and within minutes I was fast asleep.

CHAPTER SEVENTEEN

Erik shoved Byers through the hotel room door at the Hyatt, causing him to stumble and fall to the floor. "Get your stinking ass in there and get cleaned up. You smell like shit."

The Hyatt wasn't just the nearest hotel to where they'd found the little man, but one of the best on the island. It reflected GT's personality. Only the best.

Byers scrambled up from the floor and disappeared into the bathroom. Erik turned to his boss. "His clothes gotta go, GT. I swear he smells like he's been sleeping in them in a cesspool for a month. It's gonna take me hours to get the smell outta the car."

GT pulled a roll of bills from his pocket and gave Erik a hundred bucks. "I saw a T-shirt shop over near that restaurant. Go see what you can scrounge up."

Erik stuffed the bills in his pocket and strode to the door. "I'll get what I can, and when I get back, I'll go see if

I can find a carwash with a vacuum. Maybe an air freshener. Man, that guy really stinks."

GT sat heavily in a recliner. "Yeah, he shit his pants back there in the alley."

Closing the door, Erik smiled. *Maybe I'll go over to that restaurant after I get the car cleaned*, he thought.

Sitting back in the comfortable recliner, GT mentally calculated what this foray had cost him already. They'd spent nearly five thousand in bribes, gas, food, and hotel rooms. If Grabowski was here in town, he knew he had to find him and fast, before he sold off all the coke. *Find him and kill his ass slow*, GT thought. *Then we can get the hell off this rock baking in the tropical heat.*

In the bathroom, Byers stripped out of his soiled clothes, dumping his feces in the toilet. He turned on the shower and stepped in to clean himself and his clothes for the second time in one day.

He knew something the two black guys didn't know. He'd seen the coke dealer, Grabowski, coming out of *Irish Kevin's* bar earlier. After leaving the pier, he'd spotted the guy again, in the same restaurant he and the hooker had eaten at. Hurrying past, he'd circled the place, hiding in the shadows, where he could watch him without being seen. When Grabowski had left, he'd quickly returned to the parking lot to follow them and run into these two guys.

How they'd missed seeing Grabowski he couldn't figure out, unless they were just too busy checking out the girl with dreadlocks in the little yellow dress. He'd decided she wasn't a hooker after all. She was Grabowski's girlfriend. *And these two guys don't seem to know anything about her*, he thought. *I'll just hang on to that bit of infor-mation. Might need it for a bargaining chip.*

After scrubbing his clothes, Byers hung them over the shower's curtain rod to dry a little. Five minutes later, as he was just getting out of the shower, his captor banged hard on the door.

"Toss those nasty-ass clothes in the trash and get your ass out here," GT growled.

Byers shrugged. It wouldn't be the first time he'd given up his ass to save his ass. If these guys were gay, he could play the part well enough to get free. It wouldn't be the first time. He'd hang on to that one bargaining chip for when he needed it.

It hadn't taken Erik long to find clothes. As GT turned away from the bathroom door, Erik walked in. "Had to buy clothes in the boy's section, boss. Nothing in the men's clothes would fit that little twerp."

"Whatever," GT replied, pacing the floor. "Get him out here and give him the clothes."

Just then, Byers opened the bathroom door and stepped out, completely naked and resigned to his fate. He just hoped the rumors about black guys weren't true.

Erik looked at him and couldn't help a chuckle. "No wonder the hooker was laughing at him." He tossed the bag at the little man, and it hit him in the chest and al-most knocked him over. "Get back in there and put those on, asshole. We don't wanna see that pathetic excuse for a dick."

After Byers went back into the bathroom, GT sat down in the corner at the small table. "We gotta find Grabows-ki and fast, Erik. That clown knows something. If I have to, I'll beat it out of him."

"If he's here in town, we'll find him. Just a matter of time, boss. Ya know, we didn't even think of asking that waitress if she'd seen him. Waitresses and bartenders see everyone. Too bad we don't have a picture. We coulda been showing it around to all the waitresses and bartenders."

"Go get the car cleaned up, Erik. Then stop by that restaurant the little guy ate at. That waitress likes you. Maybe if she saw the guy, she'll open up to you. If not, we can ask around a few places tomorrow."

"What about the little prick?" Erik whispered, nodding toward the bathroom and grinning at his own joke.

GT reached into his pocket and handed Erik several hundred-dollar bills. "Can you camp out tonight? Me and that little turd fondler are gonna get acquainted."

Erik tried to suppress a smile. "Sure, boss, I can always find a place to crash so you can work."

Erik knew GT preferred to handle dirty work in private. He didn't fully trust anyone, not even Erik. When he'd first started working for GT several years earlier, Erik had taken it personally. Now, he realized it was just one of his boss's weird ways. Not the only one, either. The guy didn't get physical with people when they didn't answer his questions. He'd beat the guy into submission and *then* start asking.

GT jerked a thumb toward the bathroom. "I'm sure he knows something more. From the look of his face, it's a sure thing he's had a few beatdowns. I might have to change tactics, if he survives the one coming. Who knows, having a sewer rat to ferret out information might come in handy. If not, I'll dump his body in the water later tonight. Pick me up here at eight, ready to work. And if you can, find us some fucking guns."

As Erik nodded and opened the door to go back out, Byers came out of the bathroom, wearing a pair of blue jean shorts that hung to his knees and a kids' Mickey Mouse T-shirt.

Under the table, GT shoved the opposite chair out with his foot. "Sit down. We're going to talk, and if you lie to me, I'll know it and knock one of your teeth out for every lie."

Erik closed the door, knowing that the little weasel was going to experience some real pain, the mood his boss was in. At the concierge desk, he got directions to an all-night detail shop and within an hour, the horrible odor was gone from the car, replaced by a nice tropical scent.

With four hundred bucks in his pocket and eight hours to kill, Erik pulled the white Escalade into the parking lot of the Half Shell Raw Bar. Glancing at the clock in the dash, he noted that it was a few minutes past midnight and hoped he hadn't missed her. Maneuvering the big SUV through the lot, Erik circled around to the main door. When he stopped, Karly was walking out with another woman.

Erik climbed out of the car and Karly saw him. She turned to her friend and said something, then the two parted and Karly walked toward the big car, smiling. Erik hurried around the hood and opened the door for her with a big smile on his face, too.

Before she climbed in, she looked up at the tall black man. "I don't even know your name."

CHAPTER EIGHTEEN

When the smell of coffee woke me, I headed straight to the laptop, with only a thirty-second pause at the counter to pour a mug of La Minita's finest. I sat down and opened the computer, taking my first sip. Ever since I was a kid, I've always liked the taste of coffee. Until recently, it'd always been whatever's on the shelf at the grocery store. I never realized there were a lot better coffees out there.

Rusty had found this brew a few months ago and I made sure to get my order to him every two weeks since then. The distributor had even sent him a book about the farm in Costa Rica. *It'd be a great place to visit someday*, I thought while enjoying the deep, rich flavor.

Sure enough, I had an email from Chyrel in my inbox. I opened it and saw that there was a file attached. While the file downloaded, I read Chyrel's message.

Stretch,

You might want to print the attached file and study it. The background is pretty extensive and it goes back over four years.

Chyrel

Sending the file to the printer, I reached over to the entertainment center console and switched on the NOAA channel on the VHF radio to get the update on the day's forecast. I was planning to take the Cigarette boat, since it draws the attention of the kind of people I'd be looking for.

The forecast wasn't what I was hoping for. The same stagnant, hot air that had been hanging over us for days was going to get shoved out of the way by a fast-moving line of storms in the afternoon. Fast-moving as they advanced to the north, the digitized voice repeated, but the line was moving slowly east, so we were going to have stormy weather most of the evening and night.

The trip down to Key West would be easy, but coming back in the Cigarette would be treacherous, with seas forecast to six feet in the Gulf.

I switched the radio to scan to catch some cross talk from boats out on the Gulf and considered calling Dawn McKenna to cancel, but Conner's smug face invaded my consciousness. I'd keep the appointment and just take the *Revenge* instead. She'd have no trouble in the big swells.

Which means I need to get underway most riki tik.

While I filled a thermos, I made a quick phone call using the sat-phone, then I shoved the papers I'd printed into a folder and carried them out to the cockpit. Above,

I could hear the kids talking away and someone moving around in the kitchen.

The engines started instantly, settling into a low burble. I placed the folder and thermos in the second seat and clicked the key fob to open the big doors in front of my boat. Quickly removing the covers from the instruments and electronics, I stored them away and looked over the panel. All the gauges were reading normal ranges, so I went down to cast off.

The hatch to the pier opened and Carl stepped into the dock area. "I figured you'd just cancel, what with the weather coming up. Taking the *Revenge* instead?"

"Yeah, she hasn't had a chance to stretch her legs in a while. Something else came up, Carl. There's a chance I may stay the night. But I'll be back before noon."

"I can come along, if you need a hand. What came up?"

He wasn't offering to be polite. I'd talked to him about what I was going to do after I got off the phone with Dawn. "Remember me telling you about the government guy that was involved in that cluster fuck on Elbow Cay? Chase Conner?"

He nodded, and as I untied the stern line, I continued, "I came across a news headline about Bradley last night. You'll never guess who his accountant is."

"Conner? Is he down here, too?"

"I doubt it, but I'm going to try to find a way to either locate him for the authorities or, better still, get Bradley to bring him down here."

"Then you'll need help. I'll grab my bag."

I stopped him as he started to turn, and Pescador passed by him, coming in. "No, Carl. I got it covered. I woke Travis up and he's meeting me at Old Wooden Bridge."

Carl stopped and turned around, the disappointment evident in his face as I went past them toward the bow line. I knew he missed the challenge and adventure that went along with his old job as a shrimp boat skipper, but with a wife and two little kids, he was better off without the excitement.

"Be careful, Jesse. You should take the dog. There's been a rash of boat break-ins down there."

Dropping back down into the cockpit, I said, "I was planning to. You know me, always careful."

Pescador sat by Carl's feet, looking up at me like he was waiting for a bone. "Wanna go to Key Weird, buddy?"

Pescador barked once and I nodded to him. He instantly vaulted the gunwale, landing easily on the cockpit deck, before lying down in his usual spot by the transom hatch.

As I climbed up to the bridge, Carl said, "Yeah, I know you. Careful, most of the time. Just keep your head down those other times, huh?"

I nodded as I engaged the transmissions and slowly idled out from under my house. Once clear of the big doors, I clicked the lock button on the key fob, and they slowly started closing on big spring-loaded hinges.

Turning out of my little channel, I headed northeast in Harbor Channel and pushed the throttles halfway up. The stern of the *Revenge* dropped down as the big props pushed the water out from beneath the hull. A moment later, she was up on plane and I made for the light at Harbor Key Bank.

Before reaching the bank, I slowed and made the turn almost due south into Spanish Harbor Channel at marker fifty-three. Easing the throttles back up to thirty-five knots, I made it to the mouth of Bogie Channel between Big Pine and No Name Keys in just a few minutes.

Travis hadn't sounded too enthused about going to Key West, but when I offered his regular charter day rate, he didn't really have much choice. I wanted to feel him out, with the information I'd received from Chyrel, about what was going on with Charity Styles's disappearance. Or more to the point, the lack of information.

I slowly brought the *Revenge* down off plane as I drew near the markers for the entrance to Bogie Channel, and the big engines settled into a quiet burbling idle, magnified as I went under the bridge crossing over to No Name Key. Approaching the entrance to the marina, I saw Travis pulling into the parking lot in his black Ford Expedition. Mentally, I whacked myself on the head, seeing the big SUV. *What the hell kind of retired guy tools around in something like that?*

Just as I bumped the fuel dock, Pescador lifted his big, shaggy head and barked a greeting as Travis stepped aboard. I reversed the port engine, spinning the *Revenge* away from the dock and turning back toward the entrance.

Quickly stowing his go-bag in the salon, Travis came up the ladder to the bridge. "What the hell's going on down in Key West that you gotta drop everything and go down there all of a sudden?"

"Just meeting someone. Might be an overnighter. Glad you brought your bag."

He sat down in the second seat and looked at me curiously. "Come on, Jesse. You don't need me along just to visit someone in Key West. What gives?"

I gave him the Reader's Digest version of what happened at the *Anchor* and my conversation with Dawn McKenna, leaving out the detail about Chase Conner and my as-yet-unknown fake identity.

"What makes you think you can do anything to help this kid and why would you even want to help someone who ripped off a coke dealer in the first place?"

As I turned back into Bogie Channel, I brought the *Revenge* up on plane as I gave the question some thought. I really didn't know if I could be of any help and I damned sure didn't know why I'd want to, outside of the unfinished business with Conner. I steered southeast into Spanish Harbor, with the two bridges spanning the narrow channel between Scout Key and Big Pine Key. The furthest one is the new span that US-1 travels on, and the nearer one is the old arch-style causeway originally built nearly a century ago by Henry Flagler for his railroad. A section had been removed from both ends, creating fishing piers. After the great hurricane of 1935, which decimated the Keys, killing hundreds of people, Flagler's railroad went belly up and the right of way was given to the Overseas Road and Toll Bridge District to turn it into a highway for cars. The new span was built in 1982.

Once we cleared the bridges, I pushed the throttles up to forty knots and started a wide, sweeping turn to the southwest. "I don't know that I can help him," I finally replied. "But last night I looked up this Bradley guy on the Internet and saw a picture of him with someone else. His accountant, a guy named Chase Conner."

Travis scratched the side of his face, thinking. "I know I've heard the name. How do I know him?"

"You don't, but I do. Deuce may have mentioned him to you. He was the guy that bugged my boat last year and put everything into motion that cost a lot of people their lives and ended up with Doc taking a bullet in the back protecting me, not to mention getting my boat blown up."

"Ah, so you're seeking retribution."

Now was the time to test his poker face. "Yeah, something like that. If the opportunity arises. I'm going to pretend to be a big-time drug dealer, shake the trees and see what kind of rats fall out. I had Chyrel create a phony identity for me."

His expression remained unchanged. "When did you speak to her? How's she doing?"

"I videoconferenced with her last night. She was at home in Homestead. Seems to be doing okay."

We rode in silence for several minutes, then I remembered the file that I needed to read. "Take the wheel, Travis. I gotta learn who I am."

We switched seats and I put my feet up on the console, opened the file and started to read. Though he tried not to be obvious, I could tell Travis was curious. I just let him think and surmise what he wanted about my conversation with Chyrel. Usually, people will come to all kinds of conclusions, if given the time to stew on something.

Closing the folder for a moment, I said, "While we're down there, I'll be Stretch Buchannan, a medium-level cocaine distributor out of Key Largo. You're my bodyguard and we're down there to check out someone nosing into my distribution territory."

"This GT Bradley?"

I opened the file and continued reading. I hadn't mentioned Bradley's first name. *So,* I thought, *he is still tied in with the DHS.* That meant either he'd had someone else monitoring my Internet searches, or Chyrel had reconsidered and told him about it this morning. I had no doubt that my conversation with her was through a hack-proof encryption. She wouldn't have said anything if there was the slightest chance the communication could have been intercepted.

I handed him the printout of Bradley's picture. "That's Bradley on the left and his chauffeur, Erik Lowery. The guy behind them is Chase Conner."

"You sure? His face is only partly in the picture and a little out of focus."

"It's him," I replied.

"And he's in Key West, too?"

"No, I don't think so. But if I can swing it, it'd sure be nice to find out exactly where he is."

Travis looked straight ahead, glancing at the photo to commit it to memory and thinking while I continued to read the dossier. Chyrel was good. The background included all kinds of made-up details, with just enough truth to make it easy to remember. The physical description was excellent, down to the location and types of tattoos and scars.

Finally, Travis broke the silence. "I still don't understand why you wanted me along."

He'd finished stewing, time to just let him have it and gauge his reaction. "My relationship with Deuce goes back a long way. I've known the guy since he was a kid. His dad and I were friends."

Stockwell glanced over at me, holding my gaze. At first his eyes were intense, as if I'd struck a nerve. Then they went calm again. "You've totally lost me now, Jesse."

Yeah, right.

"Deuce was raised by a Marine, and he's a SEAL. There's more honor in that man than anyone else I know, Colonel."

I hadn't called him that since he'd stepped down from his position with the DHS—if indeed he ever had. It had the desired effect. His jaw muscles contracted as he stared straight ahead.

"What exactly did you and Miss Koshinski talk about last night?"

The bait's been taken, time to set the hook.

"Her orders were clear," I replied. "You don't have to worry, she's a team player all the way. But I don't like being lied to, especially by people I consider a friend."

His voice took on a serious tone, not that of the Travis Stockwell I'd hired as a casual first mate, but that of the former Army Airborne Colonel, assigned to Homeland Security to try to clean up a growing terrorist threat in the Caribbean.

"Above your paygrade, Jesse."

"Switch seats," I said as I stood up and put the file in one of the upper cabinets.

He obliged and once I was back at the helm, I slowly pulled back on the throttles, bringing the *Revenge* down to idle speed. We were still inside the reef line, just west of American Shoal, but a good three miles from shore.

Turning to Travis, I studied the side of his face. "Bullshit, Colonel. I haven't had a paygrade in over eight years now. I don't give a hairy rat's ass whose idea it was, but making Deuce lie to his friends goes completely contrary to his sense of honor. You can spout national security all you want, but I know it's about control, and you're not the controlling type. However, Deuce would never jeopardize the security of this country, and if he were ordered not to divulge something, he wouldn't. That forces him to lie, which is so against his nature, he'd alienate himself from his friends, pretty much like he's doing now. Tell me I'm off base."

Travis looked starboard, toward the distant shore. "Chyrel's good. No doubt she picked up some intel she wasn't supposed to and passed it on to you. That's not good."

So, it wasn't her, I thought, very much relieved. "Chyrel's one of the good ones. If it's even implied that something should be kept secret, she wouldn't spill. She told me straight up she wasn't allowed to talk to me about anything job related. Just because I'm a grunt doesn't mean I can't add two and two, Colonel. You've been lying to me all along. And spying on me. I never mentioned Bradley's first name."

He turned back to me quickly and started to say something, but I interrupted him. "Please don't compound that lie with a lie of denial. There's no investigation going on into Charity's disappearance. That means she's on the company clock. If you even attempt to deny it, you'll swim to shore from here."

His hands tightened on the armrests of the chair. Colonel Travis Stockwell wasn't a man accustomed to being dressed down, and I was uncomfortable doing it.

After a moment, his posture relaxed and he sighed. "It was just a matter of time until you and the other team members put it together."

"She's doing wet work for the DHS and you're her handler?"

"No, not DHS," he replied vaguely.

"You're shittin' me! The CIA?"

"You didn't hear it from me," he replied with another sigh.

"And Deuce knows, but was ordered to keep it under his hat?"

Lowering his head, he replied, "Even his wife doesn't know."

That would explain a lot, I thought. And what a strain it must be putting on their new marriage. Carl had once told me the secret to his and Charlie's happiness was that they kept no secrets from one another. Deuce was in a situation where his duty had to be placed above his honor. Lying just wasn't in his nature.

I looked out over the calm water as the *Revenge* gently rocked in the small, slow-moving swells. The sun was now high above the eastern horizon and gulls wheeled and cried above the boat, expecting a handout. Pushing the throttles to the stops, the *Revenge* nearly leaped up on plane, sending the gulls careening toward shore.

"Sometimes, Colonel, a man's honor has to be placed above his duty. Maybe not with everyone. There are plenty out there whose sense of duty easily outweighs their sense of honor. Not with a man like Deuce, though. This has to be tearing at the very fabric of his being."

"You have to keep what you know to yourself, Jesse."

Turning in my seat, I stared hard into his eyes. "Like hell I do, *Director*. Don't worry, I won't be shouting it from the rooftops, but there are people in the man's life that have a right to know. People in Charity's life too. Their friends and family. Deuce can't function at a hundred percent with a lie to his wife hanging over his head."

"This is why you brought me along? So you could threaten to feed me to the sharks if I didn't divulge a matter of national security? What Charity's doing down there is important and she's good at it."

Down there? In the Caribbean or South America?

My mind drifted back to Deuce and Julie's wedding and the explosion that had killed Jared Williams. In the short time they'd known one another, Jared and Charity had become close. A few weeks after his funeral, Charity and I had crisscrossed the Caribbean, tracking the man responsible for Jared's death. Jason Smith, the former deputy director.

"I've no doubt she is. I've seen her work up close. With your predecessor." I relaxed after a moment and pulled back on the throttles to forty knots. "Truth is, I do need you, Travis. These guys in Key West are dangerous."

Stockwell knows the kind of man I am and I hoped he knew that he could trust my judgement. He grinned. "Then let's go see the fortuneteller. We can figure the other problem out later, alright?"

That was as good as I was going to get for now and I knew it.

CHAPTER NINETEEN

Erik arrived back at GT's hotel room early, as he'd promised. It hadn't been easy to tear himself away from Karly and he was dragging from the physical abuse she'd put him through. He found his boss waiting. The little man was still there, sitting in a corner of the room. Byers had quite a few bruises on his face and his left eye was swollen nearly shut.

"Our friend Byers had another little tidbit of information that he finally gave up. He's going back to Pittsburgh with us after we find Grabowski. I fucking saw him twice last night and didn't even know it."

Erik pulled out a chair across from his boss and sat down. "Coming back to Pittsburgh with us?"

GT looked at the man slumped in the corner. "Yeah, I offered him a job and he accepted it. I always wanted to have my own ferret."

"What'd he tell you?"

"Grabowski was with a woman last night, right here in Key West. A local, from the sound of it. Short and pretty, with blond dreadlocks."

"If she's a local, we should be able to find her easy enough."

Nodding his head toward Byers, GT said, "He saw the two of them coming out of a place called *Irish Kevin's* yesterday evening. We'll start there. I saw her and him out on the pier at sunset and again later, just before we ran into this guy. Guess the little blond bitch distracted me."

Looking over at the troll-looking heap in the corner, Erik just knew they wouldn't be able to remain inconspicuous with him tagging along. "What are we gonna do with him while we go look for Grabowski and the girl?"

"He'll only draw attention we don't want," GT replied. "I told him he's free to go and to keep his eyes open." Then GT looked at Byers and laughed. "Well, one eye anyway. He'll meet us back here this afternoon. Give him your key card."

Digging the card from his pocket, Erik flung it at the guy, hitting him in the leg. "You sure he can be trusted?"

"Course not. But he knows I can find him again. Let's go."

A short five-minute drive later, GT and Erik arrived at *Irish Kevin's* bar, but it wasn't open. The sun was barely up and it was already past ninety degrees. The sign on the door of the bar said they didn't open until eleven.

"Head back to that restaurant," GT said, already feeling irritable from the heat. "When I saw Grabowski and the girl there, they were crossing the street into a neighborhood."

As the Escalade approached the Half Shell Raw Bar, GT pointed to a side street. "Turn down there. That's where they were going when I saw them. You have any trouble finding a place to stay last night?"

Erik grinned at his boss. "Remember that waitress? I stayed with her."

The big SUV idled slowly down Margaret Street, both men looking out the windows at the rows of old Conch houses shaded by tall trees, people going about their morning routine in the heat of the day.

Not seeing Grabowski or the blonde, and it being a crapshoot at best finding them on the many narrow streets of Old Town, GT told Erik to just keep circling through the neighborhood. There was little else they could do.

Eventually, the big car turned onto Eaton Street and they made their way east. It was nearing eleven o'clock and GT wanted to be at the bar when it opened.

Waiting to turn right at the corner of Duval Street, GT looked ahead, down the next block of Eaton. "There they are! Grabowski and the blonde in the green dress."

Leaning forward in his seat, GT looked both ways on Duval Street, instinctively looking for cops. When he looked back, Grabowski and the blonde were gone. "Damn! Where'd they go?"

"They went into a place on the right, boss. I got my eye on it."

Finally, the light on the pole across the street changed and the big SUV roared through the intersection. "Which place did they go into?" GT smelled blood in the water.

Slowing the car, Erik pointed. "They went in there. *Madam Dawn's Psychic Readings.* Think Madam Dawn's gonna be able to tell them two what's about to happen to them, boss?"

"Pull over to the curb, a little past it."

Just as GT was about to get out, Erik put a hand on his arm while looking in the mirror. "Wait, boss."

GT looked in the side mirror and behind them, a black Ford sedan had come to a stop in front of the psychic's shop. "Is it a fucking cop?"

"No, boss. It's a taxicab. But take a look at the two guys that just got out and are going into the same place."

"Can't be!" GT yelled, banging on the dash. "That's the tall guy from that fisherman's bar yesterday!"

Watching in the mirror, he saw the man who seemed to be the leader of the locals who had disarmed them. He was with another man about the same build but a little shorter. They opened the door of the psychic's place and disappeared inside. A moment later, someone turned the sign over to *Closed* and pulled the shades down.

GT's hand moved automatically to where his shoulder holster should have been. He felt naked and vulnerable when he realized nothing was there. "We'll wait here till they come out."

CHAPTER TWENTY

Arriving at the little marina by the Hyatt an hour later, I left the air conditioner and generator running, with plenty of water in Pescador's bowl. He was already snoozing in the salon. Pescador's only four or five years old, but already slowing down and showing signs of age, as big dogs do at that age.

Tying off to the dock, Travis and I went up to the parking lot and met my old friend Lawrence at the foot of the pier. Travis had called ahead to the marina to get a slip and I'd called Lawrence for a ride.

"Good ta see yuh again, Cap'n," the old Bahamian said, pumping my hand. Lawrence had been invaluable some time ago, providing plenty of information about a Miami drug trafficker in Key West who was attempting to smuggle arms and terrorists into the country by boat. I always found cab drivers and bartenders to be very reliable about information.

I leaned in close and whispered, "From now on, Lawrence, I want you to call me Stretch Buchannan and treat me like a big-time cocaine importer from up island. I'll explain it all when we get in the car."

Travis put both our go-bags in the backseat and climbed in. I sat up front with Lawrence. "If yuh want me to treat yuh like a druggy, Cap'n, thata mean I treat ya mighty scornful. You be knowing dat, mon."

I turned sideways in my seat and nodded back toward Travis in back. "Lawrence, this is my friend Travis Stockwell."

The gray-haired islander turned in his seat and reached a big hand back. "Any friend of Cap'n Jesse's is a friend to Lawrence. I tink I see you heah in Key West before, Mistuh Travis."

Stockwell looked at Lawrence a moment then snapped his fingers. "You have a good eye for faces, Lawrence. About a year ago, I was here in town and you took me to a restaurant for dinner."

Lawrence grinned, showing perfectly straight, big white teeth. "Di Blue Heaven, mon."

"Yeah, that was the place. Good memory, too."

Turning back to me, Lawrence said, "Whut dis business about yuh bein' a druggy, Cap'n?"

"We're looking for someone. Two big black guys, well dressed, shaved heads."

Lawrence thought for a moment and said, "Not seen two big black mons togedda, Cap'n, but I seen a mon look jes like dat last night on Duval."

"Odds are they'd be together, but if you see anyone that looks like that, will you call me? They're drug dealers from way up north."

"Miami?"

I chuckled. "Way norther than that. They're down here from Pittsburgh and have an associate there I'd like to get my hands on. That's why Travis and I are pretending to be bigshot coke importers from Key Largo, to try to smoke these men out."

"Ahh, I see, Cap'n. Somebody is movin' into yuh territory and yuh be here to show dem di error in dere ways?"

"Exactly. You know where Dawn McKenna's shop, or store, or whatever she calls it is?"

"Yah, mon! But, no way she's involved wit di druggies. Mizz McKenna a good woman, mon."

"No, she's not involved," I said. "She called me to see if I could help her niece's boyfriend. The Pittsburgh dealer is looking for him."

Lawrence put the car in gear and drove out of the hotel parking lot. "Her place is just over on Eaton Street. Be dere in jest two minutes, mon."

A few minutes later, Lawrence pulled the cab to the curb in front of a small storefront with the name *Madam Dawn's Psychic Readings* hand-painted on the door's window.

"Yuh want me ta wait, Cap'n?"

Handing him a twenty, I said, "No, that's okay. If we need you, I'll call. But let me know the minute you see these guys."

Lawrence nodded and pressed the button to put the window up as he pulled away from the curb, maneuvering the big sedan around a Cadillac SUV parked in front of him with dark windows.

When I pulled open the door to Madam Dawn's, a little bell mounted on it jingled and a blast of cold air hit me in the face. I stepped inside, with Travis right behind me. Dawn was sitting at a table in the corner with an ordinary-looking younger man and a young woman with blond dreadlocks.

Dawn got up and met us at the door, taking my hand. "Thanks for coming, Jesse. I wasn't sure you would."

She reached behind me and flipped the sign in the window over to *Closed* and pulled the shades. Then she led us into the small side room, decorated with the usual accoutrements of a psychic reader.

Heavy burgundy drapes over the windows blocked the outside light. A small lamp with a mosaic glass shade provided the only light in the room.

"You're a psychic and didn't know if I'd come or not?"

She laughed. Dawn McKenna was a tiny little woman in her late thirties, maybe. Dark hair and dark tan, she could easily pass for a gypsy, though I knew she was of north European descent.

"Being a psychic is more about observing than predicting the future," she said and waved an arm to the other two. "This is my niece, Coral, and her friend Michal. That's with no E, isn't it Michal?"

The young man stood up. "Yeah, but how'd you know that?" Extending his hand to me, I took it and noted dozens of small burn scars on his forearm.

"You're Polish," I said. "And you work with steel."

"Now who's the psychic?" Dawn asked, smiling. "That's very good, Jesse. The same way I guessed it, but I had the advantage of knowing his last name."

"You guys lost me," Michal said.

"The burn marks on your forearms," I said. "I figured you to be a welder. Knowing you're out of Pittsburgh and

Dawn saying there was no E in Michal, I guessed at the Polish part."

"Please, everyone sit down," Dawn said, dragging two extra chairs to the large table. It had a dark red cover, with a gilded fringe, and a large crystal ball mounted on a base in the middle.

Once we were all seated, Dawn said, "We each choose our destiny, so predicting what a person may or may not do depends on the situation and the person. I thought you might not come because of the nature of the problem. You're known to be sort of a Dudley Do-Right man. Knowing that, there must be some other reason for your coming."

Nodding at Travis, I introduced them and everyone shook hands. "Okay, with all the introductions in order, let's get to the point," I said.

Michal started to say something, but I cut him off. "Dawn's right. I really don't give a crap about your problem, how you got into it, or why, or how you'll get out of it. I'm only here because I learned last night that the guys that are looking for you are associated with someone that blew up my boat and got a friend of mine shot. If finding the guys that are after you and then having them lead me to the guy I want helps you in some way, I don't give a shit about that either. You're a drug dealer."

The blonde stood up angrily. "Now hold on just a minute, mister." With me still seated, she barely had to look down at me, her blue eyes filled with rage. "People can change. Michal wants out of this. He wants out of it all. He came here to start a new life."

"Calm down, Coral," Dawn said, reaching a hand across the table and taking her niece's hand. "Mister McDermitt said he'd help. Maybe not for the altruistic reasons you'd want him to, but help is help."

Travis spoke for the first time. "You're from Pittsburgh?" he asked the younger man as Coral sat back down again.

"Yes, sir."

"What's your last name?"

"Trebor," Michal replied. I could tell he was lying.

I leaned across the table toward him. "If you want my help, you'll be honest."

Michal looked over at Coral and she nodded. He turned and looked Travis straight in the eye. "Grabowski. Michal Grabowski."

What? That was the name the little cretin at the Anchor had used.

"Michal Grabowski, Junior?" Travis asked him. "Your dad was a soldier?"

"Well, yeah. But he died a few years back."

"You look like him," Travis said. "Sorry to hear he passed. We served together and he was a good man. Why are you into drugs, son?"

Eyeing Michal closer, I could see a few small scars on his face. He was a short man, and had probably been a small kid. He looked to be built pretty solid. No doubt he'd earned the scars as a little kid and grown up tough.

"I'm not really," Michal said. "I was just hanging around at a guy's house I know, drinking some beers and watching a baseball game. He's the dealer. I'd already decided to get out of town and start over somewhere, even had my stuff packed and in the car, what little I had. When the dealer went to the bathroom, I grabbed his stuff and drove to the bus station. I sold some on the way down. But this morning, Coral and I tossed the rest into the water."

Turning to me, he added, "I'm clean, Mister McDermitt. Honest."

I stared into the younger man's eyes and saw no sign that he wasn't telling the truth. "These guys aren't gonna buy that story, kid. From what I know about drug traffickers, if they don't get back what's theirs, they'll slit your throat and toss you in the water, too. Probably do it anyway, even if they do get it back. Tossing it, you lost your only bargaining chip with them."

Michal's head dropped into his hands and Coral hurriedly put her arms around his shoulders. I couldn't help but think they made a nice couple.

Lifting his head, he looked at each of us, finally stopping on Coral. "What am I gonna do? Those guys are here in Key West."

"What are *we* going to do, Michal?" the young woman corrected him. "I'm in this with you. I talked you into throwing it into the bight, remember?"

I thought it over, the sight of the two young people clinging to one another finally convinced me. "From now, until this is resolved, you two will stick with me and Travis. We're docked behind the Hyatt. That's where the guys who are looking for you are staying."

Michal started to object, but I stopped him and laid out the plan I'd come up with the night before, to pretend to be a coke distributor from up island. We improved the plan, Dawn suggesting that Michal be one of my new low-level dealers. She assured us that she could put the word out on the street faster than anyone in town. Finally, I asked Travis to join me outside for a minute, to talk alone.

Once outside, I turned to the deputy director. "Conner is wanted by a whole slew of government agencies, Colonel. Nothing of a national security nature that I know of, but wanted is wanted."

"What is it you want to do?"

"I believed the kid when he said he wants a fresh start. I want to give him a new identity."

Travis leaned back on the outside wall and crossed his arms. "I apologize for the lies, Gunny. Deuce and I were both ordered to. I assume you want to use the team?"

"Just Chyrel. She can create a whole new identity that will stick. Better than even WITSEC could do, I bet."

The US Marshall Service's Witness Security Program was a highly vaunted government program that was the best at creating new identities for federal witnesses needing protection.

"Yeah, you're probably right," Travis said. "But Deuce doesn't have the authority to lay out the resources for that."

"You mean as *acting* deputy director? The real deputy director does, though."

Travis looked up the street for a moment. Finally, he looked back at me. "Okay, I owe it to his dad. That and more."

Together, we went back inside. The three of them were huddled together over the table talking as we entered and looked up. Sitting back down, Travis took the lead.

"We're going to need your driver's license," Travis said to Michal. "We have someone that can do a better fake background than anyone you might find here."

"It was stolen in Miami. A crackhead has it, but he's here in town."

"Ugly little guy that smells like a sewer?" I asked.

"How'd you know that?"

I grinned. "I'm a psychic, kid."

"We don't really need it," Travis said. "Just the photo on it. But we can make a new one."

"I know someone that can do that," Coral spoke up. "She's a pro photographer and she's done pictures before for people to have new IDs made."

"Call her and see if she's busy," I said. "We can go over there right now."

"Ask her if she can provide a digital copy," Travis said. "On a memory stick, or disk, doesn't matter. After that, we can go back to the boat and email it to our person in Homestead and I'll have the finished ID sent down here by courier."

"All that sounds really expensive," Michal said.

"Don't worry about the cost, son," Travis said. "Your dad paid the debt a long time ago."

CHAPTER TWENTY-ONE

I think they're leaving, boss."

Sitting forward, GT looked at the mirror on his side. The tall guy from the bar and the guy he'd arrived with were standing outside talking. After a few minutes they seemed to agree on something and went back inside.

"Who the hell is this guy and what's his connection to Grabowski?" GT mumbled.

Ten minutes later, the same taxi that brought the two big guys, pulled over to the curb behind the Caddy once more. Grabowski, the blonde, and the two big men left the psychic's shop and climbed into the cab, and it pulled away from the curb.

"Follow them," GT growled. "But not too close."

Erik started the SUV and waited for a car to pass, then pulled out onto Eaton Street behind it, the black taxi about a half block ahead. The cab turned left at the next intersection onto Whitehead. Erik let the cab get a little further ahead of them and allowed another car to turn in front of them, putting two cars between them and the cab.

At the lighthouse, the cab turned left onto Truman, and Erik slowed to allow a little more space before turning after it. A few blocks later, just past a large Catholic school, the cab pulled over to the curb and all four passengers got out.

"Pull over here," GT said.

Erik eased over to the curb at the corner of the school property and they watched as Grabowski and the other three entered a photography studio and the cab pulled away, only to stop a block later at a sandwich deli.

"The cabbie's taking his lunch break," GT surmised. "Pull up to the deli. Maybe we can find out from the driver just who those two are."

As Erik drove past the photo studio, GT looked over to see if he could see Grabowski and the others, but the blinds were drawn on the windows and door. Erik eased the big SUV up behind the idling cab and GT opened the door. "Wait here, Erik."

GT made it to the door of the deli, just a step behind the cab driver. "Say, brother, the passengers you just dropped off. One looked like an old friend, the tall guy, but I don't want to embarrass myself if it's not him. You didn't get his name, did you?"

The cabbie turned and looked squarely at GT. He was an older man, with graying hair, but he still looked robust. "If you a friend a dat mon, yuh need bettah friends and I not be yuh bruddah. Dat was Mistuh Buchannan. His friends call him Stretch. He a big-time drug smuggluh from up island. Di udduh man is his bodyguard. I heah dem talking about hiring di third man."

Surprised, GT asked, "A drug smuggler?"

"Ya, mon, he brings tons of dat white powduh into Key Largo. He a mon yuh bettuh stay clear of."

Returning to his car, GT took out his phone and made a call. Climbing in, he said into the phone, "Stewie, look someone up for me. A guy named Stretch Buchannan in Key Largo. Supposed to be a big-time mover there. Call me back when you get something."

"He's a distributor?" Erik asked.

"Turn around and pull into that little hotel parking lot across the street from the studio. Yeah, that's what the cabbie said. Stewie's checking him out."

Having no more than said it, GT's phone rang as Erik wheeled into the parking lot and turned around. Checking the caller ID, GT answered his phone immediately. "You found something already?"

Listening for a minute, GT frowned as he watched the storefront across the street. Without a word, he ended the call and put the phone in his pocket, his expression growing more venomous.

"That turd fondler sold my product," GT hissed, his blood pressure beginning to pound in his temples.

Erik had seen his boss this way a few times and knew he needed to keep GT talking, so the man wouldn't explode. "The guy checks out?"

"Yeah, he checks out. The guy's supposed to be one of the biggest coke importers in South Florida. Operates out of Key Largo, and the whole Keys are like his own personal playground or something. According to the cabbie, he just hired Grabowski."

"That means..."

"Yeah, Grabowski gave him my product." GT pointed across the street. "They're coming out and the cabbie's back."

As GT and Erik watched, Grabowski and the girl got in the backseat of the cab. The two men hesitated at the front passenger-side door, the bodyguard looking around as they talked. Then he looked straight at the white Escalade and said something to his boss, who followed his gaze.

"They made us," GT said.

As GT watched, the man named Buchannan said something to the bodyguard and then got in the front seat of the cab, like he owned it. The bodyguard closed the door for his boss and then started to cross the street toward where GT and Erik sat in the big SUV. As he approached, he held his hands out to his side, showing them to be empty, and simply walked straight up to Erik's window.

"See what he wants," GT snarled.

Erik buzzed the window down as the man came up to the door. He was older, probably in his fifties, hair graying at the temples and cut short. He leaned on the car with his left forearm, tanned and corded with muscle, his hand rough-looking and scarred. He was obviously no stranger to physical altercations. Erik looked into the man's steely gray eyes and said, "What the fuck you want?"

The look on the man's face was one of idle curiosity, no sign of fear or even care. Erik wasn't accustomed to this. Bending slightly, the man stared past him, ignoring Erik completely. "Mister Bradley, I presume?"

GT's head snapped around. "Who's asking?"

The man's face changed to an expression of amusement. "I am," he replied. "Mister Buchannan is curious as to what you're doing here in his town, so far from home. He'd gotten word that you were sticking your face in places you shouldn't. Stretch Buchannan runs everything from Card Sound to Key West."

In the past, there had been a number of people who'd tried to muscle in on GT's own territory back in Pittsburgh and he remembered exactly how he'd taken care of it. Unarmed, the memory of how he'd handled those occasions caused his voice to come out strained and uneven. "The man with your boss. He stole something that belongs to me, and I either want it back or to be paid for it."

"Mister Cavanaugh? No, he didn't steal anything from you. Mister Buchannan thinks you might be trying to move in down here. That wouldn't be wise, Mister Bradley."

GT missed the obvious threat. "Cavanaugh? His name's Michal Grabowski."

"No, it's not," the man countered in a cold, flat tone, his eyes sharp and clear, showing no sign of anxiety. The man's right hand slowly moved toward his back, where GT was certain he had a gun. "Why are you really down here, Mister Bradley?"

Without having to be told, Erik slammed the car into gear and hit the gas, the big Escalade's engine roaring as he turned hard right, one of the rear tires spinning in the grass and bouncing over the curb. Afraid that the man might start shooting, Erik cut the wheel back and forth, accelerating east on Truman, causing other motorists to veer out of his way and two pedestrians to jump toward the safety of a parked car.

Turning the wheel sharply, the tires squealed in protest as Erik turned onto Windsor Street. He kept his foot hard on the gas, noting with some irony a huge cemetery on the right.

Not yet, Grim Reaper, he thought. After he'd weaved through a couple of residential streets and was sure they weren't being followed, Erik finally slowed.

"Fast thinking, Erik. You just earned your keep."

"What now, boss?"

"Head back to the hotel. I'm not leaving this hellhole of an island without my stuff, or the money it cost. It don't represent a whole lot in the grand scheme of things, but it's the principle. Word gets out that some two-bit steelworker can just run off with my stuff and sell it to another distributor, it'll hurt our accounting and collections. How fast do you think Brown and his crew can get down here?"

"From Miami? You really think we need him?"

"This Buchannan has a really nasty reputation and lots of soldiers. Our guys are two days away by car and they can't fly with guns."

Erik remembered the mile markers and how the first ones he'd noticed were after they left Miami. "Gotta be three or four hours for him to get here from Miami."

CHAPTER TWENTY-TWO

After the two black guys left, Byers slowly got to his feet. He'd been wrong. Being a punching bag for a former pro football linebacker hurt a lot more than being sodomized. He looked at himself in the mirror, turning his head so he could see out of the one eye that was still open. Moving his tongue around inside his mouth, he counted three places where he used to have teeth, the taste of blood still on his tongue.

When he breathed too deeply, he was certain the pain he felt was at least one broken rib. There was a cut above his left eye, and the whole side of his face was swollen and puffy, dark blue around his eye, which was swollen shut. Wetting one of the hotel hand towels, he carefully wiped away the crusty dried blood.

In the end, he'd told GT Bradley everything he knew. Then Bradley had surprised him by offering him a job, as if the beating had never happened. Then the man had given Byers two hundred dollars and reminded him how easy finding him had been. Byers had accepted the job offer, and Bradley had beaten him again until he was unconscious, slumped in the corner.

Strangely, Byers thought it was a good idea. Why sell bits of information now and then, when he could be on someone's payroll to root around for it? He still had his stash in the room and if push came to shove, he knew he could liquidate and disappear.

Leaving the hotel, Byers went straight to the nearest bar, which was just opening. It was only a few steps across the street, a place called the Rum Barrel.

Byers made his way to the far end of the bar as the bartender approached him. Byers laid a twenty on the bar top. "Anything you got that'll ease the pain."

"Damn, mister! You step in front of a bus? Maybe you need to see a doctor instead of a bartender."

"I've seen worse," Byers said, which was the plain and simple truth. "Just pour me a double shot of whatever's handy."

The bartender grabbed a bottle and poured a shot glass nearly half-full. Reaching into his shirt pocket, he pulled out two single packs of powdered pain reliever and placed them in front of Byers, along with the drink.

"Want me to call the cops?"

"No, no cops," Byers answered. "I'll be okay. Hey, ya know where I can buy some decent clothes?"

Noticing for the first time the kids' clothes the man had on and his diminutive stature, the bartender replied, "Yeah, try Cariloha just a couple blocks down Front Street to the left. It's on the right side, you can't miss it. They sell a cross between Caribbean and Hawaiian clothes in all sizes."

Tearing the two packets open, Byers simply poured the contents into his mouth and washed it down with what he assumed was rum. The warmth spread through his body and lessened the throbbing he felt around his left eye.

Byers pushed the twenty toward the bartender. "One more, that first one really helped."

Grabbing up the bottle once more, the bartender poured another double shot into Byers's glass and picked up the twenty. "That'll be ten bucks."

Making sure to give the little man small bills so he could leave a tip, he counted out the change on the bar, a five and five ones. Byers simply tossed back the second shot of rum and scooped up his change, stuffing it in his pocket, before walking out into the oppressive heat. The bartender glared after him, but Byers simply ignored him.

The second double shot, coupled with the intense heat, made it difficult for Byers to walk a straight line, but he finally found the place the bartender had told him about. In minutes, he'd spent fifty dollars, but had a decent pair of pants and a polo shirt. As an afterthought, he grabbed a Panama Jack hat from a rack and tried it on, careful not to pull it on too tightly. Looking in a mirror, the hat dwarfed his head, but hid the huge black eye pretty well.

"Some place I can put these on?" Byers asked the girl behind the counter.

She tried not to stare at his swollen face and pointed to the back of the store. "Changing room's back there."

Minutes later, after throwing the kids' clothes in a trash can, Byers left the store and started shuffling back toward the hotel. At least he could get out of the heat, maybe take a nap before his new boss got back.

Just turning the corner before the hotel, Byers watched as a pretty girl in a green dress stepped out of a big black taxi. He stopped. The alcohol in his brain slowed his reaction, but he recognized the girl as the one that had been with the coke dealer the night before.

Stepping behind a low bush, Byers watched as the coke dealer he'd ripped off, the guy who'd been the whole reason for his receiving a beating at the hands of his new boss, stepped out of the cab with her. Then the rear door on the other side opened and an older man got out, looking around the area. *That's someone you don't want to mess with*, Byers thought.

The front doors of the cab opened and another man got out of the passenger side. The driver, a black man with gray hair, met the taller man in front of the car, where they shook hands. It took Byers a moment to place the tall guy. He was the one in the fancy wooden boat he'd seen at the bar in Marathon. The one with the woman and kids.

Byers instinctively crouched lower, seeing the coke dealer with these two tough-looking men. He didn't want to be seen. The coke dealer was who his new boss was looking for.

After the four of them disappeared around the side of the hotel, Byers quickly followed. He cut through the parking lot, keeping low behind parked cars. Barely taller than the cars, he didn't have to crouch very low.

Surprisingly, they didn't go into the hotel, as Byers expected. Instead, they walked straight out toward the docks behind the hotel. Byers watched through his one eye as they walked out onto the dock and stepped into a big blue-and-white yacht with the name *Gaspar's Revenge* on the back of it. Waiting a few minutes to see if the boat left or if they came back out, Byers decided to go up to his boss's room. He remembered he could see the water from the bathroom window.

This might be information my new boss can use, Byers thought.

Minutes later, Byers was looking out the bathroom window and saw the big yacht, the rear of which was partially obscured by a palm tree. However, the approaches to it were visible for several yards and Byers knew if anyone came or went, he'd see them.

It was only a few minutes after Byers had taken up his position by the window when he heard the two black men come through the door. His new boss was saying, "Call him. Now! I want him and his crew down here yesterday."

Byers stepped out of the bathroom. "I think there's something you should see, Mister Bradley."

The sight of the little cretin startled GT. He didn't figure the guy would be in the room, but would be out searching for Grabowski. "What the fuck you still doing here? Why aren't you out looking?"

"I found them," Byers replied. "The guy you were looking for, the one with the blonde in dreadlocks? They're right outside, on a boat with two big guys."

GT strode toward the sliding glass door and the balcony beyond it. "Show me."

Byers had preferred the bathroom window, so he couldn't be seen. His new boss didn't seem to care if they were seen or not. GT's confidence gave Byers a feeling of security.

As Erik sat down at the table with his phone, GT slid the door open and stepped out on the balcony, which afforded a commanding view of the pool below and the dock area just to the left. Beyond the docks the sparkling water stretched out forever.

Byers stepped out and pointed to a big blue-and-white offshore fishing boat. "About ten minutes ago. The guy you're looking for and the blonde got out of a black taxi with two tough-looking guys. I'd seen one of them before. All four of them got on that big boat."

GT looked at the little man, noting his new clothes and hat for the first time. "And you've been watching them the whole time? Nobody's left that boat?"

"I watched for a few minutes from down there," Byers said, pointing to the corner of the building. "When I was sure the boat wasn't leaving, I came up here real quick for a better view. I don't think they coulda left the boat in that short a time and gotten far enough I couldn't see from the bathroom window. I'm sure they're still there."

"Good," GT said, glad that something was finally going his way. "Sit your ass down in that chair and keep an eye on 'em."

CHAPTER TWENTY-THREE

Lawrence is back from lunch," Travis said, looking out the window of the photography studio.

When Travis opened the door, I heard Lawrence say, "Dey're here, Mistuh Travis. Across di street in di big white cah."

Travis turned toward us and pointed to Michal. "You two, in the backseat." Then he looked at me and said, "Play it by ear?"

I nodded as I followed the young couple through the door. Out of the corner of my eye, I saw the white Escalade with dark windows across the street and pretended not to notice. It was the same car that had been parked in front of Dawn's place when we'd arrived there earlier.

Travis walked with me around the car, his head on a swivel. He'd already spotted them and was putting on a show. The hard-ass bodyguard.

"How you want to do this, Jesse?" Travis asked as he opened the door for me and locked his eyes on the SUV, letting Bradley know he'd been discovered.

"We disarmed those two yesterday, but that doesn't mean they haven't rearmed. How confident are you?"

"I feel good about the background Miss Koshinski gave you, if that's what you mean."

"Enough to walk over there and ask a big-time coke dealer from up north why he's in my town?"

Travis grinned. "Sure thing, Mister Buchannan."

Climbing in the front seat, I pulled my Sig from its holster at the small of my back, keeping it down low by my right hip so as not to get anyone excited.

"I did jes like yuh say, Cap'n. Told dat mon yuh a druggy and control all di Keys."

I watched closely as Travis casually strolled over and leaned on the door of the big car. A moment later, the Escalade roared out of the parking lot, kicking up grass as it bounced over the curb. Travis had his hand under his shirt, but didn't draw his gun. As the car took off down the street, it weaved back and forth, scattering people and cars from its path before nearly rolling as it turned hard, heading toward Key West Cemetery.

"Back to the boat, Lawrence," I said as Travis got in the backseat next to Michal.

"I dropped your fake name on them," Travis said and then conveyed everything he'd said and what Bradley had replied. To Michal, he said, "Your last name is now Cavanaugh, by the way. Only thing I could come up with on short notice."

Lawrence turned on Simonton Street and made good time through the lights. Soon, we were in the parking lot at the hotel marina.

I thanked Lawrence and handed him two twenties. "Dat way too much, Cap'n."

"The extra's for the risk." I peeled off five more and handed them to Lawrence. "This is to cover your time, while you sit with Dawn."

Lawrence looked at the bills in his hand and then looked back up at me, as Coral got out of the back door. "Yuh tink Mizz Dawn might be in danger?"

"Probably not, but I don't like to take chances. Would you mind just hanging out near there?"

"Me and Mizz Dawn are good friends, Cap'n. I'll watch over her, for sure and certain." Climbing out of the cab, the others waited for me under the shade of a palm tree. Lawrence met me in front of the idling sedan and we shook hands.

"Do you own a gun?" I asked him.

"Got a little pea-shootuh in my money box," Lawrence replied, nodding toward the cab.

I appraised the old Bahamian man in a new light. "Good, keep it handy. These guys might make the connection and I'd hate for anything to happen to Dawn. So why don't you go have her read your fortune and palm or whatever she does?"

"I do dat, Cap'n. But yuh shouldn't make light of Mizz Dawn's gift. She truly can see tings we don't."

The four of us hurried to the boat as Lawrence pulled out of the parking lot. I stepped down into the cockpit and offered Coral a hand. She bounded down to the deck lightly on bare feet without any help.

"My dog's inside," I told her.

"I love dogs."

"Me too," Michal offered.

Unlocking the hatch, Pescador sat just inside, waiting. He looked at the two strangers and then back to me, expectantly.

"Go," I told him. He streaked past us, bounding over the gunwale, heading straight to a palm tree that partially shaded us. "But don't be long," I shouted after him.

"That's a big dog," Michal said.

"You two go on in," I told Coral. "Make yourselves at home."

Travis and I waited while Pescador sniffed around for just the right spot and finally hiked his leg on the only tree within a hundred feet.

"No sign of a tail," Travis said. "Think they'll just give up?"

"Would you?" I asked as Pescador jumped back over the gunwale and disappeared into the salon.

"I damned sure would, but you and I don't think like criminals."

"Bourke told me once that thinking like a criminal is an important asset to have," I replied. Andrew Bourke is one of Deuce's operatives. A big, barrel-chested Coast Guardsman, with a voice like a bullhorn, he'd lost his wife and only child, a little boy, in the World Trade Center collapse. He and I had spent many hours discussing how criminals think and how best to use that knowledge.

"Well, anticipating the enemy's probable action I can do," Travis said. "I'm not a street cop, though."

"They'll be close by soon enough," I said, looking through the palm fronds to the top floor of the hotel.

"What makes you think they're that good?"

"I don't. Chyrel traced Bradley's credit card. They're staying right up there."

Travis looked up to the building, then grinned and started through the hatch. "Where's your laptop?"

I pointed to the entertainment center. "Second cabinet."

"This is a beautiful boat, Captain McDermitt," Coral said as we entered the salon.

"Thanks. Y'all have a seat anywhere. This won't take long. There's water and beer in the fridge."

Sitting down next to Travis at the settee, I watched as he powered up my laptop, inserted the thumb drive and clicked on the *Smooth Jazz* icon. A moment later, Chyrel's face appeared against a plain white background indicating she was in her office in Homestead.

"Travis?" Chyrel asked, unsure. "Where's Jesse?"

Leaning over closer, I said, "Hi, Chyrel. Director Stockwell and I need your help." Travis glared at me.

Chyrel looked puzzled. "I'm not sure I follow you."

"We need you to create another fake identity for someone," Travis said. "A deep one, that'll withstand any scrutiny. Permanent. Before you start, call Deuce and tell him what I'm asking for. Tell him I said *green mushroom*, then call me back on vid-comm."

"Green mushroom?"

"He'll know what you mean. Call me right back."

Without waiting, he closed the video feed and pushed the laptop aside. Looking at the young couple sitting on the sofa, Travis said, "What I'm going to tell you doesn't leave this boat. The only reason you're here is your dad, Michal. I work for the federal government, and right now

that's all you need to know. You'll have a new identity before morning. It'll be so complete and in-depth that even
the CIA wouldn't be able to find out who you really are.
Michal Grabowski Junior dies today. You can stick with
Cavanaugh, or any name you like."

"Robert Trebor," Michal said. He looked at Coral and
she smiled.

"Trebor?" I asked, remembering he'd used it earlier.
"That have some kind of meaning?"

"Just to the two of us," Coral replied.

"You got a notepad and a pencil?" Travis asked me.

I got both from a drawer in the galley and knowing
what he wanted it for, I handed them to Michal.

"Write down everything about you physically," Travis
said. "Height, weight, hair and eye color, scars, tattoos,
anything that would identify you. Do you have a criminal record, or ever served in the military?"

"No, I never served," Michal replied. "Got some traffic
tickets, nothing more than that."

"He's meaning fingerprints," I interjected. "Total honesty time. Your new identity is going to be placed over
your old one wherever there's a fingerprint or DNA record on you."

"You can do that?" Travis nodded and Michal thought
for a while. "No, I've never been fingerprinted in my life."

"Good," Travis responded. "That'll make it easier."

As Michal began to write down the information, I sat
back down at the settee. "Green mushroom?" I whispered.

"Means the charade is over, Jesse," Travis replied in a
low tone, glancing at the two younger people, who were
talking quietly between themselves. "When Chyrel tells
Deuce I said those words, he'll open a file on a secure

server, located in Quantico. In that file will be a document from me outlining what he can divulge going forward. It means the truth about what Charity and I have been doing can be talked about within the community of the team. It was known from the start that the cover wouldn't last forever, but it needed to be sold that way to get her in place. Steps were taken early on to release the information when the time was right. You just pushed up the schedule a little."

A ping came from the laptop as Michal walked across the salon deck and slid the notepad to Travis, who picked it up and scanned what Michal had written. Turning the laptop back around, he clicked the blinking video icon and Chyrel's face again appeared. She was smiling now.

"What can I do for you, Director Stockwell?"

Over the next hour, Travis gave Chyrel the physical information and the five of us came up with dozens of small details to complete the background for Robert "Bob" Trebor. Some facts were real, some exaggerated, and some completely made up.

When we were finally finished, Chyrel said, "I'll have a Florida driver's license, Social Security card, birth certificate, and debit and credit cards sent down by courier in the morning. How much money in the accounts?"

Travis looked at Michal. "Do you have any money, son?"

"Not a lot," Michal replied. "My credit cards were in the wallet that was stolen. But they were maxed out and I only have a few thousand in cash."

Turning back to the laptop, Travis said, "Set up the bank statement with an odd balance around fifty thousand in savings and a couple grand in checking, Chyrel.

Show six years of regular mortgage and utility payments, plus the sale of a house with a profit to bring it to that balance. Give him a fairly decent credit rating and show activity that would be consistent with the score."

"Will do, Director. It's good to have you back, sir."

When Travis closed the laptop, Michal looked at him with an expression that could only be described as shock. "Fifty thousand dollars?"

"Did your dad ever tell you about Mogadishu, son?"

"I know he was there," Michal replied. "He was with Special Forces then."

Travis looked out the port-side porthole for a moment, thinking. When he looked back at the young man, his face appeared calm. "Bravo Company, Third Battalion, Seventy-Fifth Ranger Regiment, to be precise. Your dad was my platoon sergeant, I was his CO. Long story short, he saved my life. I guess that's worth fifty grand, don't you, Jesse?"

I grinned. "Absolutely, Colonel. I'm sure there's strings attached that you haven't mentioned, though."

"Strings?" Coral asked.

"Yeah, strings," Travis replied. "From now on, you're Robert Trebor, resident of Key West. You'll go about whatever life you chose to make here, but anytime you hear of anything, no matter how small or insignificant, that has to do with arms smuggling, terrorism, anything like that, you'll have a number to call and report it."

"A snitch?" Michal asked.

"More like a concerned, patriotic citizen. The part of the government I work for is tasked to investigate and deter terrorist activity in South Florida and the Caribbean. We don't care about petty crimes or drug trafficking, at least not as it pertains to our mission. That's the job of other agencies, like DEA. We're interested in possible terrorist activities only."

"I can do that," Michal said.

"It also means you can't be involved in anything illegal, son. If you get yourself picked up for trafficking, I never heard of you and you become useless to me. Think you can do that?"

Michal and Coral looked at one another, smiling. "Yeah," he said, "we can do that."

"Alright, Robert," Travis said. "Or do you prefer Bob?"

CHAPTER TWENTY-FOUR

In the back office of a small gun store in South Miami, a black man with weathered skin, a deeply lined face, and a permanent scowl picked up the phone on his desk. Dialing with hands that were scarred and knotted from years of working as a cattleman when he was a younger man, he waited. Though only thirty-seven, he had the appearance of a much older man. Until you looked at his eyes. They were hazel and danced with the light of youth. The color of his eyes looked even lighter when set against his dark ebony skin.

"We got a job," he muttered into the phone, his South Florida redneck accent belying his African-American heritage.

After a moment, he said, "You, me, and three more oughta do it. Meet me at the gun store in half an hour. Bring your van. We're going to Key West."

Without waiting for a reply, Austin Brown hung up the phone, rose quickly from his desk, and went to the counter out front. His only employee, his wife of twenty years, was sitting on a stool, reading another crime novel. There weren't any customers in the store, located just off US-1 in Naranja, on the southern outskirts of Miami.

Mary-Beth Brown looked over her glasses as her husband entered. "You got that look in your eye, Austin. Where you off to now?"

"None a your business, woman."

Mary-Beth took off her reading glasses, leaving them dangling on a chain on her ample bosom, and slid off the stool. At just a fraction over five feet tall and more than a fraction over two hundred pounds, Mary-Beth looked up at her husband, her face flushing nearly as bright as her copper-colored hair.

"Ain't my business? Now, you just hold on, Mister High and Mighty. I'm the one what pays the bills around here. I have a need to know where the money's comin' from."

"Just a job for that guy up in Pittsburgh I tole you about."

"The drug dealer? What kinda job?"

"He's down to Key West and needs reinforcements, that's all. Me and a few of the guys are goin' down there. He's payin' five grand under the table."

Mary-Beth had met Austin when they were in high school. He was a local high school rodeo star who worked summers and after school as a cow hunter for a big ranch near their hometown of Clewiston, on the shore of Lake Okeechobee. Mary-Beth had been nominated for Homecoming Queen, but when news got out about her unplanned pregnancy, it ruined her chance to win. Her parents became livid that she'd become pregnant by a black boy and threatened to disown her if she didn't

have an abortion. Instead, the two had run off to Fort My-
ers and married before dropping out of school.

"Five thousand dollars?" she asked. "How much of that
do we get to keep?"

"Half. Claude gets a grand and whoever he brings will
get five hundred each. He's bringin' three other guys."

"Well, none of 'em better be that no good Billy Ray,"
she said as he walked past her behind the counter and
looked through the glass top at the different handguns
on display.

"Where's my Python?"

"It's in the back," she replied. "You was changing the
grips, remember?"

Austin opened the case and took out two matching
Colt 1911s and put them on the counter. "Oh, yeah. Would
you run and fetch it for me? I just sold these two Colts.
Got a grand each for 'em."

Mary-Beth headed to the back room muttering, "You'd
likely forget your dang fool head if I wasn't around to
keep it glued in place under your hat."

Turning, Austin opened the rifle case and took out
two AK-74s and his own Armalite AR-10 and laid them
on the counter. "Hey," he yelled through the open door.
"Grab me that green bag under the desk while you're
back there."

When Mary-Beth returned, Austin took the bag from
her, placed it on the counter and put the three rifles in it,
along with a pair of Remington pump-action shotguns,
two boxes of buckshot and three boxes of Winchester
.308 ammo.

"That's a lot of firepower, Austin. Who the hell you
goin' up against?"

"Erik said it's just some rival that ripped his boss off up north and ran off to Key West." Austin looked at his wife's worried expression. "Now Mary-Beth, you know the hardware's just for show. We go down there, scare the bejesus outta them boys, get Erik's boss's stuff back, collect our pay, and be home before sunrise."

"You better make sure you do. No playin' around while you're down there. I know what goes on in Key West. Here's your Python."

Austin took the big .357 Magnum revolver from her, opened the cylinder and spun it. Austin liked guns and was known in South Florida to be one of the best gunsmiths. Ten years ago, he'd been thrown from his horse while hunting cows for his employer and suffered two fractured discs in his back. A cracker who couldn't sit a horse and crack a whip to move cows, wasn't much good on a ranch, but his boss liked him. Even paid for his rehab and put him to work fixing the guns for the other cow hunters when he got out of the hospital. The old gunsmith on the ranch was getting on in years and needed an apprentice. Austin was smart and had a natural gift for intricate mechanical things.

Cow hunters were to South Florida what the cowboy was to the Wild West. Florida was one of the leading beef cattle states, raising more beef than Wyoming, North Dakota or New Mexico, but its ranchers had to use different methods to round up the herds than in those big, wide-open states. During roundup, cattle had to be hunted individually and in small groups through the dense palmetto and underbrush common in south central Florida. Sometimes you could hear a cow but not see it, so the original cow hunters used long bullwhips to crack the air above where the cow was hiding to drive it out. Early cow hunters called each other crackers for that reason, and the term is still used today.

Austin reveled in being one of the few black crackers in the state and he was good at his job. Right up until a pygmy rattler had spooked his mount and left him lying across a palmetto root, forever ruining any chance he had of riding the circuit of the Professional Rodeo Cowboys Association.

Within minutes, Austin heard the sound of tires crunching on the gravel lot out front and looked up. It was Chet in his Dodge van. The passenger and cargo doors opened as Chet climbed out of the driver's seat. Ace got out of the front seat and Claude and Billy Ray jumped out of the cargo door.

Great, Austin thought, glancing quickly toward the back, where Mary-Beth had disappeared. Billy Ray was a little on the wild side and Mary-Beth didn't like Austin associating with people like that.

"Chet's here, Mary-Beth," he shouted. "We're gonna get goin'. See ya in the morning."

"You be careful," his wife called from the storeroom.

Austin quickly stuffed the two Colts in the bag and flung it over his shoulder. The men outside had their own handguns. The Colts were for Erik and his boss.

Austin reached the door before the men came in, striding quickly toward the van, hoping to get out of the lot without Mary-Beth knowing that Billy Ray was going.

"Let's get on down the road," Austin said, twirling his finger in the air.

"I gotta take a piss," Billy Ray said.

"We'll stop at Mickey D's on the way," Austin replied, shoving the gun bag into Billy Ray's hands. "We're in a hurry."

Billy Ray grumbled something, but carried the bag to the van and put it inside. A moment later, the five men were on the road to Key West.

CHAPTER TWENTY-FIVE

E rik looked up as GT came back inside. "Brown said he'd get a few guys together and be here before dark, boss. I still don't like having to use those guys."

"He's your buddy. You recommended him for that last job. What's wrong?"

"Austin's okay, but some of the white trash he associates with makes my skin crawl. They're a bunch of loose cannons. He's bringing us a couple of clean Colts, though."

GT offered an evil grin. "That's good. I don't like not having a gun nearby. And sometimes a loose cannon is just what you need."

It hadn't escaped Erik's attention that his boss was getting more and more irritable and hadn't even asked about the price of the guns or the backup. GT didn't think straight when he was in one of these moods. This whole trip down here was costing more than the stolen coke was worth. In Erik's mind, he thought it would have been better to write it off as a business expense. But GT didn't think that way. He was always concerned with appearances and not giving anyone the impression he was weak.

Erik looked up at his boss. "It's just that some of the guys Austin hangs around are real unpredictable, especially that Goodrich character."

GT sat down across from Erik. They'd known each other for many years, and GT trusted Erik more than anyone else, considered him a brother. They'd grown up on the same tough streets of Pittsburgh's slums and gone to school together up until high school, when redistricting had put them in different schools even though they'd lived only two blocks from each other. Erik would have gotten a scholarship to college like GT had and probably would have made the NFL too, if he hadn't suffered a fractured hip in his senior year of high school. An injury that GT himself had caused.

"I've only met Brown that one time and only briefly," GT said. "But I trust your judgment. How is it you know him, anyway?"

"Rehab," Erik said, not wanting to bring up the incident on the gridiron that had changed his life forever. "Mom threatened to sue the school district, so they spared no expense and sent me to a rehab hospital in Tampa, since the cold weather at home would be hard on rehab. Austin was there recovering from a broken back. I guess being the only two black guys on the floor, they put us in a room together and we kind of hit it off and stayed in touch after."

"And his crew?"

"Crew," Erik snorted derisively. "A bunch of rednecks with more guns than brains and no self-discipline."

"So why'd you contract them for that other job?"

Erik stared out the window a moment. "Figured they'd be like Austin, hardnosed, smart, and would do what they were told. Austin plays like he's one of them, but he's sharper than all his buddies combined. They only hang around him because he finds easy work for them." Erik stood up and walked to the far side of the room. "Just looking at those two guys out there on that boat, I know this won't be easy."

"It's just two guys!" GT said, getting excited. "And I don't care if Brown's crew kills all of them. I just want back what's mine."

Erik turned around. "GT, it's just us two here. Back home, you got a good many foot soldiers you could round up in a hurry. Good ones. We're in this Buchannan guy's backyard here. I'd bet he has more than just him and that bodyguard. And that guy's a pro, all the way. Probably some kind of mercenary."

"Well, they can't be too smart. Showing up in a flashy boat and not even pretending to hide. Wonder why Buchannan took Grabowski in and is trying to shove us out? Grabowski had to look just the same to him, someone outside his network selling coke. Maybe they knew each other before that little turd fondler ripped me off."

"Yeah, you're probably right on both counts," Erik said, deciding not to bring up GT's own proclivity for driving around in flashy cars and staying in high-priced hotels.

GT knew Erik was a thinker and admitted, if only to himself, that Erik was smarter than him. Always had been. GT would never have made it through middle school if it wasn't for Erik helping him.

"What about that place where Grabowski met with Buchannan, and where they went afterwards?" GT asked. "What did you make of that?"

Erik thought it over for a moment. "I don't see a connection between a fortuneteller and a photographer, besides their both being locals." Nodding toward the balcony, Erik continued. "He said he saw Grabowski coming out of that bar with the girl. You saw them later coming out of the restaurant and they're still together today. Girlfriend, probably. My guess is she's a local too."

"That reminds me, we still don't know who she is. We need to get to that bar and see if we can find out. The connection is they're all locals and so is Buchannan. We should visit the fortuneteller and photographer, find out what they can tell us about him. These people all know each other, it seems like."

"Both of those places will be closed before Austin gets here," Erik said. "We only have the two of us and the one car. Someone needs to stay here and watch the boat. How you wanna do that?"

GT considered it. "Both places aren't too far. I'll stay here with the car, in case Grabowski rabbits. One other thing. That cab driver didn't seem to like Buchannan much. You go to the bar and keep your eyes open for the cab driver. See if you can find him and pump him for more information. We'll send the ferret to the fortuneteller and the photographer. See what they know."

"I don't know," Erik said. "You think you can trust him?"

"He coulda bolted this morning. Instead he found where Grabowski's holed up and came back here."

Byers appeared in the doorway. "You're wrong about the cab driver."

GT turned in his chair. "What do you mean?"

"When the taxi dropped them off at the boat, the tall guy and the driver acted like old friends, shaking hands and what not."

This news surprised GT. "Probably just being cordial," he said dismissively.

"I was close enough to hear, once they got out of the cab. The tall guy asked the cab driver if he had a gun and then sent him to the fortuneteller to watch over her."

Looking at GT, Erik could see that he was mulling this new information over. Finally, Erik spoke up. "They were onto us before they came out of the fortuneteller's place. The cab driver fed you a line of bullshit."

GT frowned. "All that means is that you won't get any information from him simply by asking. And it puts the two of them together, the cabbie and the fortuneteller. That's convenient. You go there, Erik. Find out whatever you can, using whatever means you have to."

Turning to Byers, GT took his dwindling money roll out of his pocket and peeled off two twenties. "And you go to the bar you saw Grabowski and the girl coming out of. Use this to grease some palms and find out who she is and how she might be connected to Stretch Buchannan."

Rising, GT strode past Byers and sat down in the balcony chair. Over his shoulder, he shouted, "Go now!"

CHAPTER TWENTY-SIX

My sat-phone chirped and I looked at the caller ID. Recognizing the number as Dawn's, I answered it.

"I don't need a babysitter," she nearly shouted.

"Just indulge me, okay. Y'all wanted my help and there's always a chance they connect you and Coral. I don't like loose ends."

"I'm closing up in an hour anyway, Jesse. And Lawrence has rounds to make."

"I gave him enough to cover any loss of income," I said.

"No, it's not that, and thanks for that by the way, it was sweet. But I have a schedule worked out with a number of places so the waitresses and bartenders leave work at different times. Lawrence picks the girls up and drives them around the island, before dropping them off at their homes, just in case of stalkers. We've had more than a few overly amorous tourists follow girls home, but not since we set up the schedule."

"Knowing Lawrence, I completely believe that," I said. "Would you at least have him do the same with you? Then he can make his rounds."

"Why is it that all of you strong, silent types are always so damned overprotective?" she said with a sigh. "Never mind. You already got Lawrence rattled to where I couldn't beat him out of here with a broom. Besides, my daddy's Mossberg is in the closet."

"Good. Call me if anything comes up and tell him to call me when he drops you off at home."

"Aye, aye, Captain Bligh," she responded and hung up.

I looked over at Coral, sitting on the couch with Michal. "Your aunt's a character."

Coral looked up and smiled. "She is that. Her and Lawrence sort of watch over a bunch of us girls. They see us as vulnerable."

My sat-phone chirped again. It was Deuce. "I'm gonna step outside to take this."

I answered the phone and told Deuce to stand by, while I made my way to the salon hatch. Once outside, I said, "If you say one word of apology, I'll hang up, then come up there and kick your ass."

"The director explained?"

"Yeah," I replied. "The CIA, man? How the hell did you guys let them rope you in?"

"I'm not supposed to say, but I'm going to anyway. It was the secretary's idea and the president agreed. The secretary personally sends a courier down there, who hand-delivers information about a possible target to Travis. He then arranges whatever assets Charity needs, flies to wherever she is and hand-delivers the target information."

"How many times?" I asked, probably with a bit too much ice in my voice.

"Three so far."

Three? I thought. *Charity's good, but that's pushing the bounds of chance.*

"I don't like it, Deuce. The woman's not completely stable. Have you told Julie?"

"Just now. She knows everything I just told you."

I grinned. "Put some raw meat on that black eye. She'll calm down in a while and forgive you."

Deuce laughed. It was good hearing him laugh again. "She was pissed about the cover-up for sure, but after I explained everything she understood. These last few months have been hard enough on her, with the move and everything. Once I explained, I guess she sort of figured out why I've been such an ass lately."

"You're always an ass, man."

"Yeah, well we both learned it from the same man," he responded with a chuckle. Then he became serious again. "Look, Chyrel has all the physical stuff ready for your man down there. I won't even ask how or why. I'm sure the director has his reasons. I'm sending it down by chopper with Scott and Germ. By the time they get to you, she'll have everything on the electronic side completed and can email the dossier. They should be there within the hour and if you need them or the chopper, they'll stay on station."

"Thanks, Deuce. I'll explain everything when I see you. Are y'all coming down any time soon?"

There was silence for a moment. Finally he said, "No time real soon, brother. Maybe in a week or two, I can get away."

We said goodbye and I stood there in the cockpit for a moment. A slight breeze had picked up, but did nothing to quell what had become a historic heat wave. Through the gently rustling palm fronds, I could just make out someone sitting on the balcony I'd already determined to belong to the room GT Bradley was in. Though he had a good view of the whole dock area and most of the boat, the palm obscured any direct view of the cockpit.

Chance favors the prepared mind, I thought, looking toward the sun, now halfway down to the horizon. I went back into the salon.

"Get Chyrel back," I said to Travis. "I have a small change in our plans."

"What's up?" Travis asked as he opened the laptop.

"We're going to pull a switch," I said, nodding to Michal and Coral on the couch.

Travis glanced at them and I could see he knew right away what I was talking about. "We have two couriers coming?"

"Germ and Scott," I said. "Should be here in an hour, just before sunset."

A moment later, Travis had Chyrel on the video feed and I asked if Germ and Scott had left yet.

"No, in fact they're right here, just about to leave."

Jeremiah "Germ" Simpson and Scott Grayson had both been Marine Recon dive instructors, before being approached by Deuce to work with the Caribbean Counterterrorism Command. Germ was a sergeant and Scott a staff sergeant. Over the past two years, the team had been cross-training, teaching one another new skills. All the team members were now accomplished scuba divers, among the many other skills each had taught to the others.

The two men joined Chyrel behind the monitor and I laid out my plan to them and to Michal and Coral at the same time. When we finished, Scott said that he had his doubts they could pull it off, but would give it a shot.

Travis ended the video connection as Coral stepped up to the settee. "And where are we supposed to go?"

"Don't worry," I said, taking out my phone and typing in a message to send to two people. "You'll like it there."

CHAPTER TWENTY-SEVEN

Leaning forward in his chair, GT watched as the lone figure came out the door to the boat's cabin. All he could see was the guy's feet, so he couldn't be sure if it was Buchannan himself or his bodyguard. GT quickly moved to the balcony's rail and went to the far end, but it didn't afford any better view. The guy stood on the back of the boat for a few minutes and then disappeared back inside. At least the rest of the dock area was visible, so nobody could come or go without being seen.

For the next hour nothing else happened on the boat. Then GT heard the hotel room door close and looked inside. It was Byers, returning already.

"Find out anything?" GT asked as the little man stopped in the open balcony doorway.

"The guy working the bar was tight-lipped. Wouldn't even look at your money. After I left, another guy came out of the bar, said he'd overheard and knew who the girl is. I gave him forty bucks and he told me that she's the usual day bartender there. Name's Coral, but he didn't know her last name. Guy's a tourist and she shot him down when he hit on her yesterday. Said she took a cab home after work, so didn't live very close by."

"Coral, huh?" GT said, standing up. "Keep watch on the boat."

Without waiting for more, GT went inside and sat down in the deep recliner to think. Knowing who she was and where she worked was a help. When she and Grabowski left the boat, they'd be able to follow more discreetly, at least, knowing where she'd be the next day. If they couldn't get Grabowski and the girl tonight, he'd have a couple of Brown's guys waiting when she went to work tomorrow, figuring that not many bars gave bartenders two days off in a row.

A few minutes later, Erik returned. "Struck out both places, boss. The sign on the photography store said they don't close until six, but they must've closed early. It was locked up. Just as I got to the fortuneteller's place, she was getting into the same black taxi. I asked around about the taxi driver at a couple of places, but nobody I talked to would tell me anything about him, besides his name. Lawrence Lovett."

"These locals are tight," GT said. "Byers found out who the girl is. Name's Coral something and she works days at *Irish Kevin's* bar."

Erik glanced out the open glass door to where Byers was sitting, watching the boat. "Be dark soon. Brown'll probably be here in about an hour. What do you wanna do then?"

"Whatever it takes," GT growled. "Maybe we can make up the loss of the product with the girl. I know some people that'll pay top dollar for her."

"Something's going on down there," Byers said from out on the balcony.

Rising quickly, GT and Erik joined him. Below, another boat had pulled up alongside Buchannan's yacht. There were three people on it, but it was hard to distinguish any features because of the palm tree.

"You see what they look like?" GT asked.

"Yeah, the guy at the wheel is tall and skinny, light brown hair almost to his shoulders. The other two had their backs turned, but they're both dressed in black pants and shirts and carrying black bags."

"Sounds like a buy," Erik offered.

They watched as someone came out of the cabin on Buchannan's boat and the three people on the smaller boat climbed over the rail and joined him. All four disappeared into the cabin.

"Sure looks like it," GT rumbled. "A buyer and a couple of hired muscle, carrying cash for my stuff."

Plopping down in another chair, GT leaned on his elbows. "I'm gonna cut Grabowski a whole bunch of times. Real slow. But first, he's gonna watch me screw that little girlfriend of his."

A few minutes later, the door to the cabin opened again. And just like before, the palm tree, coupled with the glare from the setting sun, prevented them from making out anything more than the legs of four people as they came out onto the back of the boat.

A moment later, the smaller boat pulled away and started out of the little marina. All three men on board

had their backs turned, so it was impossible to see much more than what Byers had described earlier.

"They left the two black bags," Byers noted.

"That means there's probably enough cash on that boat now to cover what Grabowski took," GT surmised, looking at his watch. "Erik, call Brown and find out how long till they get here. We can wrap this up as soon as they arrive. Those turd fondlers don't have any idea we know where they are."

Erik disappeared into the hotel room to make the call. A moment later, he stepped back out onto the balcony. "They'll be here in less than an hour, boss. Brown said they were on the Seven Mile Bridge. That must be that really long bridge before the island with all the deer and cops."

"Good," GT said quietly. "We can move in on them after it gets dark. There aren't any other boats down there and I've only seen a handful of people walk by. I want Buchannan and that bodyguard of his dead. But I want to kill Grabowski myself."

Returning to the air-conditioned comfort of the room, GT said, "Why don't you call down and see about getting some food sent up here? And call Brown back and tell him to park in the side lot and call when they get here. You can meet them down there at the side door. We'll wait until it gets good and dark."

CHAPTER TWENTY-EIGHT

O nce away from the little marina and moving north in Key West Bight Channel, Doc Talbot brought his small skiff up on plane and circled around to the east, heading back to the Coast Guard station where he'd picked up Scott and Germ. The three hadn't had much time to catch up before arriving at Jesse's boat just beyond the bight.

"We're out of sight now," Doc told his passengers. "Jesse said to drop you two off at the chopper and it'll take you up to his island."

Shrugging out of the oversized black sweatshirt and sweatpants, Coral neatly folded them and set them on the seat next to Doc. "Thanks, Bob. I don't know if it's possible that those guys would mistake me and Michal for those two you came in with. They're pretty big guys. Michal, meet my good friend, Bob Talbot."

The two shook hands, and Michal quickly shed the sweat clothes Jesse had given them both as the boat slowed down, entering the dock area of the Coast Guard station. "Mister McDermitt kept calling you Doc," Michal said.

"Nickname," Doc answered. "I used to be a Navy Corpsman."

"And the two men you brought out?"

Doc glanced at Michal, then looked at Coral and shook his head. "Probably best that you don't know who they are. And forget that I was here, too."

"Where's this place we're going?" Coral asked.

"Jesse's little oasis. It's an island about thirty miles northeast of here. Nobody around for miles, except the island's caretaker and his family. You remember Carl Trent, he owns the shrimp trawler I run? He and Charlie and the kids live up there."

"I'd wondered where they moved to. I see Charlie now and then, but never bothered to ask."

"You'll like it up there," Doc said as he brought the little skiff up alongside the northernmost pier, where a ladder extended up from the waterline to the top. He nodded to a small black helicopter sitting at the foot of the pier. "That's your ride. Just tell him who you are and he'll have you there in ten minutes. Don't bother asking him any questions, though. Likely he knows less than I already told you."

Once tied off, Doc opened the storage box under his seat and took out a small briefcase, which he handed to Michal. "This is for you," he said. "I'm told it holds your future."

Michal looked at the small case, then reached out and took it. "What about my belongings at the motel?"

"I don't know anything about that," Doc answered. Then to Coral he said, "Nikki's gonna stop by your place and grab a few things for you. She can go to the motel and get his stuff too, if you like. We'll all be up at the island tomorrow for a big shindig Jesse's putting on. Can you manage until then?"

"Oh, sure," Coral replied. "Charlie and I are about the same size and Carl might have something for Michal. Thanks, again, Bob."

Coral turned and started climbing up the ladder as Michal and Doc shook hands. "I'm at a loss as to why all these people are doing so much," he said.

"Simple," Doc replied with a shrug. "Jesse asked. Now get going. I'll see you guys tomorrow."

Coral was nearly to the top of the short ladder as Michal waited to hand the briefcase up. He saw that she once more hadn't worn anything under the loose-fitting green dress. Coral turned around at the top and reached down, taking the briefcase as Michal quickly climbed up to stand beside her.

"Do you ever wear panties?" he whispered.

"Don't own any," she said with a smile.

Below, Doc untied the single line and shoved off. As the little outboard sputtered away from the pier, he turned and waved. The two of them waved back and then turned toward the waiting helicopter.

As they approached, the pilot climbed out and opened the rear door for them. Moments later, they were settled into the backseat, and the pilot started the engine. They were soon airborne, flying out over the water and turning slightly away from the setting sun. They leaned toward the window on the left side, watching as the last of the sun disappeared below the horizon.

They both closed their eyes for a brief second, each mouthing a silent wish. When they opened them again, the sun slipped away below the horizon and a brief but dazzling green flash enveloped the cockpit.

Coral smiled and hugged Michal tightly. "I hope you wished well, Michal."

"If I tell it, will it still come true?" She nodded eagerly in response. Michal looked deeply into her bright blue eyes. "I wished for just one more day in paradise," he said. "With you."

"Hate to interrupt," the pilot said. "This is where I'll be dropping you off."

Michal and Coral leaned between the seats and saw a small island ahead. In the low light of twilight, they could make out the roofs of several small buildings and what looked like torchlights flickering in a square around the cleared interior of the little island.

Seconds later, the small helicopter touched down lightly in the middle of the square and the pilot climbed out and opened the door for them, the engine still running. He helped them both down and pointed to where Charlie and Carl stood beside a pair of large tables with their two kids.

Coral took Michal's hand and led him away as the pilot climbed back in and brought the engine speed up. Once the two of them were well clear of the spinning blades, the tone changed from a high-pitched whirring sound to a heavy whump and the helicopter lifted off. Turning southwest, it quickly disappeared.

"Welcome," Charlie said, stepping toward the two and hugging Coral. "So good to see you again."

"Good to see you too, Charlie."

Coral introduced Michal and was about to explain why they were there, but Carl interrupted. "No need to explain. Jesse texted me everything. Are y'all hungry? We were just about to eat."

Michal suddenly realized they hadn't eaten since breakfast and his stomach growled at the mere mention of food. "I know I am," Coral replied for both of them.

"Have a seat and relax, then," Charlie said. "I bet you guys are exhausted. Hope you like seafood."

Charlie hurried off to a little house on the west side of the island with the two kids. "We're having grunts and grits with janga soup," Carl announced, turning to a large stone grill, a smile on his face.

"Anything I can help with?" Michal asked.

"Thanks, son, but everything's ready. Just take a load off. We don't have guests here very often. There's beer and water in the cooler there."

Sitting down on the big bench in front of the table, Coral took two bottles of water from the cooler, then noticed a small plate with lime slices and squeezed one through the neck of each bottle. "Exactly where is here?" she asked Carl. "I wasn't paying much attention."

"The Content Keys," Carl said. "Jesse owns this little island and Charlie and I help him take care of it."

There was a light breeze blowing out of the west, carrying the scent of iodine and brine from the sea. Coral smelled something else, but couldn't place it at first. Then she realized it was ozone, just as a low rumble of thunder came rolling in off the water.

"We'll get some rain before this night's over," Charlie said, returning with a small pot in one hand and a carving board with a loaf of fresh bread in the other, the two kids walking carefully behind her. The little boy carried a stack of plates, bowls and silverware, and the little girl carried a large salad bowl.

"We grew the vegetables ourselves," Carl Junior said, beaming.

Later, as Michal was helping himself to a second bowl of the delicious soup, he turned to Coral and asked, "I've never heard of janga soup. What is it?"

"Janga are freshwater crayfish in Jamaica," she said. Turning to Charlie with a knowing smile, she asked, "How'd you get them up here?"

"We raise them," Charlie replied, noting her smile. "We'll show you in the morning, it's too dark now. They're actually just Louisiana crawfish, but Rufus calls them janga and I guess they're closely related, or maybe it's more the ingredients he uses for the soup, because it seems to have the same effect." Smiling at her in the light of a tiki torch, Charlie nodded toward a house set high on stilts. "Jesse said to put you in his house for tonight."

"Same effect?" Michal asked.

The three other adults laughed and Coral leaned over and whispered in Michal's ear. "Janga are a natural aphrodisiac."

Michal nearly choked on a spoonful and coughed. "Really?"

"That's what they say," Carl replied. "And I, for one, believe them. Y'all run along, I know you gotta be tired. We'll get the dishes."

Coral wiped the corners of her mouth with a napkin. "Are you sure we can't help you?"

"Y'all go ahead on," Charlie said. "The house is unlocked and the windows are open. With that cooling breeze, it should be plenty comfortable up there." The wind picked up then and another roll of thunder washed over the little island, closer now. "The shower is fed by a reverse-osmosis unit and all the electricity is twelve volt. Jesse never put his house on the grid, though, so use the oil lamps to save on the batteries. Do you have any clothes?"

"Only what we're wearing," Michal said.

"Come with me, Coral," Charlie said, getting up from the table. The two of them walked toward the little house on the western shore.

Once they were out of earshot, Carl said, "Jesse told me most of what was going on, son." Then, in a serious tone, he added, "Nothing like that goes on here, though."

"No, sir," Michal replied, knowing exactly what he was referring to. "We threw it all in the water this morning. I'm starting fresh now."

"Good idea. New place, new way of life. You'll like it down here after a time. The heat and humidity takes some getting used to, but the people here are genuine and can be counted on when trouble comes. Especially people like Jesse."

Charlie and Coral returned, carrying two small bundles. "Y'all just run along," Carl said. "We get up with the sun here, so get some rest. If you want to help, I'd be glad to have some in the garden tomorrow."

They said goodnight and Coral took Michal by the hand, leading him toward the tall house on the other

side of the clearing. At the top of the steps, away from the flickering light of the tiki torches, Michal looked out over the water to the south and the sky above it.

"Whoa," he whispered, coming to a stop halfway across the deck and looking up into the sky.

Coral looked up into Michal's face and saw the light of a billion stars sparkle in his eyes. "I bet you never saw a sky like that back home."

Michal blinked, sure that his mind was playing tricks on him. "It's beautiful. Is that janga soup some kind of hallucinogen, too? I've never seen so many stars."

"You have to be away from the city to see them," Coral whispered, taking his hand in hers. "Do you remember my rules?"

"Rule one: Coral makes the rules."

He could see her smile in the brilliant starlight as she twirled one of her dreads. "Rule two," she said. "Coral always comes first."

CHAPTER TWENTY-NINE

Once the sun went down, I doused all the lights except the one in the guest cabin and closed the door. The interior was almost totally dark inside. Outside, I wanted the appearance that nearly everyone had gone to sleep. I'd gotten the gear we'd need from under my bunk after Coral and Michal had left, and the four of us were nearly prepared.

"Think they went for it?" Scott asked. "I mean, I'm at least a hundred pounds bigger than that girl."

"The eyes see what the mind tells them to," Travis answered, looking through the slits in the blinds over the porthole using my night vision spotting scope. "You couldn't have been more obvious with the bags and they were all out there when the kids left. One of them had to have noticed they didn't have the bags when they left. They're drug dealers. I'd say that Jesse was right on the money and they saw that little charade as a drug deal. It's what their minds are accustomed to seeing."

"Let's hope so," I said. "There's three of them now, though."

"No sign of any movement anywhere outside," Travis said. "One person on the balcony, and lights on inside the room."

"Another couple of weeks, lobster season opens," I said. "Every room in that hotel will be full then, as well as every square foot of dock space. You about ready, Germ?"

"Yeah," Germ replied. "Your gear's in excellent shape." Both Scott and Germ were wearing the black tactical clothing they'd arrived in and now had scuba masks hanging around their necks and wore Drager LAR V rebreathers. Different from scuba tanks, they're less bulky and don't release bubbles in the water.

"Won't they see the hatch open?" Scott asked.

I made my way to the port side and lifted the cushions off the sofa. Raising the lid, I said, "You'll go down through the engine room and out onto the deck. If you hug the gunwale, they won't see you."

I moved a few things out of the way in the storage compartment and lifted the panel for the false bottom. "Give me a hand here, Scott."

Both Germ and Scott were wearing Pulsar Edge night vision headsets so they could visually check out the equipment. Scott looked down in the hidden compartment, which could be accessed from here or down in the engine room. "You got it set up just like the old boat?"

"Better," I replied, lifting out the M-2 machine gun receiver and handing it to him. "On the old *Revenge*, you could only access this from the engine room."

Scott laid the receiver on the cushions and, leaning over, he looked down inside. I felt around until my hand found the release mechanism. When I pulled it, the underside of the compartment dropped open with a quiet hiss, from the two hydraulic pistons. "Now, it can be accessed from above or below. Should be wide enough for you."

Scott studied the small opening. From experience, I knew he could easily make out the narrow space between the port engine and the hull, and the footholds he'd need to use to get down to the lower deck.

"Yeah, I think we can get through there easy enough."

"Once you're down there, move forward around the engine, then aft to the hatch. Just lift the upper part enough to get the hatch open. There's little light out there, doubtful they'll see the top move and they can't see the bottom at all."

Scott reached up and switched on the tiny earwig I'd given him. "Comm check," I heard him say through the device in my own ear.

"Roger," I said. Travis and Germ repeated the affirmation and Scott stepped over the side of the sofa and placed his feet wide inside the storage area. Using his arms, he slowly lowered himself until his foot found the engine manifold, then he stepped on down into the engine room. A moment later, Germ followed him and I went to the rear porthole and peeked through the blinds.

What little light there was from the dock area was shaded by the gunwale, but I could see Scott crawling toward the transom door. Within seconds, both men were through it and in the water.

"They're submerged," I said to Travis. The masks the two men wore were full face masks, which would allow them to communicate underwater. Being the highly trained underwater combat instructors they were, I didn't expect any conversation.

It was a long ten minutes later before Scott said anything, but finally he reported in. "We're ashore. Give us ten minutes to get into position."

"Too bad you don't have two more headsets," Travis said.

"Yeah, that wouldn't draw much attention. Us walking along the docks with night vision."

"Even with this scope, I can barely see them." Travis moved the scope up to the balcony of Bradley's room. "Still just the one guy outside. No reaction."

A few minutes later, I heard Scott's voice over the comm. "We're in position."

My eyes had adjusted to the near darkness inside the salon and I looked over at Travis. "Okay, Colonel, time to take a stroll."

"Wait," he said. "I have movement inside the room."

"What are they doing?" I asked.

"One of them is leaving. Let's wait a minute and see where he goes."

A moment later, Germ's voice came over the comm. "A van just pulled into the lot. A white Dodge."

I instinctively put a hand to my right ear, where the earwig was, trying to hear what was going on, but I knew the bone-conductive mic of the transmitter didn't pick up any outside noise. "Hang loose, everyone."

"Somebody just came out the side door of the hotel where the van's parked," Germ said. "Black guy, shaved head. People are getting out of the van."

I released a slow breath, realizing I'd been holding it.

"Five guys in the van, shaking hands with the bald guy. This isn't good."

"Reinforcements?" Scott asked.

"Looks that way," Germ replied. "Too far away to hear what they're saying. One lanky, older-looking black guy dressed like a cowboy. The others are all white, dressed the same. Wait one."

"Eight of them now," I muttered, not liking it.

"One of the guys is getting a long bag out of the back of the van. Looks heavy and bulky. I think it's a tactical gun bag."

"Change of plans," I said. "Travis and I will go for a walk like we'd planned on, but instead of capturing them in the open, we'll wait and let them get aboard."

I quickly put the machine gun's receiver back into the hidden compartment and closed it, replacing the cushions. "Let's go, Colonel. When we're outside, yack it up about going out for food. Loud enough so the guy on the balcony can hear."

"What are you going to do?" Scott asked.

"We'll play it by ear," I said. "When they find nobody aboard, they'll likely go off looking for Travis and me. Remember, Travis and I are a couple of smug drugglers."

Travis stuck the night vision scope in his pocket and we left. Knowing they'd board after we left, thinking Michal and Coral were now alone, I left the hatch unlocked. They'd just bust it anyway.

Pescador waited just inside. Leaving him here might cause the guys to shoot. "You stay with me, Pescador."

Vaulting the gunwale, I shouted, "Hurry up. I'm hungry."

Following right behind me, Pescador hiked his leg on the palm tree again as Travis asked in an overly loud voice, "Where we gonna eat, Stretch?"

"I feel like a steak, how about you?"

"Whatever you say," Travis replied.

Walking along the dock, I heard Germ's voice over the comm. "The little guy on the balcony went to the door and is now standing at the rail watching you. The other black guy just stepped outside and is looking back and forth from you to the boat. I think they bought the switch."

Walking quickly, we approached the corner of the building. Around it would be where the van had parked. Germ was hunkered down in some vegetation just to the left of the sidewalk, away from the building. If I hadn't known he was there, I'd have never seen him. He whispered, "All six men went inside a few seconds ago. You're clear."

"Good," I said. "They'll probably come out that way in just a few minutes. Let us know when they do. I'll sprint around to where Scott is, and Travis will duck down between some cars here as your backup."

I ran around the corner, Pescador loping beside me. Nearing the main door to the hotel, we slowed to a walk, not wanting to draw any unwanted attention.

A minute later, I squatted down next to Scott, who was hidden behind the dangling roots of an old banyan tree. "I'm with Scott now."

"Roger," came Germ's voice over the comm. "Four men on the balcony now. The little guy and the three black guys. They're looking all around the dock area."

"We should have put a bug up there as soon as we got here," Travis said.

"They'll attempt a pincer movement, meeting at the boat from two sides," I said. "We should be able to take them from behind."

"They're going inside," Germ said. "All but the little guy."

Travis said, "They'll be coming out our way in just a second, Germ."

A slow minute ticked past. "So much for being tactical," Germ said. "Seven men, five with long guns, heading straight for the boat."

When they came into view, Pescador's ears came up, on full alert now, and a low rumble came from deep in his chest. I reached down and stroked his flank, noting the coarse hairs on his neck and back were standing up. "At ease, boy," I whispered quietly.

Within seconds all but one man swarmed onto the deck of my boat and a loud blast shook the night. "Son of a bitch," I snarled.

"You shoulda left the door unlocked, Gunny," Scott said.

"I fucking did."

With the *Revenge* pointed in our direction, Scott and I couldn't see the cockpit. But it was visible and only a short distance from Germ. "Five men entered the cabin. One on the dock, one in the cockpit. Engage?"

I wanted to blow their heads off. I could hear shouting from inside my boat.

"Wait until they come back out," Travis said, taking charge.

A moment later, four of them stepped up onto the dock, looking around. When the other three came out, Travis said, "Scott and Germ, engage."

Scott was already prone, using the night vision goggles to aim the silenced MP5 submachine gun. Not an easy task, and it made for an uncomfortable position, but I knew he and Germ had trained with both pieces of equipment before.

Two quick puffs came from the ugly little gun and I watched as three men went down, one falling in the water. Another spun, but remained upright, as he and the remaining three sprinted toward us, shooting wildly in all directions.

Scott and I rose in unison and I pulled my unsilenced Sig from the holster behind my back. A few yards apart, we advanced toward the onrushing men, Scott's gun spitting quietly and my Sig barking loudly with every footfall, both sending a rain of nine-millimeter lead at the startled men, now only fifty yards away and closing.

Two more went down and the other two turned and charged toward the building. The lead man crashed through the glass of a sliding door and the second followed right behind him.

Pescador charged after the two fleeing men, until I called him off. We heard muffled screams from inside the room followed by two quick gunshots. Then all went completely quiet. A moment later, I heard sirens in the distance.

"Report!" Travis shouted.

"Two tangoes down, two got away through the building," Scott said as we approached the two men on the ground. "We're okay here. There may be casualties inside the hotel room."

"Three tangoes down at the boat," Germ added. "All dead."

Scott knelt by the two men on the ground and quickly checked for a pulse. "Got one still alive, here. But he's not gonna make it."

I knelt beside the injured man, Pescador right beside me, his hot breath coming out in a series of short low growls. The man was about thirty, wearing jeans, cowboy boots and a western shirt. His hair was scraggly, his goatee unevenly trimmed. I grabbed him by his shirt collar and lifted his face close to mine, snarling, "Who are you?"

"Billy," he replied, coughing up blood. "Billy Ray Goodrich. Please don't kill me."

I looked down at the blood flowing freely from a chest wound. Lower, his jeans were soaked and quick bulges appeared in his pants from a wound in his thigh, a large pool already forming around his legs. His femoral artery.

"Too late," I said, dropping him to the ground. "You're already dead." The man's body convulsed once, the flow from his leg wound stopped, and his eyes went glassy.

"Back to the boat!" Travis shouted. "I've got some serious explaining to do."

A Key West police cruiser came roaring into the parking lot toward Travis, lights and siren going full blast. Travis stood in the glare of the headlights, his left arm up, holding his credentials, and his empty right hand stretched out beside him. When the siren stopped, two police officers hurriedly stepped out of the car, guns drawn and aimed at Travis.

"Federal agents! Stand down!"

CHAPTER THIRTY

Byers watched with anticipation as GT and the other six men swarmed toward the boat. One of them held back on the dock and in the dim glow of a small light shining up from the ground into the palm tree, he saw that it was the bodyguard, Erik.

With that many guns, the three men and the girl on the boat didn't stand a chance. Hearing his boss's plans for the girl, he was hoping that he might be allowed a small portion of the fun that was in store.

With a single shotgun blast, one of the rednecks blew the lock off the door to the boat's cabin and five of them rushed in. There were a few shouts and then they came back out.

As they climbed back up to the dock, several of them seemed to stumble and fall, one falling into the water with a loud splash. Suddenly, the four still on the dock started running toward the far side of the building. Then all hell broke loose, the four men shooting in all directions.

Out of the corner of his eye, Byers saw two men stalking steadily toward the four men. Both of these men had their guns up, spitting flame, but Byers could only hear one. Two of the four from GT's group fell to the ground and the remaining two ran toward the building.

Time to get the hell out of here, Byers thought. Ducking back inside, he spotted the open bag that the rednecks had brought their guns in sitting on the bed. Going through it quickly, he found only one gun, a huge chrome-plated revolver with white grips that reflected the light in shades of pale pink and light purple.

He shoved the big gun into his pants and pulled his shirt down over it. GT and Erik had left their jackets on the bed and Byers quickly went through the pockets, smiling as he pulled out GT's wad of cash. Shoving that in his pocket, he opened the door and headed straight for the stairs, not even considering waiting for the elevator.

There were only two people in the lobby when he got there. Both were at the door, looking outside. One was the desk clerk, the other an older blonde lady. Byers pulled his Panama Jack hat lower on his face and passed the desk, going out a side entrance.

Once outside, Byers heard a door open and close far down the side of the building. Crouching by a large anchor, he saw two men running across the parking lot. He recognized one of them as the black cowboy who had arrived just minutes earlier. The other was either GT or Erik, they looked so much alike that Byers couldn't tell for sure in the dim light. He waited half a minute as the two men sprinted across the parking lot. As sirens approached, he quickly made his way through the nearly empty front parking lot, ducking behind a car whenever he could.

Looking back, the desk clerk and the blonde were both looking in the opposite direction, toward the docks. Byers headed straight for a bunch of trees with long dangly roots hanging from the branches. Wedging himself deeper among the thicker tangle of roots near the main trunk of the tree, he got down low to the damp ground. The side parking lot quickly filled with police cars.

Byers was good at waiting. His small size and cowardly nature made him very good at hiding as well. So he sat there on the wet ground while the police searched the parking lot. He heard one say that he'd found a trail of blood, and several others joined him, headed off toward town.

When it looked clear, Byers finally extricated himself from the tangle of roots and crept around the edge of the parking lot. A narrow opening in the fence at the corner of the property was no problem and he was soon out on the road. A large crowd had gathered near the entrance and Byers lost himself among them, moving cautiously backward as more people came running up.

Hearing thunder in the distance, Byers turned and casually walked away from the hotel on Simonton Street. When he reached Caroline Street, he turned left and hurried past the restaurant he'd eaten at the night before, suddenly realizing he was hungry.

Sneaking around the side of the restaurant and reaching the deck area, he stole a quick glance and saw there were two tables that hadn't been bussed yet and nobody around. Moving quickly, he climbed over the low railing, grabbed a half-eaten fish sandwich from one plate and a fistful of cold, greasy fries from another and half rolled, half fell across the railing, retreating to the bushes along the side of the parking lot.

Eating while he walked down Grinnell Street to Eaton, he then turned left, knowing the last bus of the night would be coming that way. He hadn't quite made it two blocks when the bus came around the curve and he flagged it down.

A few minutes later, the bus rolled slowly past the hotel, where police and now a firetruck and several ambulances filled the lot with red and blue flashing lights. Half a dozen people stepped away from the crowd, waving at the bus. When it stopped, they got on, all talking at once. Byers had his hat pulled low and pretended to be dozing.

He caught snippets of the conversations around him, mentions of five men shot in an apparent drug deal gone bad. Someone else said something about federal agents, another mentioned terrorists, and still another said something about an alien invasion.

Thirty minutes later, Byers made his way up the aisle from the backseat as the driver pulled over at his regular stop on the east end of Stock Island. It had just started raining and the wind was blowing as Byers ran down the road to the little motel.

The same old guy was at the desk when Byers stepped inside, dripping wet. Rising up on his toes to the holes in the glass, he said, "Lost my key, man. Do you have another one?"

The old man looked at him, clearly irritated. "That'll be ten bucks for a duplicate key."

Peeling one of the twenties off the roll of bills he held below the counter, Byers slipped it under the glass. A moment later, the man shoved a ten and another key back to him. "Lose that one and there ain't no more."

In his room minutes later, Byers took his stash from under the mattress and fired up a decent-sized rock, then sat down on the edge of the bed. The crack seemed to settle his nerves enough that he was able to get the big gun out of his pants without shooting himself. He admired the shiny gun, which looked even larger in his small hands. Along the side of the barrel was engraved *Colt Python .357 Magnum Ctg.*

Guns were foreign to Byers, but he knew what the .357 meant. The barrel was long, he guessed it to be six inches at least, with a rail on the top that ran the length of it. He figured out how to release the cylinder and turned it, noting that two of the cartridges had tiny dimples in the center.

He pulled them out and saw there was no bullet in either. He dropped the empty cases in the trash can and pulled one of the others out, marveling at its size and weight. Over an inch and a half long, it was much larger than he'd expected. He slid the cartridge back in and closed the cylinder. Looking closer, he saw that each cartridge housing in the cylinder had a small picture engraved in it. Horses, cows, cowboy hats and other redneck stuff.

Placing the gun on the table, Byers took the wad of cash out of his pocket and counted it, his grin growing broader with each bill. He now had a little over two thousand dollars in cash, plus his coke stash that he was sure he could sell. Somewhere. Anywhere other than here.

Figuring he was at least safe in the motel room, he decided to take a nap, then catch a bus north, away from Key West.

CHAPTER
THIRTY-ONE

The rain came down in sheets as the ambulance crews loaded the bodies of the five dead men. One ambulance had already left with a middle-aged couple from Indiana. They weren't badly hurt, a flesh wound in the woman's arm, and a shoulder wound that went through cleanly for her husband.

Welcome to Key Weird, I thought. *Remember to send a post card home.*

"He'll come up with something," Scott said, standing next to me and Pescador. Travis was still talking to one of the sheriff's investigators, who'd arrived ten minutes after the first patrol cars.

"Yeah," Germ said, standing next to Scott in the driving rain. "Travis is a good man. Pissed me off, when I first heard about that whole Charity thing, but I'm betting it came from higher up."

So we stood waiting, as the rain poured down on us and the wind whipped at our clothes. Three Marines and a water dog. We could easily have taken a few steps to the left to stand under the palm tree, shielding ourselves from some of the rain. But clothes dry and the human body is waterproof, so we waited in the rain.

Finally, Travis and the investigator, clad in a rain slicker, walked over toward us. "This is Lieutenant Morgan, from the Monroe County Sheriff's Office. He has a couple of questions, but I've already explained that he'll get only one of your names."

Travis winked as the investigator stepped forward. "Which of you is the DEA agent?"

Scott stepped forward and produced a sealed plastic bag from his front pocket. Inside it, there was an open wallet with his credentials. "Special Agent Scott Grayson, Lieutenant. Drug Enforcement."

The lieutenant looked closely at the ID and at Scott's face. "You're operating here without notifying the sheriff, Agent Grayson."

"*Special* Agent Grayson," Scott corrected him. "Nothing to notify. Simple joint surveillance between two federal agencies. The dead guys obviously wanted it to be something more."

The lieutenant glared menacingly at Scott. He looked to be in his mid-thirties, balding, and already losing the battle of the bulge. Under normal circumstances, he might have pulled off the threatening cop look, but with his hair drenched and hanging over his forehead, he just looked tired.

"Did you identify yourselves to the suspects?"

Scott took a slow step toward the investigator, his broad shoulders and thickly muscled arms a sharp contrast to the lieutenant, though they were about the same age.

"Lieutenant, I've been in law enforcement as long as you, probably longer. Of course, I did. Idiots like these don't react like law-abiding citizens and because of that, they're dead. No sweat off my balls."

The lieutenant held Scott's gaze for a moment, then looked at me and Germ. Finally he turned to Travis. "Director Stockwell, y'all are free to go. The sheriff's office would like to get a heads-up any time another agency is investigating something here in Monroe County. Just as a professional courtesy."

Without waiting for a reply, Lieutenant Morgan stomped off toward the growing throng of people, now joined by the lights and camera of a news crew.

Travis looked at Scott and said, "Good job. Can we get in out of the rain?"

Pescador rose and shook the water out of his fur, then leaped across the gunwale into the cockpit. Germ and Travis boarded and, looking over my shoulder at Scott as I stepped down to the deck, I said, "DEA?"

"Or FBI, CIA, FDLE, hell, I carry a whole damned Scrabble board in my pockets now."

Inside, Travis switched on the salon lights. "At least one person on any mission now carries multiple IDs, courtesy of Homeland Security. Makes it easier to smooth things over with the local law enforcement."

"Two got away," I said after grabbing some towels from the head and passing them around. I began setting up the coffeemaker.

"Not for long," Travis responded. "Only one way on or off the island. Local and county law enforcement will be checking anyone leaving."

"Unless they steal a boat," Germ said, echoing my thoughts.

"A cowboy and a Pittsburgh drug dealer? Doubtful. At any rate, I think our new friend doesn't have anything to worry about as far as GT Bradley is concerned. If he does get away, he'll head home as fast as he can and be picked up there."

"Then we're done here?" I asked.

"I'd say so."

"Then let's get the hell outta here. You want to catch a cab home or ride back and spend the night on the island?"

"I'll get the dock lines," Travis said, looking at his watch. "We'll be there before sunrise."

Up on the bridge, I watched while Travis and Germ untied the lines. Scott sat on the port bench, watching me. "You're wanting to stay gone, aren't you?"

The rain had quit and as I watched the moon come out from behind the scudding clouds, I thought about it for just a moment.

"It used to be nice here, back when I was a kid. It's still mostly nice up in Big Pine and Marathon. But it's getting worse, Scott. I find myself wanting more and more to do nothing but fish, dive, eat good food with good friends and, well, just live."

"I hear ya, Gunny," Scott said with a low sigh. "Sometimes, I'm just tired of it all, man. And you've been doing this for what? Almost thirty years?"

"Twenty-eight years, a month, and twenty-two days."

"You deserve a rest," he said with another sigh.

I did deserve a rest. When I came down here after retiring from the Corps, all I wanted to do was get drunk, chase women, fish and dive, and eat and sleep. Not necessarily in that order. Things happened that I couldn't ignore, things that spiraled out of control. Friends got hurt, terrorists changed our way of life, and I lost my wife. Somewhere along the line, I'd also lost my direction.

I'd grasped onto Deuce's team like it was a lifeline. I found friends among their tight-knit community, the camaraderie of warriors. More bad things happened and more friends were hurt. It just didn't seem to make much difference what I did about it. Now, I had my daughters back in my life, a good woman that I loved, and my little island to escape to.

To hell with the rest of the world, I thought and started the engines.

Minutes later, the *Revenge* slowly idled away from the dock in the moonlight, once more leaving carnage in my wake. In the channel, I checked the radar and turned north, bringing the big boat up on plane, going through the process like an automaton.

The clouds were nearly gone and stars now filled the sky as we made the turn to the northeast and home, but it didn't have the same effect it usually does. Still, it was beautiful, and in the back of my mind the same three words scrambled for purchase, trying to fight the oncoming rush of island time. *No loose ends.*

CHAPTER THIRTY-TWO

Pescador's barking woke me. From the angle of the sunlight streaming through the open window, I could tell it was already midmorning. Knowing that Michal and Coral would be in my little house, the four of us had gone straight to the eastern bunkhouse when we returned last night. The rain had cooled things off a lot and I slept comfortably, not losing a single wink for the events of the night before.

Rising from my bunk, I saw Travis just starting to stir, but Scott and Germ were already up and gone. "I think we're getting old, Colonel."

Travis pulled on a clean shirt from his go-bag and stood up. "Speak for yourself, Jarhead. My rank allows me to start the day later." He stretched and, hearing more than one vertebrae pop, we both laughed. "I'll go to the other bunkhouse and get Chyrel on vid-comm to find out the latest news."

I rose and went bare-chested to the pier out back. The sudden shock of the cool Gulf water after last night's storm broke through the fog in my brain in half a heartbeat and I soon lost myself in the rhythm of the swim for the next thirty minutes.

When I finally got back to the pier, Coral was waiting with a towel. "Your friends said to talk to you or your first mate, but I can't find him. What happened last night?"

I took the towel from her and rubbed my face and hair vigorously. "Have you talked to your aunt?"

"Yeah, Charlie let me use her phone and showed me where I could get a signal. Aunt Dawn said there was a shooting last night in Key West. The news hasn't confirmed anything, but the coconut telegraph says that four men were killed."

"Five," I replied. "Bradley's bodyguard, and four of five redneck wannabe-mercenaries Bradley hired. He, the little man, and one of the cowboys got away."

"Little man?"

"The guy who stole Michal's wallet in Miami. Somehow, Bradley was tracking Michal's credit card usage, but it was the pickpocket they were following. He and Michal both just happened to end up in Key West and now the pickpocket's joined up with Bradley."

"So what happens now?"

I turned, leaned on the rail and watched as a flock of pelicans flew in a tight formation out over the Contents, peeling off and diving one by one on the baitfish in a narrow channel between two islands. Coral leaned on the rail next to me and waited.

"Now, I suppose you two go on with whatever life it is you choose," I said. "Bradley will be caught either trying to get out of Key West, or when he gets to Pittsburgh."

She stared off to the far horizon for a moment, then looked down into the water below the pier. "Five men dead. That's not what we wanted to happen."

Taking her by the shoulders, I turned her toward me. "None of that's on you, kid. Those men made a conscious decision to follow the life that *they* chose. If people like that are lucky, they spend half their life in prison. If not, they spend the rest of it just being dead. What you need to ask yourself is this. Is that young man worth it?"

She smiled a little, but there was moisture in her eyes. "Aunt Dawn was right about you. She said you had a reputation for ending problems before they started, then rationalizing what happened in a way that makes perfect sense."

"I barely even know your aunt."

"Yeah, she said that too. But down island, you're pretty well known as a problem solver." We both turned toward the island and could see Michal and the Trents' kids throwing a ball to one another in the clearing, Pescador bounding after it when little Patty dropped it. "I think Michal's worth it. Deep down, he's a good man. Aunt Dawn told me weeks ago that he would arrive in my life soon and she thinks he's worthy, too."

"If he keeps on the right side of the line," I said.

She turned to me, eyes now blazing defiantly. "Because of the drugs? We threw the coke into the bight. He's done with that."

"And the pot?"

"Everyone smokes weed, even Aunt Dawn on occasion. That's no big deal."

I looked at her, surprised. I'd known only a handful of people who ever smoked marijuana and they were all young people, like Michal, Coral, and Jimmy. "Your aunt does?"

"That surprises you?"

"Well, yeah."

"Not often and don't tell her I told you."

Travis stepped out of the shade of the gumbo limbo next to the western bunkhouse and motioned to me. "Excuse me," I said. "Make yourself at home here until we're sure it's safe to go back down island. We're having a sort of party here later. Y'all are welcome to stay."

I trotted after Travis and followed him around to the far side of the west bunkhouse and into Chyrel's little field office there. The two bunkhouses had originally been built identical, but Carl remodeled this one. It now has a desk to accommodate Chyrel's computers and bunks for up to four women, separated from the rest of the bunkhouse, where the men from Deuce's team stay from time to time, as needed.

Once inside, Travis closed the door. "Chyrel hacked into the local PD and sheriff's computers. None of the three men who escaped last night have been apprehended. And there was a report of a stolen boat sometime overnight."

"What kind of boat?"

"An eighteen-foot Mako center-console. The owner said it had less than half a tank of gas on board."

"They couldn't make it more than fifteen or twenty miles without stopping for gas somewhere."

Travis nodded. "Word went out from the marina the boat was stolen from to every other marina in the Keys. If they buy gas anywhere, it'll be reported."

"Local cops have more roadblocks up, besides the Stock Island Bridge?"

"Yeah, but not until after the theft was reported."

"Damn," I said. "Always reactive, never proactive. They could be all the way to Daytona by now. All they had to do was get past Stock Island in the boat and then steal a car. What about the five dead guys?"

Travis went to Chyrel's desk and picked up a notepad. "Erik Lowery, age thirty, resides in Pittsburgh. Known bagman and bodyguard for Gerald Tremont Bradley. Did a few years in Attica, up in New York. The other four are from the Okeechobee area. Small-time hoods, but well known to the authorities in Hendry, Glades, Palm Beach, and Dade counties."

I looked at the list of names, but none were familiar. "Let me call someone I know up there. See if he has any idea who the black cowboy is that these guys were with."

Travis tore the page off and handed it to me. "Your daughter and her family are coming down today?"

"Yeah, I'm picking them up at the *Anchor* at noon. You staying for the cookout?"

"Is that an invitation?"

"Unless you prefer the Wooden Spoon."

"Sure," he replied. "Thanks."

Aboard the *Revenge*, I used the sat-phone and called a friend in LaBelle, just west of Lake Okeechobee. He answered on the first ring.

"Figured you'd be calling, Kemosabe," Billy Rainwater said by way of answering the phone. Billy and I went to school together, though he was a couple of years behind me, and later served in the Corps together. His dad was one of the last of the Calusa, the original people that had inhabited South Florida. His mom was Seminole. I occasionally buy guns and a few other toys from him.

"What do you mean you knew I'd be calling? You don't even know this number."

"You're looking for a black cracker name of Austin Brown, originally from Clewiston. He called me less than an hour ago for help. I figured you'd find out who his buddies were and call me."

"He called *you* for help?"

"Said he and the guy he was working for needed guns and off-road transportation. When he mentioned the name of your boat, I cut him off and told him he was on his own and better get shed of the guy he was with, muy pronto."

"He say where they were?"

"Nope, and I didn't ask. He ain't a bad guy, Jesse. Just has some redneck, trailer-trash friends. Or had some, anyway. The average IQ in Naranja went up a bit after last night. That's where Brown lives now, owns a gun shop down there. I could tell he was on a payphone, though, and near water. Heard cars going by on the highway and gulls crying."

"He say how many people he was with?"

"Nope, but the way he talked it sounded like just him and the one guy he was working for. I won't even ask what happened down there, Kemosabe. His white trash buddies got shot to shit and you're involved. That's enough for me to know they probably deserved it."

"Anything else you can tell me about him?"

"He's smart. Way smarter than he lets on. He knows me and knows if I'm warning him away, the guy he's working for is like kryptonite to Superman. As soon as the opportunity presents itself, he'll ditch the guy he's running with. Odds are he's traveling solo already. His wife's name's Mary-Beth, a white woman. The two of 'em run his gun store on Old Dixie Highway, near Biscayne Drive. Mean woman."

"Thanks, Billy. I appreciate it. If he calls you back, see if you can find out where the other guy is. I'm only interested in that guy, so long as your friend keeps his ass up there on the mainland."

"Never said he was a friend. Just a business associate."

I ended the call and went back out to where Carl, Germ, and Scott were working in the garden. "Shouldn't you be headed up to get your daughter?" Carl asked.

"Leaving in a minute," I replied. "Got a second, Scott?"

I walked toward the steps leading up to my house, and Scott followed, wiping his forehead with the tail of a sleeveless workout shirt. "What's up?" he asked when I turned around.

"You and Germ mind hanging out here a day or so?"

"The Pittsburgh drug dealer got away from Key West PD?"

"Apparently," I replied. "The hired gunman he's with is an amateur out of South Miami, Austin Brown. They probably stole a boat last night and could have made Saddlebunch Keys before running out of gas. They'll probably get picked up today. If not, I might know where at least one of them is headed."

"Sure, Gunny. We'll hang out, unless the director says different."

"You know a gun shop on Old Dixie up near the base?"

Scott laughed. "About a dozen. Shooting's a pretty popular pastime up there."

"Owned by a black guy named Austin Brown and his wife, a white woman, Mary-Beth."

"Yeah," Scott said. "I know the place. At least by reputation. It's said you can buy clean guns there. By clean, I mean they've never been registered, have had the serial numbers removed, and never been used in the commission of a felony."

"The black cowboy last night was Austin Brown, and the trailer trash were his buddies. Bradley probably hired them, no idea how they knew each other."

Scott rubbed the back of his thick neck. "I thought a couple of those guys looked familiar. I've probably seen them around Homestead."

"I gotta head up to Rusty's place to pick up my daughter and her family. Let Travis know what I told you?"

"Sure thing, Gunny. See ya in a bit."

Cutting through a path around the steps, I waded out to the foot of the pier, climbed up and went through the door to the dock space. After a quick rinse under the shower on board, I was dressed in clean clothes and pulling out from under the house in the big Winter center-console, *El Cazador*.

Twenty minutes later, I had to heave to in the shallows by the channel to the *Anchor* to let a boat pass that was coming down the canal. As it got closer, I recognized Mac Travis at the helm. He turned toward me as he approached and, coming alongside, he reversed his engine, bringing the boat to a stop.

Mac nodded. "McDermitt."

I stepped over to the rail and leaned on it, ready to fend his boat off if need be. "How are ya, Mac?"

"Same old shit," he said. "You hear about that shootout down in Key West?"

"Heard something about it," I said. Mac was a decent enough guy, kept pretty much to himself most of the time. "Some bad guys got killed and a few of them got away."

"Three got away, but one of 'em went back to the scene of the crime. He's dead now, too."

"Hadn't heard that," I said.

"Some ugly little crackhead about five foot nothin' that was supposed to be involved."

The guy that tried to sell crack to Charlie, I thought. *No great loss there.*

"Cops get him?" I asked.

Mac laughed and took off his fisherman shades, revealing the white rings around his eyes, where the skin wasn't exposed to the rays of the sun.

"Weirdest thing I ever heard. You know that little footbridge near the aquarium?" I nodded. "The guy that pedals the Key West Mobile Library was crossing it on that three-wheeled bookstore thing of his. Apparently the little crack monster was crossing it from the other direction and must've tripped over something. The bookmobile bumped him right off the bridge. It was feeding time in the shark pen just thirty feet away."

"He fell in the shark pen?" I asked.

"No, but when they feed the big sharks in the pen, a bunch of little ones, mostly spinners and bonnet heads, come into the tidal pond area that the pen gets its clean water from. What I heard was, the guy wasn't any bigger

than a ten-year-old girl, easy pickings for the five or six three-footers that usually show up for scraps."

"Guess he missed the sign," I said.

"What sign?"

"'Don't feed the sharks.'"

Mac laughed, putting his shades back on and reversing his boat back into the channel. "Thought you meant the one on the bookmobile."

"What's that?"

"Says, 'Be nice, or I'll kill you in my next book.'"

CHAPTER THIRTY-THREE

T ied up to Rusty's big barge at the end of the turning basin a few minutes later, I walked across the deck and up to the dock, where I stopped to look around. The air was a little cooler, in the high eighties maybe, but the humidity was through the roof. The only cars in the lot were Rusty's old pickup, my Travelall, and an older Toyota that I knew belonged to Angie, Jimmy's girlfriend.

I crossed the yard to the front door of the bar, the smells of something good cooking from out on the back deck filling my nostrils. Opening the door, I stepped inside, waiting a moment for my eyes to adjust to the dimmer light inside.

"Hey, Jesse," Jimmy said from behind the bar. "Ya just missed Rusty, man. He headed out about ten minutes ago."

"Hey, Jimmy. He take his skiff?"

"Yeah, some bonehead tourists went aground off Sandy Point. Wanna beer, dude?"

"Sure," I replied. "In just a minute. I want to see what Rufus has back there."

When I returned, I took a seat on my usual stool at the end of the bar and Jimmy placed a frosty Red Stripe on a coaster in front of me. "That was you in Key West last night."

It was a statement, not a question. Word spreads quickly among this small island chain community. Still, I didn't want any details out there. "No idea what you're talking about, Jimmy." I took a long pull on the cold Jamaican beer as he watched me.

Jimmy winked. "Sure, dude. Whatever you say."

"Where is everyone?"

"It's Friday, man. Everyone's working."

"Why aren't you working?"

Jimmy wiped the bar top with a towel. "I am, man. Just not working for old Joe anymore. He bent another prop shaft. Why's a near-blind skipper hire a mate and not listen when the mate tells him he's plowing into skinny water? Anyway, Rusty's giving me some hours here. Not much, but enough."

That was Rusty's way. Half the people in Marathon worked for him at one time or another and it was likely another of Joe's crew would be stopping by today. If a fisherman lost his boat in a storm, or a lobsterman fell on hard times, he'd put them to work doing odd jobs that really didn't need doing, just to put a few bucks in their pockets without taking a handout. They were prideful people.

"Hey," Jimmy said. "You hear the news about the school?"

"Cindy's school?"

"Yeah, it opens next week, man. Me and Tru took the sign up and helped install it. Guess what she's calling the school."

"I figured it'd be the same as Alex's school in Oregon, *Catching It?*"

Jimmy laughed and stopped polishing the bar. "It's gonna be called the *Alex DuBois McDermitt Fly Fishing Lodge.*"

Just then, Rufus brought my cobia sandwich in and placed it in front of me. "Really? Well, that ought to bring in some customers." As Rufus turned to leave, I touched his arm. "Got a second, Rufus?"

The little Jamaican man turned around and showed his big, gap-toothed grin. "What can Rufus do for yuh today, mon?"

I took a quick bite of my sandwich as he sat down, the explosion of flavors tickling my taste buds. "Man, this is good. Hey, I meant to ask you about the other day?"

"Seen many udduh days, mon," he said, still grinning. "Which day be dat?"

I wiped my mouth and searched his smiling eyes. "With those two smug drugglers? I was right over there, both eyes open, and I still don't know what I saw."

His grin widened. "It nuttin', mon. Jus di suspension of time and space is all."

Looking into his eyes, I didn't see any sign of subterfuge. "A suspension of time and space? I've watched you out in the water a few times. Come on, what's your style?"

He looked puzzled. "No style, mon. It just what I and I say. A momentary suspension of time dat allow Rufus to be in more dan one space at di same time. In di whole cosmos dis kinda ting happen all di time."

Without another word, the old man got up and strode to the back door. "He's an old-school mystic, dude," Jimmy said. "I bet he's two hundred years old."

The door opened and we both glanced over. A man and woman were silhouetted against the bright sunlight behind them, the woman carrying a small bundle.

"Eve!" I got up and walked quickly toward them.

"Hi, Father," my oldest daughter said, smiling and stepping through the door.

I met her halfway across the floor and gently hugged her, so as not to disturb my sleeping grandson in her arms. She turned and said, "Nick, I'd like you to meet your father-in-law, Jesse McDermitt. Father, this is my husband, Nicholas Maggio."

I looked into Nick's eyes for the first time since I'd held a gun on him and his father in their Miami office. There was a little hesitancy there. Holding out my hand, I said, "Really nice to finally meet you, Nick. Eve's told me a lot about you."

He took my hand in his, with a grip that was firm at first but instantly softened when I returned it in kind. "Nice to meet you, Mister McDermitt."

I waved toward the bar. "Let's not be so formal, huh? Just call me Jesse. And Eve, really? How about Dad?"

We walked over to the bar and I introduced them to Jimmy. "I wasn't expecting you for another half hour. Would y'all like some lunch? Rufus makes the best fish sandwich in the Keys."

"No thanks," Nick replied. "We left Miami a little early so we could eat lunch before we got here. The restaurant we stopped at had really fast service. Please, finish your lunch."

While I quickly ate the rest of my sandwich, Jimmy continued with his news of Cindy's school. "Anyway, dude, me and Cindy got to talking about fishing. She'd been so busy getting the school ready, she hadn't had time to wet a line. We went out just before sunset and I put her on some redfish. Long story short, I work for you again, mi hermano!"

I nearly choked on the last bite of my sandwich. "Huh?"

"She offered me a job, right there from the casting deck, dude. Said she was taking resumes to fill staff positions and all that, but she liked to do interviews for guides on the water."

"Congratulations, Jimmy! You're a perfect fit for that."

"The school is even providing me a skiff, man."

"They couldn't find a better guide," I said. Then, with a sidelong glance, I asked, "Rules?"

Jimmy glanced at Nick and Eve quickly. "We didn't talk about it, but I know, same rules as on the *Revenge*. Es no problema, dude."

Nick spoke quickly to Jimmy in fluent Spanish. Jimmy grinned and replied back in rapid-fire sentences, leaving me far behind. Nick smiled and said, "Your Spanish is exceptional. You are Cuban?"

I laughed, knowing what was coming next. "No, dude," Jimmy replied, falling back into his usual southern California surfer routine, although he'd never been to California that I knew of. "I was a Conquistador in one of my past lives, man. Not some Spanish admiral or anything, just one of the troops, ya know. What I do is meditate for an hour and I can go back to one of my past lives and just sort of look around and listen for a few days. It all comes in super-fast motion, but I've learned to retain everything I see and hear."

"It's true," I said, getting up. "The man has a photographic memory."

I laid a ten on the bar, even though I knew Jimmy had already recorded my lunch in the bar's tab book. "Hey, tell Rusty I was here and left, but I'll be back later, or tomorrow. Also, spread the word. The guy Rufus did the little time hop thing with? He may be coming back through here, or maybe he came through last night and is further up island. I'd sure like to continue the conversation I had with him in Key West last night."

Jimmy grinned and winked. "Will do, Skipper. If I hear anything, I'll let you know. Thanks."

Shaking Jimmy's hand and congratulating him again on the job, I led Eve and her family down to the turning basin. I made a mental note to call Cindy and find out if she needed anything. I'd been bankrolling the school's initial expenses, but a lot of local businesses were now stepping up. Still, I wanted to thank her for using Alex's name. Made good business sense, really. She'd been known as one of the best guides in the Keys, and her name was widely known in the fishing community all across the country.

"A boat?" Nick asked as we approached *Cazador*. "I thought we'd be going in the car."

I grinned. "Not unless your car's amphibious, Nick. The only way to my house is by boat or chopper."

"I don't know about taking little Alfie on a boat."

"He's a waterman," I told him. "Just like his pappy, great-grandpap, and great-great-grandpap before him."

I stepped down and quickly started the big diesel engine. Reaching up, I took my grandson and helped Eve over the gunwale before handing him back to her. "You weren't here when I baptized him, Nick."

"Is that what that was all about?" Eve asked. "That night out on Cape Sable?"

I glanced at her as I untied the bowline. Eve was a lot like her mom and so different from her sister. Where Kim was tall, Eve was short. Eve also had her mom's dark hair, which she wore short in back, tapering to longer in the front. She'd also inherited her mom's more formal manners.

"I did the same with you," I said. "I offered you up to Neptune in Pamlico Sound, just a week after you were born. And Kim not much longer after her birth."

Coiling the bowline and hooking it in place, I moved aft and untied the stern, holding the dock until Nick was aboard. He was holding a small baby carrier and had two bags hanging across his shoulders.

"You did?" Eve asked.

"So did my dad. You might not accept a life on the water, kiddo, but you were born to it. My dad offered me to the god of the sea on the day I was born and his dad did the same for him."

Eve looked around the boat. Seating aboard *Cazador* is limited to only the two spots at the helm and two forward of the console.

"Nick, put the carrier right here next to me at the helm," I said and shoved the boat away from the barge. "You two can sit forward."

Nick looked all around the seat and finally said, "There's no seatbelt."

271

"Nope," I replied. "You don't want to be belted into a boat if it overturns."

His eyes shot up at me, concerned. I hoped it was concern for his son and not himself. I still didn't have a good read on him yet.

"Relax, Nick," Eve said. "Nothing will happen."

She took the carrier from him and placed it on the wide helm seat, then put the baby in it, sleeping soundly.

"You think he has enough sunscreen?" Nick asked, gently touching the boy's arm.

I smiled and pointed at the hardtop over our heads. "He's fine, son. We'll have the sun directly overhead all the way."

Nick looked at me and smiled. "Thanks, Jesse."

Once they were seated I toggled the bow thruster, turning the thirty-two-foot boat's bow toward the end of the canal and engaging the transmission.

A minute later, we entered the channel and I pushed the throttles forward, one hand on the baby carrier sitting next to me. When I looked down, his eyes were open. I located a release on the side and set it up a little, using the handle as a brace.

"There ya go, little Jesse. Now you can see the water."

Looking back through the small windshield, Eve said, "Did you say something, Dad?"

I smiled back at her. "Just talking to my grandson."

I basically ignored Eve and Nick all the way to Harbor Channel, talking mostly to my grandson in the seat next to me, telling him everything I knew about the different islands and channels we passed. Where we would go to catch grunts, when he got older and where we could dive on some lobster honey holes I knew about.

272

Approaching the canal to the house, I slowly brought the *Cazador* off plane and turned into it. The big door on the east side was already open and Germ was on a ladder propped precariously on the center dock.

Reversing the engine and toggling the bow thruster, I turned the boat around and backed into her berth. Germ climbed down and was ready to tie off when I killed the engine.

"Back sooner than we expected," Germ said, taking the stern line and making it fast to the dock. "We're almost done with the ladder well."

I introduced him to Eve and Nick then we all climbed up to the dock. "Follow me," Germ said and led them to the far side of the dock area and the door.

I glanced up at where he'd been working, surprised to see that the whole thing was done and there was even a railing around the opening, up inside the house.

Taking a quick detour, I climbed up the new ladder and into my living room. The rail looked custom made, fashioned aluminum railing just like around the bow and pulpit of the *Revenge*.

I almost ran into Travis when I opened the door and stepped out onto the deck, just as Germ led Eve and Nick up the steps from the pier.

"Carl's idea," Travis informed me. "Said he picked up the pulpit and railing from a boatyard on Islamorada where they were dismantling a big Viking that'd had the bottom ripped out of her."

When the others joined us, we stopped by the railing overlooking the island. "Mi casa es tu casa, Nick."

Looking down from the deck, Nick took everything in. Michal, Coral, and the kids were out on the sandbar in front of Carl's house with buckets, gathering clams. Charlie and Scott were busy in the garden, picking spinach to use in a salad and Carl was scooping a few of the biggest crayfish out of the tank.

"This is unbelievable," Nick said. "How many people live here?"

"Just Jesse and the Trent family," Travis said. "Scott, Germ, and I just dropped by for a visit, and the young couple out there are staying over for a day or so."

Nick turned around, apparently recognizing the voice. Travis stepped forward and held out his hand. "I'm Travis Stockwell, Mister Maggio."

Nick looked confused for a second, then shook Travis's hand. "Pleased to meet you, sir."

Charlie noticed us, put down her basket and rushed up the steps. "So nice to see you again, Eve." They hugged and Charlie took the baby from Nick, rubbing her face on his belly and getting a laugh in return. "Come on down to the house, Eve. I don't get many women visitors. We'll leave the men to talk about fishing."

Eve took one of the bags from Nick. It was bright yellow and covered with blue and red balloons.

"Come on inside, Nick," Travis said, leading the way back to the door. Once inside, Germ closed the door. "Have a seat, son," Travis said, pointing to the little-used table and chairs in the corner of the galley.

Germ waited by the door as the three of us sat down. "This is the first time we've had a chance to talk in a while." Travis said. Nick looked nervously from him to me. "I'll get right to the point. You and your dad owe me and from time to time, I've contacted him with a question, or maybe something he could help me with. By default this quid pro quo extends to you."

Nick thought over what he said and slowly nodded. "You mean like some kind of informant?"

"Let's call it legal advisor," Travis said, with a disarming, fatherly grin. The man could charm the panties off a nun. "I'll get right to the point. Have you ever heard of a cocaine distributor from Pittsburgh by the name of Gerald Tremont Bradley?"

"I've heard of him," Nick said. "Goes by his initials, GT, former pro football player. Now he's a big-time cocaine distributor up there. I know his attorney personally. We went to law school together."

"We're more interested in his accountant," I said.

"His accountant? I don't know anything at all about who his accountant is," Nick said, turning to me.

I looked in his eyes and believed him. "His name is Chase Conner and he once worked for the state."

"Chase Conner?" he asked, thinking. "What capacity did he work for the state in?"

"Department of Revenue," I replied.

"No, I don't recall ever hearing the name."

I sat down next to him. "I'll be straight with you, Nick. I'd like to believe you and I'm leaning toward that. Chase Conner bugged my boat about a year ago, learned about an old Spanish treasure a friend found a clue to, and then gave that information to some pretty bad people. Because of Conner's actions, a lot of people were killed. Some probably had it coming, but there were a few innocent people killed, and a good friend took a bullet meant for me."

Nick's Adam's apple bobbed. "Valentin Madic."

"Yes, Valentin Madic."

The level of discomfort was obvious on Nick's face. "I wish I did know something about him. I truly do. I'd love to be able to help you in some way, if for no other reason than to make amends. Madic was one of our clients and Father and I were the ones responsible for sending some of those people after you."

It pleased me that he admitted this. Travis's brow furrowed. "That's unfortunate, but we'll catch up to him sooner or later." Then to me, he said, "One of the men who got away last night is dead."

"Killed by baby sharks," I said with a grin. "Learned about it on the coconut telegraph an hour ago."

"I need to subscribe to this thing," Travis said. "Seems like it's faster than the Internet and more reliable."

"Last night?" Nick asked, putting two and two together. "That was you guys in Key West?"

"Does this coconut telegraph extend all the way to Miami?" Travis asked. "Yes, that was a joint forces DEA and DHS raid on a suspected distributor attempting to expand in south Florida." Coming from Travis, it sounded not only true, but plausible.

"DEA, sure. But DHS? I though you guys were strictly national security stuff, with no policing powers inside the borders."

Travis nodded. "Strictly speaking, yes. However, the Caribbean Counterterrorism Command is a badged police force within the DHS. The DEA's agent down there needed backup in a hurry and part of my team was here for a little break and readily available." Travis nodded toward Germ by the door. "Agent Simpson there, along with Agent Grayson, myself and Jesse, went down to lend a hand."

"And Bradley's still on the loose down here in the Keys?"

"You're quick," I replied. "Bradley was in the company of a low-level gunman from up your way. Austin Brown."

Nick's demeanor changed and he became more serious. "Him I know. From back before we first met. I wouldn't discount him as low-level."

"Doesn't matter," Travis said. "I have it on good authority that they've more than likely parted company. We're only interested in Bradley, primarily to get to his accountant. DEA can have Bradley and the sheriff can have Brown."

Nick considered it. "Like I said, I knew Brown from a couple of years ago."

"Back before you met Jesse here."

"Um, yeah. I knew him in sort of a professional capacity."

Travis grinned again. "What you're so deftly trying to tiptoe around is that Brown moved guns for you and your father. Guns purchased illegally on the black market and brought in through Miami."

Nick tensed.

"Relax, Nick. What's done is done and you're not involved in that anymore."

It was a statement of fact. I had no doubt that all of Nick and his father's business dealings and movements had been closely scrutinized for nearly a year.

"Yeah," Nick said with a sigh. "He moved guns for us."

Travis grinned again. "Still have his number?"

CHAPTER THIRTY-FOUR

W hat do you mean he won't help?" GT shouted, drawing the attention of a small group of tourists launching a boat.

Austin turned slowly toward the Pittsburgh dealer, slipping easily into his usual cracker demeanor. "Mister Bradley, you might want to try *not* making a scene here. In case you ain't noticed, we're the only *brothers* around here."

Austin sat down on a bench outside Cudjoe Gardens Marina and contemplated his plight. GT finally calmed down enough and sat down next to him.

"You led me and my friends into a trap, Mister Bradley. Erik said all we'd have to do was show up with superior numbers and you'd get your stuff back. We did and now they're dead. My friend on that payphone just now told me about the guy you were trying to muscle in on. We're lucky to be alive. And we'll be damned lucky to stay this way."

Having spent most of the night and morning adrift with GT, Austin was beginning to tire of him. *Maybe Billy's right,* he thought. *Maybe it'd be best to just cut my losses and ditch this clown.*

Knowing that the police would have road blocks set up, Austin had insisted they steal a boat. However, they'd run out of gas after only twenty minutes of fast running, then drifted until the current carried them into Cudjoe Bay just a few minutes ago.

Looking around at the people nearby, GT realized the cowboy was right and lowered his voice. "Listen, Austin, it's no longer a matter of getting my property back. Now it's about revenge. Erik and I went way back. I'm talking playground friends here."

"I don't know," Austin replied. "From what my friend just told me, that guy's one of the most dangerous men in all of South Florida."

"I can make it worth your while," GT said. "You know a safe place? Somewhere I can bring my guys down from Pittsburgh? Get us some guns? You do this and there's twenty large in it for you."

Slowly lifting his head, Austin turned and looked GT in the eye. "Guns? Yeah, I can do that. If we can get up to Miami, we'll be safe at my place. But I don't know about coming back down here. This guy's got serious money and can hire the best."

"I know, I know. This is his territory. I'm sorry I didn't tell you who he was upfront. Somehow they knew we'd be coming for them." Scratching the hundreds of mosquito bites he'd suffered through the night, GT reconsidered. "I'll make it twenty grand and pay for the guns separate, plus any other expenses you incur."

Austin watched the tourists for a minute. "Ya sure ya wanna do this?"

"Just get me someplace safe. I'll have money wired to your account and my soldiers will be on the next plane out of Pittsburgh. You won't even have to come along after that."

"Lemme make another call," Austin said, already dreading it. "We'll need to find a place to lay low for a few hours until my wife can get down here and pick us up."

"You sure you can get us guns?" GT asked. "I can make one call and have my guys on a plane in two hours, but they can't even bring a nail file."

With the guns he planned to sell Bradley, Austin knew he'd clear twenty-five or thirty thousand dollars. All pure profit. "Yeah. I own a gun shop."

"I'm not talking about hunting rifles or revolvers here."

"Neither am I," Austin said, starting to rise.

"Let me call first," GT said, passing him and picking up the receiver on the payphone.

While GT talked on the phone, Austin watched as a man came walking up the road from the nearly vacant neighborhood where they'd beached the boat.

GT's call lasted only a minute before he came back over to where Austin waited. "Money's coming with my guys. My accountant doesn't like paper trails and refuses to wire it. Sometimes, I don't know why I keep his ass around."

"For exactly that reason if you're smart," Austin said. "He's looking out for your best interests, but until the money's in my hand, we don't have a deal. I'll get us a ride."

Picking up the receiver, Austin dropped a quarter in and dialed. A moment later, his wife answered and he gave her the short version of the previous night's events, telling her that Chet, Ace, Billy Ray and Claude were all dead.

"You just stop right there and listen," his wife said. "That lawyer called, the one you and Billy Ray, God rest his soul, did some gun deals with. He has something cooking that can mean big bucks."

Turning around to keep GT from hearing, even though he was ten feet away, Austin watched the man who'd just walked up, now heading back the way he came. Another guy who'd been working on a boat out back was with him.

After a moment, Austin said, "Okay. That can work. I'll call him when you get here. Bring my backup cell phone. But I gotta go, things are developin' fast. You get here quick as you can and drive slow on US-1 before the turn to Cudjoe Gardens Marina. We'll be hiding in the mangroves and flag ya down, 'member where that's at?"

He waited a moment and then hung up without another word and walked casually to where GT stood. "We gotta go now!" he whispered urgently. Looking back over his shoulder, he saw the two men walking briskly back toward the marina.

Austin's strides were long, his cowboy boots clicking on the asphalt as he ambled hastily toward the main road, GT following close behind him. "What's the hurry?"

"That guy back there found the boat. We gotta get up to the highway and find a place to hide out for a coupla hours. Think you and your boys can use a helicopter?"

"Your wife's picking us up in a chopper?"

Austin kept looking back over his shoulder, but nobody was coming out of the marina. "No, she's coming in my Power Wagon, but I'm working on a gun deal with a guy out of Miami that has a whirlybird. If you got cash, I might be able to arrange a borrow."

CHAPTER THIRTY-FIVE

W‌alking with Nick around the perimeter of my island, I showed him the aquaculture system behind my house. Taking a narrow path through the trees, I pointed out the reverse-osmosis unit and heavy-duty diesel-powered generator, both mounted at chest level on stilts halfway between my house and the bunkhouses.

"Over there's the battery shack," I said, pointing along the shoreline. "Carl has thirty deep-cycle marine batteries there that power an inverter for the things that need one-ten voltage. But most things are twelve volt or run on propane or alcohol."

"How long can you last here if a zombie apocalypse happens?"

Laughing, I said, "If you mean the government, that's already happened. But if things get bad, we can last more than a month. Much longer if we ration energy usage. A friend delivers diesel, alcohol, and propane once a month. With enough fuel, we can survive here indefinitely."

Nick stopped and glanced back up to the house. "Is that why you had us come out, Jesse? To see if I'd play ball?"

"Don't flatter yourself, Nick," I said flatly. "That was impromptu. You're here because like it or not, we're family. Regardless of what your mother-in-law might have told you, I'm not a complete monster. Unless you piss me off. Rule six."

"Rule six?"

I grinned as I started back through the trees toward the bunkhouse. "You're a smart guy, you'll figure it out."

Trotting to catch up, Nick looked through the trees at the interior of the island. "What besides those water pumps requires high voltage?"

"Come on, I'll show you."

Minutes later, we entered Chyrel's comm-center. Scott was sitting at the desk in a video conference with two men I didn't recognize. At least, I didn't recognize their faces. Their demeanor, glimpsed for only a second before Scott closed the laptop, I did recognize. A couple of new young snake eaters.

After I'd introduced the two men and explained to Scott how Stockwell was using information from Nick and the phone call that he'd made to devise a plan, Scott opened the laptop again and the two men reappeared on the screen. One was obviously inside a car and the other appeared to be in a dense wooded area.

"These men are members of Bravo Team out of Largo," Scott explained, zooming his camera out so that all three of us appeared in the tiny screen in the corner. "They're conducting surveillance on the gun shop in Naranja and the fortuneteller's place in Key West." Turning to the screen, he said, "Gentlemen, this is Jesse McDermitt and Nick Maggio. Please introduce yourselves."

The man on the left half of the screen spoke first. "Afternoon, Gunny. I'm Bill Guthrie, I was Jared's spotter in Iraq."

"He mentioned you a time or two."

"Mostly sea stories, I bet," the young man said, grinning. "Right now I'm getting eaten alive in the woods across from the gunsmith's store." He was mid-twenties, with unkempt collar-length dark blond hair and dark blue eyes. Beads of sweat were visible on his forehead and he wore a goatee, with a two-day stubble covering the rest of his face. I liked him instantly.

"Anything goin' on there?"

"The wife left in a hurry just a few minutes ago in a beat-up vintage Dodge Power Wagon. Franklin picked her up a block later, headed south on Highway One."

"When all else fails, call the wife," the second man said. He looked less military than Bill. I guessed he was probably a cop. He had long dark brown hair, parted down the middle and hanging past his shoulders. Also in his mid-twenties, his skin was tanned dark by the sun. At first glance, you'd think surfer, but his eyes were old and had obviously seen a few things. "I'm George Hamilton," he said. "No relation to the guy in Hollywood. Formerly with San Diego PD, narcotics. Guess I was chosen to watch the fortuneteller because I kind of blend in down here."

The background out the back window of the car didn't look familiar. "She's not at her shop?"

"No, sir, she's at her home on Porter Lane, just a couple blocks away. It's a cul-de-sac. The Jamaican taxi driver just left. They sat on the porch talking for about twenty minutes."

"He's from Andros, not Jamaica. Any other approaches to the neighborhood?"

"I scouted it on foot before bringing the car in. There's a pedestrian path that leads to Thomas Street, by the post office. A shortcut for folks who live here, I'm guessing. Well used, but too sandy and narrow for anything other than walking."

The camera jiggled and turned away from Hamilton. He zoomed it in and showed a narrow path between banyan trees and a stand of bamboo.

"The director's idea," Scott said. "Miss McKenna is taking a day off. She didn't much like that."

"No doubt," I said. "Where's Franklin?"

"He doesn't like messing with video," Scott replied, tapping a few keys. A map of South Florida appeared, showing a red dot in the center and a small dash-cam video in the corner. After a moment, the map moved, but the dot remained centered. "He's southbound on the turnpike extension, traveling about seventy miles an hour, nearing US-1. Where's the suspect, Jim?"

A voice came over the speaker. "About half a mile ahead, left lane. The big jacked-up four-by-four." Scott moved the mouse and clicked on the dash cam. The video feed and map changed places, showing a larger video. Jim Franklin had already been a legend with the CIA and a surveillance instructor at Langley when he was recruited to teach Deuce's team the finer points of watching someone without being seen. Far ahead of him, I could see the big off-road machine.

"Hope your tank's full, Jim," I said. "She's probably on her way to pick up her husband."

"That you, Jesse? Yeah, both tanks are full."

"Yeah, it's me. Keep us posted on where she's going, but I'm betting she won't stop for another hundred miles."

"I'll need help, then. Tailing someone that far is asking to be spotted. Particularly when we get to the two-lane."

"Already on it, Jim," Scott said. "Sherri's at a pull-off near Lake Surprise. Coordinate with her on when and where to swap out. But it's just gonna be the two of you."

Sherri Fallon was one of the few women on Deuce's team. Formerly an armorer for Miami-Dade Police, she was also an accomplished stage actress. Her job with the team, besides her proficiency at maintaining weapons, was to teach acting to the members of the team, particularly improv. Being able to think fast in a changing scenario and convey ideas to one another in a subtle way has proved helpful on more than one occasion.

"Copy that," Franklin replied. "I'll contact her right away. Anything unusual comes up, we'll let you know."

Scott minimized the screen and the two men on surveillance reappeared. "Sorry, Bill," Scott said. "But you're going to have to hang tight there. We don't know enough to pull you off. Someone else may have access to the building. We'll get someone there to relieve you before nightfall."

"No problem," Guthrie said. "I have an unobstructed view of three sides of the building. It's surrounded by cleared vacant land and the only thing behind it is marsh."

"Same for you, George," Scott said. "We can't be certain the subject won't come directly there, if and when the wife picks them up. Keep your eyes and ears open."

"Roger that," Hamilton replied.

Scott closed the laptop and swiveled the chair around. "What kinda plan are you and the director cooking up?"

I spent the rest of the day mostly fussing over my grandson, making sure he stayed in the shade for the most part. Or in the water. Though he wasn't walking yet, he quickly learned to swim. Experts call it the Mammalian Breath-Hold Response. Infants instinctively hold their breath when submerged for a second or two. I figure that in the grand scheme of things, we're just not that far removed from our air-breathing cousins in the sea and if a person allowed themselves, they'd quickly adapt to life on or in the water. Little Jesse sure did. After the first shock of going under, and much to Eve and Nick's astonishment while watching me dunk him, he quickly began to enjoy it, laughing hysterically when I lifted him up. After just a few minutes, he taught himself to kick with both feet and pull with his hands, to swim underwater as I backed away from him. A born waterman.

At some point in the early afternoon, Travis and Nick disappeared for a while. Eve had asked where they might have gone and I'd told her that Travis probably needed to ask him some legal advice. Not far from the actual truth, but enough that I felt guilty about it.

In my mind, I'd accomplished what had been asked, since it looked like Michal was free of the chain around his neck that was GT Bradley, and I'd told Travis about the connection to Chase Conner. A part of me wanted to be there when he was taken down, but a larger part was more concerned with continuing my life and enjoying it.

Later in the evening, after we'd eaten and were enjoying a few ice-cold beers, Travis asked Nick's opinion on Michal's new identity. Eve gave Travis a curious look, but didn't say anything.

Nick considered the information Travis had told him for a moment. "So, Michal Grabowski will just cease to exist?"

"He pretty much has already," Travis replied. "First, we already know that when his credit card records are checked, they will show usage from Pittsburgh to Key West. Second, when the police finally pulled what little was left of the crack dealer out of the tidal pool, the only ID on him was Michal Grabowski's Pennsylvania driver's license and the very credit card that brought him to Key West. The head and face were far too mangled to make a picture ID, but the coroner estimated the body was about the same height and weight shown on the license even though both legs were missing and at least half the rest of the body mass was gone in big chunks. Based on what he had, the coroner felt comfortable making the preliminary identification as Grabowski, pending DNA analysis. Michal Grabowski didn't have a DNA sample on record anywhere and both parents are deceased, so that'll come back negative. The coroner's initial identification will then stand. Michal Grabowski, a tourist vacationing in Key West, died in a horrific accident."

Charlie had taken the kids to put them to bed. Scott and Germ took advantage of her absence and quickly gathered the dishes in a tub, disappearing toward the north pier to wash them. Under the flickering flame of three tiki torches, Carl, Travis, and I sat across from Nick and Eve, Nick gently rocking the baby carrier. Standing behind them, Michal and Coral held hands, listening closely.

"How good are the documents you had created?" Nick asked, his legal mind already racing ahead.

"Even the CIA wouldn't be able to disprove that the man behind you isn't in fact Bob Trebor. And by the time we're through, there will even be fingerprints on file, dating back to when his parents had him fingerprinted in grade school."

"You can do that, Dad?" Eve asked.

"Me?" I said, laughing. "I can't even compose an email without help. If Travis says it's done, it is."

Michal sat down next to Eve and Coral put her hands on his shoulders. He looked up at her and smiled. "So, we can start a new life?"

"If you mean between Bob and Coral," Nick said, "that's pretty much up to you two. But, from a legal standpoint, it seems as though Bob Trebor started his life twenty-five years ago. Now, how good is yours, Coral?"

She looked shocked. "I don't know what you're talking about."

"Coral La Roc and Robert Trebor? Please."

I nodded in agreement. "As my friend Rusty would say, it's a bit of a co-inky-dink."

Coral smiled defiantly. "I had mine legally changed several years ago and the records are sealed."

"Sealed to casual inspection," Nick said. "I could get a court order to produce it without very much trouble."

For the first time since I'd met the young woman, I saw fear in her eyes and couldn't help but wonder what she was running from. People come to the Keys on the run from something all the time. I was running toward something, a life of leisure. Or so I thought.

"Do you think Chyrel can do a little surgery there?" I asked Travis.

He gave it a moment's consideration and said, "I'm sure she can arrange for the electronic copy of the sealed document to disappear. It may take a day or two for the physical copy. And she can beef up Coral La Roc's background and check her old identity to make sure there aren't any holes and no trail to Florida." Then he grinned at the young woman. "But you really need to work on that Southie accent."

"What time do you need to head back?" I asked Eve. "Y'all are welcome to stay over. The *Revenge* is connected to shore power, so it has air conditioning and all the comforts of a small hotel room."

"We can wait and leave in the morning," Nick said. "You nearly wore Alfie out in the water. He doesn't usually sleep this soundly."

"If you're sure we won't be putting you out," Eve chimed in.

"Not at all. Come on and I'll show you around. Nick can watch after the little guy for a few minutes."

When I opened the hatch to the salon and switched on the indirect lighting, Eve gasped softly. "This looks a lot nicer than any hotel room."

Going forward, I showed her the stateroom and private head and how to operate the marine toilet. "I need to tell you something, Eve," I finally said when we returned to the salon.

"Your first mate and the two black guys aren't just here for a visit, are they?"

"He's not exactly my first mate."

"I sort of got that impression. He's with the government? And the other two are Marines, like you used to be."

"Once a Marine, always a Marine," I chided, sitting down at the settee. "You have good observation skills. The truth is, Travis is a deputy director for the Department of Homeland Security. I sometimes help them out with transportation."

She looked somewhat surprised. "They're like spies or something?"

"Naw, that's CIA. He's the director of the Caribbean Counterterrorism Command for Homeland Security. Germ and Scott work for him and, yeah, they came from the Corps. Recon Marines, like myself."

Sitting down at the settee, Eve considered what I'd told her for a moment. "Why are you telling me all this? Couldn't you, like, get in trouble?"

I sat down next to her. "Kim told me all the lies your mom fed you girls about me when you were growing up. I wanted you to find out on your own what kind of man I am, but something's happened to move the timetable up a little."

Eve's eyes grew wide. "What?"

"Did you hear about the shooting last night in Key West?" She nodded. "The four of us were involved. The guy we were after got away. It's his accountant that's wanted by DHS."

"Look, I understand that Mother lied. I understand what kind of man you are. Kim and I talked about it a lot and today, I saw for myself while you were playing with Alfie. Why the need to give me details on what happened last night?"

"Nick's helping us catch the guy."

Eve's head jerked up. "Oh, no, you don't. You're not getting my husband involved in some kind of Wild West shootout."

"It's nothing like that, Eve. I wouldn't put you or him in any danger. It's just that he has contacts and was able to make an arrangement that might put the guy we want right in our hands."

"How does he know these people?"

I was hoping that question wouldn't come up. Eve didn't need to hear that her husband had been responsible for nearly getting her father killed and had once been a notorious gunrunner. At least, not from me.

"Even guilty people deserve representation," I said. "And sometimes lawyers provide it, even if they know their client isn't a good person." Another true enough statement, leaving me feeling guilty.

"Is that why you asked us down here and insisted Nick come?"

"No. We just uncovered this information night before last. The only reason I went down to Key West to help Michal was the connection between the guy that was after Michal and the guy that we're after."

"So the only thing Nick is doing is providing information?"

"A bit more than that," I explained. "Through his contacts, he might be able to arrange for the bad guys to be in the wrong place at the wrong time. I just wanted you to know this. Carl once told me that the best thing for a relationship was complete honesty, so I'm being as honest as I can with you."

"Too bad you didn't know Carl when you and Mom were still together."

"Totally different," I said. "There were times back then when I was ordered to go somewhere and wasn't allowed to say where or when. Sometimes, I didn't even know where or when and didn't have time to tell your mom goodbye when the orders came. I probably hated it more than she did. But there are times when a man's duty has to come before his honor. She just never understood that." I looked deep into my daughter's eyes. She has my mom's eyes. "Do you still want to stay the night? Charlie usually makes pancakes in the morning. And she doesn't let me help."

Eve began laughing and I knew she remembered the time I once helped her make pancakes for Sandy, just after Kim was born. We'd nearly burned down the kitchen.

"Yeah, Dad," she said when she finally got control of herself. "We'll stay."

"Good. Because little Jesse's already scheduled for a second swimming lesson in the morning."

"You have to stop calling him that around Nick, Dad. Family is important to Italians. It was his idea to name Alfie after you and his dad, you know."

"No," I replied. "I didn't know that. But, come on, Alfie? You want the kid getting a black eye at school every day? How about I call him Fred? That's short for Alfredo, too. And it's a tough-guy kind of name."

"I like Fred."

I grinned. "Okay, Fred it is. Now, let's get back to the party. It's almost sunset."

"Ooh, yes. Kim told me about your sunsets here."

CHAPTER THIRTY-SIX

B y the time Mary-Beth arrived on Cudjoe Key, GT was nearly delirious from the heat and loss of blood to mosquitoes. Finally, Austin spotted his old Power Wagon coming around the curve just north of the sheriff's substation. Finding that right at the end of Drost Drive on the corner of Highway One, the two men had quickly cut through a vacant lot overgrown with a thick tangle of vegetation and then moved several blocks up the highway until they came to a large wooded area on the right.

There, they'd hidden out in a dense thicket of palmetto and scrub oak, slowly baking in the hot afternoon sun, with little shade. It'd taken Mary-Beth three hours to reach them, and though Austin was used to the climate, GT was near heat exhaustion.

Austin waited until the truck was just a hundred yards from them before he stepped out of the underbrush, waving at his wife. She pulled off on the shoulder at the end of the southbound merge lane and waited until a white van with dark windows passed before turning the big truck around.

Austin had to help GT get to the road and into the truck, then he ran around to the other side and slid in, pushing his wife to the middle. Mary-Beth reached down on the floorboard and opened a cooler, handing both men a bottle of water, which they immediately emptied.

"Thanks, hon," Austin said. "This is Mister Bradley. He wants to buy some guns."

"You have any more water?" GT said, his tongue so thick he sounded drunk, talking through cracked lips.

Taking two more bottles from the cooler, she handed each man one. "Go easy," she warned GT as he started to chug the water. "Too much, too fast will shut down your kidneys. Now, one of you want to tell me what the hell happened?"

"Doesn't this heap have air conditioning?" GT asked.

"Sure, it's two-by-fifty-five air conditioning," Mary-Beth replied. "Roll down both windows and drive fast. Now what the hell happened last night?"

Austin filled her in on the gun battle from the night before and what GT had offered if Austin would help him.

"My guys should be arriving in Miami pretty soon," GT added. "How soon before we get up there?"

"A coupla hours," Austin replied.

"Probably longer than that," Mary-Beth added. "I passed two checkpoints where the cops were looking over every car headed north. One was in Islamorada, but it's in the middle of town, so we can take the neighborhood roads around it. The other one was halfway between Card Sound Road and Blackwater Sound. That's why it took me so long gettin' here. I went up to North Key Largo to Card Sound Road. There's a third one set up just past Alabama Jack's."

"Dammitall," Austin muttered. "Yeah, we're gonna have to do some four-wheelin'. That'll add an hour. Got my phone?"

Mary-Beth handed her husband the spare phone he'd asked her to bring. He was constantly losing his phones, so she always had a spare, with all his contacts already loaded on it. She'd gotten on a first-name basis with several Verizon customer support people. Activating the replacement phone while driving was child's play. While she had Verizon support on the line, she went ahead and ordered a new replacement.

Austin handed the phone to GT and said, "See if your guys are in Miami yet. Tell 'em to rent a car or a van with GPS and go to twenty-seven three forty-one Old Dixie Highway in Naranja. It'll take 'em close to an hour to get there. But we won't get there until after dark."

"How you gonna get around the road block?" Mary-Beth asked while GT made his call.

"That road block south of Card Sound Road? Was it before or after Southern Glades Trail?"

A smile crossed Mary-Beth's face. "Definitely north of it."

"We'll hafta go a few miles west of the highway. That first canal road is too close to the highway. They'd see our lights. Maybe just follow Southern Glades all the way to the airport?"

"Yeah, that'd probably be a lot safer."

GT ended his call. "They just touched down in Miami and are gonna rent a big van and meet us there after they get something to eat. Probably get there a little before we do."

"Store's closed," Mary-Beth said. "They'll hafta wait in the parkin' lot."

As they drove into Key Largo nearly an hour later, Austin's phone rang. Mary-Beth picked it up and looked at the caller ID. "It's that lawyer guy again. He must be really hard up to sell some guns."

The mention of guns got GT's attention. "What kind of guns? Is that the guy with the helicopter?"

Raising a finger to silence GT, Austin tapped the button to accept the call. "Brown."

GT could hear a man's voice on the phone but couldn't make out what he was saying over the whine of the truck's big tires and the buffeting wind. After a few seconds, Austin said, "Well, I'm not in Miami right now, Mister Maggio. I'll be at my shop in about an hour, if you wanna stop by. Or I can come to you."

He listened for a few more seconds and said, "I don't know about that. You know I like to deal one on one. Who is this guy?"

After nearly half a minute, Austin replied, "Okay, I'll see him. But he's gotta come to my shop. Not that I don't trust ya, Mister Maggio, I do. I just don't know this fella and never heard of him. I'd be a sight more comfortable in my own shop."

Austin listened for a moment and said, "Okay, midnight, then? The door'll be locked. Tell him to just tap on the glass."

Ending the call, Austin glanced over at GT as they passed the Key Largo city limit sign. "You might just be in luck, Mister Bradley."

"That was the guy with the chopper?"

"Yes, sir, it was. But I won't be meeting with him. He's sending one of his guys, an Australian fella named Donnie Hinkle. He has a case of AK-74s he needs to unload in a hurry."

"You mean AK-47, right? I know what those are."

"Nope, the seventy-four is the forty-seven's little brother," Austin replied. "Five point four five millimeter."

"He say what he wants for them?" GT asked, already liking this turn of events.

"Never talk numbers on the phone. But you can rest assured, I'll negotiate a good price for ya. And I got tons of ammo for them. When we make a deal with this Hinkle guy, I'll ask him to contact his boss about borrowing his whirlybird and pilot."

Slowing down, Austin kept looking nervously in his rearview mirror. "That white car's been behind us since we got back on the highway in Islamorada." Mary-Beth started to twist around and Austin stopped her. "Don't turn around."

"Can ya see the driver?" she asked.

"Not too clear," Austin replied. "Pretty sure it's a woman, though. But cops use that same kinda car."

GT was watching the mirror on his side as the car came into view under the sparse streetlights. "Speed up a little and see if she does too."

"No way, man," Austin said. "Cops here in Largo'll stop you for one mile over the limit."

Squinting his eyes, GT said, "That's a Mercury Marquis. Same body as Ford's Crown Vic, though. Cops drive the Fords. It's turning off, anyway."

Ten minutes later, the big truck turned north out of Key Largo. A few miles further, Austin slowed as they approached the bridge over yet another canal. When oncoming traffic cleared, he crossed over and turned onto the maintenance road down to the canal. All three failed to notice a white van with dark-tinted windows pull off the road on the opposite side of the canal.

At the bottom of the low incline, Austin reached down and shifted the truck into four-wheel drive, then switched on the bright driving lights mounted on the roll bar behind the cab and on the brush guard of the front bumper.

"It's gonna get a bit bumpy now," Austin said as he turned right onto a double rut, running west, startling an eight-foot crocodile that slid down the bank into the canal.

CHAPTER THIRTY-SEVEN

Scott and Germ joined us on the north pier to watch the sun go down. Carl and Charlie had taken the kids to bed and I could see them sitting in their rockers on their porch. Michal and Coral were up on the deck watching from another set of identical rockers.

Hearing my sat-phone chirping from where I'd left it in Chyrel's office, I knew it was probably Linda, so I excused myself and trotted toward the bunkhouse. It'd stopped ringing by the time I got there and Travis handed it to me, so I pulled up the recent calls and hit the redial button.

"I was beginning to think you'd forgotten about me," she said when she answered. "How's the little family reunion going?"

Stepping back outside, I stood at the foot of the pier, looking out at my friends and family. "We're out on the pier. Hey, I taught little Jesse, er, I mean Fred, how to swim today. That's what Eve wants me to call him around Nick."

"He's only what? Four months old?"

"Yeah," I said. "But he's a little fish. I sure wish you were here."

"Me too," she whispered. "I'll be back in another week and I plan to take a few days off to unwind."

Teasing her, I said, "By unwind, do you mean having wild and crazy sex?"

Linda laughed, which made me miss her all the more. We talked for a few more minutes, as the sun neared the horizon and then she told me to get back to my family and we said goodbye.

When I returned and sat down next to Eve on the pier, she looked up and asked, "What's she like?"

"Who?" I asked evasively. I wasn't real comfortable talking to my daughter about Linda's and my relationship.

"Your girlfriend," Eve replied. "Scott said she's a badass."

Laughing, I glanced over at Scott on the far end, his feet dangling in the water, and he just shrugged. "She works for FDLE," I replied. "Right now she's up in Tallahassee for a few weeks working."

"Dad, that's what she *does*. What I asked you is what's she like?"

"Well," I said, grinning, "Scott's right. She's a badass." Eve punched me on the shoulder, like her sister always does. "You met her. She's a nice lady and she makes me laugh. That's all you need to know."

As the sun slowly disappeared from sight, I looked over at Eve and Nick. He had a sling over his neck and shoulder, with the baby hanging in it like he was in a hammock. Nick held Eve's hand, as they both watched the sun disappearing. I thought back to when Eve was a baby and the sunsets Sandy and I had watched together. Like my daughter and her husband, we were crazy in love, but didn't really know a lot about one another.

As the last of the sun disappeared, we got up and headed back to the tables. I caught Travis out of the corner of my eye, motioning me to join him.

"Why don't you take the baby and get him tucked in the guest cabin?" I said to Eve. "I need to talk to Travis for a bit."

Scott and Germ headed toward the far end of the bunkhouse, as Eve and Nick started across the clearing. I called after them, "Hey, Nick, can I talk to you a minute?"

Eve looked back with a concerned expression and I winked at her. She took the baby from her husband and stood on her toes to kiss him. "Don't be long."

Together, Nick and I followed the two Marines. In the office, Travis had the laptop opened, the screen segmented into four parts.

"Jesse just walked in," Travis said. "Tell me where you are again, Sherri."

In the top right corner of the screen, Sherri Fallon's face was illuminated by the dashboard lights of the car she was in. "About a mile south of where the Sheriff's Department has a checkpoint set up. I'm pretty certain they didn't make either me or Jim. We traded off several times. The truck turned off the highway onto a dirt road that runs alongside a canal. There's no way either of us can follow it in these cars and they'd be sure to see another vehicle turn off and follow them."

At the top left was a map, showing the empty landscape that is the southern Everglades, with the same red dot at its center. I pointed at the map and said, "Zoom in a little."

Travis clicked a couple of keys and the map tightened on the area between Card Sound Road and Blackwater Sound. "There," I said. "That's Southern Glades Trail. It's built on the spoils of the drainage canal and there are dozens of other canals off it. The roadblock was probably in place when the wife came down."

Travis glanced up at me. "Where's that trail come out?"

"It doesn't. It's a maintenance trail for the canal, which disappears in the Glades. Other canals off that main one crisscross and intersect most of the roads in the area, each one with its own rough maintenance trail alongside it. With that truck, old as it is, he could surface anywhere."

The screen below the map was from inside a van and I recognized the man sitting at a small desk in back, in the low light of the displays in front of him. William Binkowski used to be with the FBI and had been part of the investigation into my wife's abduction and murder, nearly two years earlier.

"Is that Binkowski?" I asked Travis and saw the man's face come up from what he was looking at.

"Captain McDermitt?" he asked.

"Yeah, Bill. Where are you?"

"I'm parked at the business across from the gun shop in Naranja. It's an adult video store, open till three. Guthrie left thirty minutes ago and will be back at four."

"He has a parabolic mic in the van," Travis said. "If Brown and Bradley go there, he should be able to hear what they say, even through the glass. We have a takedown team ready in Homestead that can apprehend them both."

"Wait one," Binkowski said. "A van just pulled into the parking lot."

Binkowski's screen went black, then switched to an exterior view. A full-size gray Chevy passenger van came to a stop next to the front door of the gun shop. The camera zoomed in on the back doors of the van to get the tag number. Next to the tag was an Avis car rental sticker.

"So much for running back to Pittsburgh with his tail between his legs," I said as the camera zoomed out and six men climbed out, stretching arms and legs.

"Think they drove all the way down?" Travis asked.

"Doubtful," I said. "Even driving straight through, that'd take nearly a full day. He hired local muscle last night instead. They probably flew. Which means they didn't bring guns."

Over the speaker, Binkowski confirmed it. "Tag's registered to Avis and was rented an hour ago at Miami International by Malik Phillips, with a Pittsburgh address."

Travis looked over at Nick. "Do you really want to help?"

Nick looked from me to Travis and back again. "What do you want me to do?"

"Make another phone call," Travis answered. "Tell Brown that you have a guy with a case of AK-74s that he needs to unload in a hurry."

"I don't know, Colonel," I said. "You're talking eight men and a woman in a gun shop. Try to take them down there and bullets could be flying into every house for miles around."

"Wasn't planning to," Travis said. He turned to Scott and said, "Get Hinkle on the horn. Call the base armory, too. They have until morning to crate up eight AKs with the firing pins filed down just enough to make them inoperable."

Spinning around in the chair, Travis spoke into the desk mic next to the laptop. "Sherri, get to the base and help Donnie. Those pins have to be just short enough to not work, but can't show any obvious flaw to a casual inspection by a gunsmith. Can you make that happen?"

"Yes, sir," Sherri's voice came over the speaker. "But if he mikes the pin, he's sure to know."

"We'll have to hope he doesn't do that," Travis said. "Bill, keep an eye on the new players and let me know if they go anywhere."

I was watching Binkowski's video feed. "Bill," I said, "zoom in on the guy holding the bag on the right side."

The camera zoomed back in again as the man turned toward the highway's streetlights. "Conner."

Chase Conner stood in the middle of the group of men. He stood out from the others, with his slight frame and more distinguished features. The others were all gorillas, by comparison. While Conner seemed oblivious to his surroundings, the street muscle he was with appeared to be on full alert, scanning the area.

"Scott, tell Donnie the plan. If we can make this work, he'll meet Brown with a single fully operational AK-74 in a regular gun bag. He'll arrange to deliver a full case of eight rifles at sunrise. Tell him we'll get back to him on where the meet will take place."

Travis stood up, stretching his back. "Better get some coffee on, it's gonna be a long night." Turning to me, he said, "We need a place for the exchange, away from the gun shop and any innocent civilians. Odds are they'll bring the muscle and hopefully Conner to the exchange and we can take them all down there. Someplace secluded, since they'll likely rearm from Brown's store, but at least they won't be carrying anything heavy, knowing they'll have the AKs after the meet."

"I know just the place," Nick said. Travis and I both turned around. "The same place Brown will likely recommend. It's where the water from the Everglades flows into a large narrow lake thirty miles west of his place. He can get there in his airboat. There's a high clearing right next to the eastern finger of the lake, big enough for our pilot to land the company helicopter in."

"Can we get a takedown team to it?"

"With an airboat or helicopter, yeah."

"A lake?" I asked. "Can you point it out on a map?"

"Sure," Nick replied. "It's the only water not covered with sawgrass, exactly twenty-six miles west of the little Homestead general aviation airport on a heading of two hundred and sixty degrees. That's why we both liked it. Impossible to get to except by him in his four-wheel drive, or by helicopter."

I went to the computer and enlarged the map image and dragged it further north from where Binkowski and Sherri had stopped following the truck. I pointed to two landmarks on the nearly featureless plain that is the river of grass. It was a satellite image, with no markings.

"Here's the Homestead airport," I said. "Do you mean this river due west of it?"

Nick looked closely at the scale in the corner and said, "Yeah, the clear spot where we used to meet is right there on the north side of the east end of that finger. He gave me the GPS coordinates. I never realized it was a river."

"That's the headwaters of Shark River, which flows into Tarpon Bay, then into the Gulf."

CHAPTER THIRTY-EIGHT

When Austin finally turned off the endless miles of trails, it was after ten o'clock and GT had absolutely no idea if they were even still in Florida.

"We'll be there in fifteen minutes," Austin said.

GT was rubbing his right thigh. He'd banged it on the unpadded door more times than he could remember. "Where the hell are we?"

"About ten miles west of Florida City," Mary-Beth replied.

They rode in silence until they pulled into the parking lot at *Brown's Guns* and climbed out of the truck. GT strode quickly to the passenger door of the van as his accountant opened it and stepped out.

"You got the money I told you to bring?" GT asked.

"Forty thousand in nonsequential small bills, just like you said," Conner replied. "What happened to you, GT?"

"Been playing fucking Tarzan in the swamps," GT growled. He turned to Austin and said, "Please tell me you got A/C inside."

"Y'all come on in," Mary-Beth said, leading the way to the front door and unlocking it.

Once inside, GT turned to the man who had been driving the van. "You bring me some clothes, Malik?"

The tall, broad-shouldered man handed him the bag he was holding. "Where's Erik, Mister Bradley?"

Taking the bag, GT said, "Erik's dead. Killed by a cracker in Key West." Then he turned around to Austin. "You got a shower here, brother?"

"That man weren't no cracker. I'm a cracker. And I ain't your damned brother. There's a shower in back, first door on the left."

Conner and the five black men stared at Austin, confused, as GT went toward the back of the store. Austin went behind the counter and picked up a Colt 1911 that he kept there, knowing without checking that it was loaded and a round chambered. He thrust it in his jeans behind his back and came back around the counter.

"There's a sort of break room in back," he said to Malik. "You guys can relax there for a while. I arranged for some heavy-caliber guns for your boss. Better'n any of the huntin' rifles I sell here. Till the guy gets here with 'em, y'all keep your paws off the merchandise."

Malik took a step toward Austin. "Who the hell are you?"

Austin met his gaze, his steely eyes never faltering, and his voice dropped to a menacing snarl. "I'm the cracker that can feed your parts to the gators, boy."

Seconds ticked by as the two men glared at one another. Finally, Malik shrugged. "You wanna call yourself a cracker, who am I to argue?" He turned to his entourage and said, "Come on."

The five men moved toward the door to the back room, but Conner held back. When they were through the door, Conner said, "I assume you're Mister Brown?"

"Yeah, I am. And you are?"

"Chase Conner, Mister Brown. I handle Mister Bradley's finances. What happened down in Key West?"

Austin clapped an arm around the smaller man and said, "Long story." Then, leading him toward the back room, he added, "Fortunately, we got about an hour."

Once GT finished in the shower and was dressed in clean clothes, Austin got cleaned up himself, leaving Mary-Beth to keep an eye on their guests. Then he sent her home, telling her that he'd stay until the sale was made and he could send GT and his crew on down the road.

An hour later, sitting on the stool behind the sales counter while cleaning an old German Mauser rifle, Austin saw the lights of a car pull into the parking lot. He quickly went through the door to the back room. Most of the men were asleep in lounge chairs, or watching an old episode of *Dragnet* on the little TV. Austin nudged GT's shoulder and said, "He's here."

GT tapped Conner's shoulder, asleep in a chair next to him. When Conner opened his eyes, GT jerked his head toward the door. "Let's do this, then you can fly on back to Pittsburgh."

As the two men stood up, Malik started to rise. "Wait here," GT said. "We don't want to spook the guy."

The two men followed Austin back to the sales floor, just as a light tapping came from the front window, which ran the width of the store and was covered with iron bars. Austin went to the door and looked at the man on the other side. He was smiling.

"You Dinkle?" Austin asked through the glass.

"Hinkle, mate," the man answered in an Australian accent. "Donnie Hinkle. Mister Maggio said you might be interested in buying something."

Austin unlocked the door and opened it. The man named Hinkle stepped inside. "You must be Mister Brown, right?"

Hinkle carried a single hard-shell rifle bag. Austin looked out the door at what looked like a brand-new bright red Mustang. Still holding the door open, he looked back at Hinkle. "Need help carrying the rest in?"

Hinkle stopped at an empty display table and placed the rifle bag on it. "Oh, I only brought the one, mate. I don't know you from Adam, but Mister Maggio vouched for ya, so 'ave a look."

GT started to say something, but Austin cut him off. "Mister Bradley here is buying. I'm just his advisor, ya might say. I own this place. Maggio said you'd be deliver-in' a case."

Smiling, Hinkle took a step away from the bag on the table. Lifting his arms wide out to the sides, his coat fell open and Austin instantly recognized the Sig Sauer P226 tucked neatly in a cross draw holster in his pants. "Ya might say Mister Maggio is my advisor. But I make my own deals, my own way, mate."

"How soon can you deliver the rest?" GT said.

Hinkle slowly lowered his arms. "I *can* deliver them in twenty minutes, but I won't. Mister Bradley, is it?"

"GT Bradley, from Pittsburgh," he answered, as though the name carried weight all its own.

"Never been to Pittsburgh, mate. I'll get right to the point. You want eight of what's in that bag, it'll cost ya fifteen even, but I never deal with people I don't know but in the broad light of day, somewhere private." Looking around the sales floor, he smiled and added, "Someplace where I'm not outgunned a thousand to one. Crikey, you got a lot of firepower here!" His eyes settled on the German rifle Austin had been cleaning. "That a model 98 Karabiner?"

"Yeah," Austin said, closing and locking the door. "Let's see what you got."

"Before we start any negotiations," Hinkle said, turning toward Austin and running both fingers through his sandy hair, "I guess I ought to tell you something."

Austin waited, watching the man closely, when he saw a red dot appear on GT's forehead.

"We talk right here in your storefront. Is that acceptable to you, mate?"

The red dot on GT's head disappeared. Austin wanted desperately to turn around and look out the window, but knew he wouldn't see anything. He seemed to come to a decision and walked slowly toward the table. "Sure, Hinkle. Open the case."

Hinkle stepped slowly toward the table. "Let's see the money first. I don't want to be wasting my time."

Looking at GT, Austin nodded and GT pointed to the table. Conner stepped forward, the black briefcase in his hand. Conner's hands were shaking as he placed the case on the table and opened it. His voice cracked slightly as he said, "There's more than enough here to cover all expenses."

GT quietly added, "But not a nickel leaves here, unless I have what I came here for."

Hinkle slowly opened the rifle case and stepped back. "What you're buying are eight Russian-made SGL21 AK-103 rifles, chambered for seven-point-six-two-by-thirty-nine-millimeter cartridges. They were converted and rebuilt by Arsenal firearms. Each one has a riveted bullet guide, Tapco G2 trigger assembly, threaded muzzle, bayonet lugs on both the gas block and front sight, and an ACE Limited side folding buttstock."

Hinkle slowly stepped away from the table as Austin picked up the rifle. He gave it a quick cursory inspection, checked the chamber and slowly raised it to his shoulder, the muzzle pointing away from everyone and away from the window. He didn't want the sniper outside to get the wrong impression.

Lowering the rifle, he placed the butt against his hip, his right hand on the bolt, and looked at Hinkle. "May I?"

"Please do," Hinkle replied confidently.

In quick easy movements, Austin flipped down the safety and ratcheted the bolt back, releasing it with a crisp snap of finely machined steel. With his thumb on the hammer, he pulled it back slightly and removed the dust covers, then quickly removed both the recoil spring and bolt carrier group. His movements were practiced and fluid, having torn down AKs thousands of times.

Inspecting the trigger assembly and chamber, he quickly reassembled the rifle, looking at both the spring and bolt assembly before putting them back in.

"Not a penny over ten grand," Austin said. "For eight, just like this one."

"Did I mention each one comes with four mags and a hundred rounds?"

"Look around ya, *mate*," Austin chided. "Mags and ammo I got plenty of."

"I can come down to twelve, Mister Brown. You obviously know the weapon, so you know that each one'll retail for an easy fifteen hundred, without the mags and ammo."

"This here ain't no retail transaction. Eleven."

Hinkle glanced over at GT and grinned. "You picked a good advisor, Mister Bradley. Eleven thousand it is."

"When and where?" GT asked.

"Sunrise," Hinkle replied. "Somewhere private."

"Call Maggio," Austin said. "Ask him if he can give you a lift to our usual spot."

Leaning to his left and looking out the front windows of the shop, Hinkle clapped his hands together. "Got my own car, mate. Just give me the address. I'll be there."

"Can't get to it by car. He'll fly you out. We've used the same spot a bunch of times. Tell him there's an extra five grand if you can give Mister Bradley and five of his men a ride to Key West."

"Key West, eh? This wouldn't have anything to do with what happened down there last night, would it?"

"Probably best if you don't know anything more than you do now," GT said.

"Mind if I step outside to make the call?" Hinkle said, heading toward the door.

Austin unlocked and opened it for him. Hinkle went to the back of his car and turned around. Holding a cell-phone in his hand, he waited until Austin closed the door before dialing.

Austin slowly walked back to the table. With his back to the door, he said in a low voice, "Don't look at me and don't say a word. The man has a sniper outside somewhere. I'm sure he's on the up and up. Mister Maggio's a good man. He just has the guy outside so he don't get taken advantage of."

CHAPTER THIRTY-NINE

I woke with a start, as Travis put a hand on my shoulder. "They took the bait," he said. "I spoke to Donnie a little while ago."

I stood up and stretched. "What time is it?"

"Oh one hundred. Sunrise is in less than six hours."

I thought for a moment. "Did you get the takedown team moving? It'll take them an hour to get here to pick us up and then insert us at least an hour before sunrise."

"Pick us up? They can be there from Homestead in a lot less time. Why do they need to come here?"

"I'm going. You probably shouldn't, but I need to see this through."

"Okay, but Scott and Germ will go with you."

"Then have the chopper bring two extra ghillie suits. There won't even be a tree stump to hide behind out there in the Glades. Oh, and bring plenty of bug spray."

Scott and Germ were lying in two other bunks in the cramped little office. Without opening his eyes, Scott said, "Maybe rebreathers would be better, then?"

"Good idea," I said. "Black wetsuits and rebreathers. That water's so dark, we won't be visible just below the surface even from a few feet away, and so far, mosquitoes haven't adapted to underwater life."

"You three get some more rest, then," Travis said. "I'll have the chopper arrive here in two hours. Another of our own pilots will be flying the Maggio bird, along with Donnie and two others from Bravo Team."

Scott and Germ both rolled over, their backs to us, and I motioned Travis to follow me outside. Carl had moved one of the large commercial coffeemakers out to the table and I poured two cups. The two of us sat down and discussed contingency plans.

During his short talk with Donnie, when the Aussie was pretending to talk to Nick, Travis had instructed him to tell Brown that he'd fly to the spot that Maggio's pilot knew with two other men besides the pilot and they'd arrive at zero seven hundred, just after sunrise. Donnie was to tell Brown that he could bring only himself, Bradley, the accountant and no more than two others. He would also tell Brown that Maggio had agreed to have the chopper fly Bradley and his crew to Key West, but not until after they returned to Brown's store. It didn't have room for that many people.

Travis had assigned a second takedown team that would raid the gun shop at the same time the chopper landed on upper Shark River and apprehend the remainder of Bradley's crew.

When I'd walked Nick to the *Revenge*, I'd retrieved my go-bag before taking the short nap. I went back to the dock and grabbed my wetsuit, my Drager rebreather, and the rest of my dive gear from the storage locker near the bow, trying to be as quiet as possible.

Sitting at the table with Travis, both of us drinking another cup of Rusty's special Costa Rican coffee, he and I had our first real chance to have a long talk about Charity Styles.

"She's damaged goods," I said finally. "She might do well at not showing it, but she could have some sort of flashback to her time in the hands of the Taliban."

"Everyone on the team undergoes a lot of psychological testing, Jesse. Charity went through even more after I submitted her name to the secretary. All the shrinks say she's okay in the head. Maybe not perfect, but well enough for the duties she was chosen for."

"How does she get around from target to target?"

Travis looked at me over the rim of his mug. Finally, he set it down and said, "Only three others have that information. Deuce, the secretary and the president. I know you well enough to know you can be trusted with it. She's on a forty-two-foot Alden sloop, equipped with the latest nav and comm equipment and anything else she might need for a mission. I'm the only one that has contact with her. I fly to where she is and deliver a target assignment and any specialized gear she'll need. She can choose to decline any target she wants, but so far she's three for three, without a single hiccup."

"An Alden sloop?"

"Her own choice. She only agreed to take the assignment if that's how she would travel. It was originally built eighty years ago, but underwent a two-month refit, sparing no cost. Her assignment area is the whole Caribbean Basin, so she can usually get to where she needs to in less than a week. During that time, she makes her own plan as to when, where, and how to eliminate the target."

"Did the shrinks take into account that she'd be alone at sea? Just her and her thoughts?"

The door to the office opened, just as I heard the heavy thump-thump of a chopper inbound and flying low over the water. Scott and Germ came out and split up, heading to the four corners of the clearing, where they placed strobes on the ground and activated them. Both men were already wearing black wetsuits and jump boots.

I began pulling my own wetsuit on and checking my rebreather. "I don't like it, Travis. Not even a little bit. Probably because I know her better than most. While she and I were on the *Revenge* last year, she opened up to me. Took her a week, but she finally talked about what happened to her in Afghanistan and how devastated she was when Jared was killed."

Scott was on the far side of the clearing, two flashlights with red cones over the lights in his hands, ready to direct the chopper down.

"But she took care of the problem then," Travis said. "Just as she's doing now."

"You weren't there, Colonel. You didn't see the look in her eyes when she did it."

The chopper flared as it approached the island, bleeding off speed. The pilot noted the illuminated flagpole, the colors hanging limp below the solar-powered light on the top of the pole. He made a straight-in approach and seconds later, the bird was on the ground. I grabbed my gear and trotted toward it, Germ and Scott joining me at the open door.

"Good to see you again, Gunny," Scott Bond shouted, offering a hand. Bond had been a SEAL lieutenant and a supervisor at their dive school. I'd always found him to be cool and level-headed.

"Good to be seen, Eltee," I replied, handing him my fly rod case.

The chopper was a UH-1, commonly called a Huey, solid black with no markings. In back were seats for up to eight men. I took an empty seat and looked at the others on board. The only one I recognized was Bill Guthrie seated across from us and I nodded to him.

As Scott and Germ sat down, two of the men across from us handed them rebreather cases, and then the chopper lifted off, spinning slowly until it faced north. Looking out the open door, the moon illuminated my little island and I saw Michal and Coral at the deck rail of my house. He was wearing only boxers and she had a sheet wrapped around her, whipping in the turbulence caused by the chopper's blades. Nick and Eve came running up the steps from the dock area and joined them.

I switched on the tiny comm unit in my ear and as Eve broke apart from the others and started running down the rear steps, I said, "Colonel?"

"I copy," I heard Travis say through the earwig.

"Tell my daughter I'll be back in time for Alfie's swimming lesson."

"Roger that," Travis responded as the chopper's nose dipped and the pilot added throttle.

Bond tapped me on the arm. "Gunny, meet Bravo Team. To expedite things, we'll just use numbers for now. There'll be time for introductions later. You, Scott and Germ are Alpha One, Two, and Three and I'm Bravo One." Pointing to Guthrie on the end he said, "You already know Bravo Two. Next to him are Bravo, Three, Four, and Five, all from SEAL Team Four."

I reached across and shook hands with the four men, noting that the one seated next to Guthrie held an MK11 sniper rifle between his legs. Placing my fly rod case on my knees, I started to open it.

"Planning to do some fishing?" the man with the sniper rifle asked.

"Roger that, Bravo Three," I replied, removing my own M40 and snapping the Unertl scope into place on the Picatinny rail. "I hear illegal arms smugglers are biting."

As we flew through the darkness, Bond outlined a basic tactical plan, where Guthrie and the SEAL sniper would take cover on the river's bank if we could find a suitable place during a flyover. Scott and I would do the same in another spot at a ninety-degree angle from them and the island. The rest of the team would surround the clearing on all sides. We'd try to use our rebreathers sparingly at the water's edge, breathing on the surface if the mosquitoes cooperated. Brown would be coming by airboat, so we'd hear them for miles just before sunrise. The chopper would fly due west and land on a sandbar near the mouth of Shark River and wait there until we had the men in custody.

Using the coordinates Travis got from Nick and verifying the clear spot using satellite imagery, the pilot located the high clearing and had no trouble landing in the middle of it. Everyone fanned out and hugged the water's edge, until the chopper lifted off and flew west. Then we regrouped in the center of the little island.

"Bravo Two and Three," Bond said, "Did you see that log on the river bank, two hundred meters southwest?"

"Affirmative," Guthrie said. "That'll make a decent hide."

"Hey, Bill," I said as the two men turned to go. He stopped and turned around. "Just make sure that log isn't a gator or python."

Both men turned and trudged off toward the southwest. Having doused all the lights on the chopper long before we arrived, our eyes had adjusted to the light of the moon and stars. There wasn't a cloud in the sky, but all of us had night vision headsets, just in case.

"Jesse, you and Germ move southeast," Bond said, pointing to a small cypress stand just a hundred yards away. "The rest of you fan out and take cover in the water."

We didn't have a long wait. Germ and I lay prone on a sandy spot at the edge of the cypress head, our bodies completely submerged in the dark tannin-filled water. We tried to keep our heads up, but with no wind, the mosquitoes were fierce.

All of us wore full face masks, to enable communication through the use of the bone-conductive mics and earwigs, so we mostly stayed submerged, breathing through the rebreathers and taking turns keeping an ear above the surface.

"I hear an airboat," one of the men said.

I lifted my head out of the water and listened. Knowing that sound travels better over water, even when the water's covered with three-foot-tall sawgrass, I could tell the boat was still a long distance away and slipped back below the surface.

"Bravo Three and Four," I said between breaths, "This is Alpha One. He'll probably come from your direction. An airboat only needs a couple of inches of water, so stay deep and if he passes over you, you'll be okay."

"Roger that," one of them responded.

A few minutes later, I could hear the roar of the air-boat engine under water and knew it was close. Knowing that the stand of cypress behind us would keep the men on the airboat from seeing me, I raised my head up high enough to see over the sawgrass, ignoring the mosqui-toes that swarmed every inch of exposed skin.

The sky to the east was already a bright pink, sunrise only minutes away. "This is Alpha One," I whispered. "I have eyes on them, four hundred meters due east and closing fast." I raised my rifle and flipped open the front and rear sight covers. Looking through it, I counted two men in the high rear seats and three in the lower front seats. "Five men on the boat. Guess they're getting here ahead of time. It's only zero six-thirty."

Over my headset, I heard Travis's voice. "Alpha One and Bravo One, this is Six Actual. Maggio's helicopter is twenty minutes out." He was using the satellite to con-nect to our comm, beaming instructions from space.

"Roger that," Bond said. "Everyone stay low and get small. We're doing this by the book. Six Actual has eyes in the sky and he's recording everything. We don't take them down until he confirms that the money and weap-ons have changed hands."

The airboat made a direct approach to the island, the engine roaring as it rode its own bow wave up onto dry land before the driver shut the engine down. The five men on board stepped off, one of them carrying a briefcase. All five stayed close to the boat, but two men with bolt-action hunting rifles stepped a little further away than the others. These two would be my and Bravo Three's targets.

Five minutes later, Donnie's voice came over the comm as he passed the five-mile mark, about the maximum distance the comm units worked for a direct connection. "This is Air One. I'm five minutes out."

Bad guys just don't stand a chance these days, I thought as I slowly slipped back below the surface and drowned at least a dozen mosquitoes. We waited patiently, Donnie giving a play-by-play as the chopper approached, confirming only five men on the tiny, bare island and nobody hiding on the boat.

"Crikey! Where are you blokes? There ain't even a strand of grass on that little sandbar."

"We're close by," Bond said. "Underwater."

"Touching down," Donnie said. "Going covert."

I slowly lifted my head until I could just see them through the sawgrass. The chopper had circled and landed facing the airboat. The engine went silent, the only sound was the whisper of the blades as they slowed.

The back door of the Bell commuter chopper opened and a man climbed out, dragging a large case behind him. Another man got out of the far side and came around the front of the bird with Donnie to join the first man. The pilot remained in the chopper.

Watching closely, I recognized Brown by his western-style clothes as he separated from his group and strode toward Donnie.

"Good mornin', mate," Donnie said to Brown, his voice coming over my headset. I was too far away to hear Brown's response, but it didn't sound pleasant.

"Eight just like the one I showed you last night," Donnie said. "Feel free to look for yourself."

The two men with Donnie stood off to the side, each one carrying the rugged AK74s on a sling around his neck and shoulder. The muzzles were pointed at the ground, but in a manner that would enable them to be brought to bear on a target very quickly.

Brown opened the case and lifted out one of the rifles at random. He quickly field-stripped it, using a small penlight to inspect the trigger assembly, chamber, barrel and finally the recoil spring and bolt assembly. Putting the rifle back together, he ratcheted the bolt and, with the muzzle facing down at the ground, pulled the trigger. Both sounds were clearly audible a hundred yards away. Brown put the rifle back in the crate and waved a hand, and I heard him shout, "They look fine."

The two guys standing off to the side of the boat stepped a little further away, a movement that was then matched by Donnie's two men. The sporting rifles the two goons carried were a poor match for the automatic Kalashnikovs of Donnie's men, and far less than the high-powered rifles Bravo Three and I carried.

"Where's Mister Bradley and Mister Conner?" I heard Donnie ask. Then a moment later, he said, "That's too bad, I was hoping to see them again."

Shit, I thought. *He sent his damned hired muscle.*

Travis's voice came over my comm. "This is Six Actual. Stand by for the exchange, go on my word only."

Slowly raising my rifle, I silently flipped up the lens covers again and took aim. "Alpha One, I'm covering the tall rifleman on the right."

Scott, now kneeling beside me, whispered, "Range one hundred and twenty meters, zero windage."

"Bravo Two. We have the shorter rifleman on the left. Range is two hundred and fifty meters, zero windage."

The man with the briefcase opened it and turned it toward Donnie, who picked up one bundle of cash and thumbed it, then quickly counted the others.

"Looks like it's all here, then," Donnie said and took the case from the man.

I had my other eye open and saw the pilot's door move slightly as he made ready to exit the chopper.

"Wait one," Travis said. "Wait for them to pick up the crate and move away from the bird."

Brown and the second man bent and picked up the crate, carrying it sideways toward the waiting airboat.

"Move now!" Travis's voice came over the comm.

In my peripheral vision I saw three men to the left of and on the other side of the chopper rise as one. Bond's voice boomed, "Don't move! This is Homeland Security and you're all under arrest!"

I heard the crash of the crate falling on the sand as my left eye slowly closed, my attention now fully on the man in my reticle. As he started to bring the weapon up, I heard two shots ring out. The man's rifle continued coming up, the cross hairs in my reticle were center mass, and I squeezed the trigger. The impact of the bullet lifted him off his feet, like a spring was attached to his back and suddenly recoiled.

Sweeping the scene for another target, I heard more gunshots and shouting, then everything went quiet. Lowering the rifle, I saw four men down on the ground and one kneeling by the crate. Donnie was directly behind him, his Sig pointed squarely at the back of the man's head, as he shouted orders at him.

Scott and I sloshed quickly through the knee-deep water, arriving just ahead of Guthrie and his shooter. Donnie and the pilot had Brown down on the ground, the pilot's knee planted squarely in the middle of his back as Brown screamed in agony.

"Six Actual to Alpha One! The takedown team in Naranja reports that there is nobody at the store! Repeat. Negative contact at Austin Brown's gun store."

CHAPTER FORTY

Driving on US-1, the sun now high behind them, Malik asked, "How'd you know we were being watched?"

GT was in a surly mood and Conner was asleep in the back of the old Volkswagen van. "You gotta pay closer attention to details, Malik, if you want Erik's job. When we first got there a white van with dark windows was parked at the video store across the street with four other cars. Three hours later, the van and one of the cars was still there, when the place was closing. You ever take three hours to pick out a fuck-flick? I remembered seeing a van just like it pass by when Brown's wife picked us up, and again later coming through Key Largo."

"The guys should have the guns by now," Malik said, checking his watch. "Brown said it'd take less than an hour to get back and the Maggio guy would fly them from Homestead airport, where they left the rental van. That means they oughta be in the air pretty soon. It's almost nine o'clock."

Clicking the end button on his phone, GT said, "Brown's still not answering. You got one of the guys' numbers in your phone?"

"Yeah, I got all four. Hang on." Holding the phone on the steering wheel of Brown's wife's decrepit van, he scrolled through his contact list and tapped on a name. A moment later, he scrolled again, then a third and fourth time.

Putting the phone in his pocket, he said, "No answer from any of them."

Crossing the bridge onto Stock Island, GT shouted back at Conner. "Wake up! We're almost there."

Conner moved up to one of the plush swivel chairs just behind the front seat. "Key West?"

"Yeah," GT replied. "I need you alert."

"I really don't know what good I'll be, Mister Bradley. I've never even been in a fight before."

"Maybe not, but an extra pair of eyes and ears can't hurt."

The van rolled across another bridge onto the island of Key West. "Go right," GT instructed.

Malik made the right turn onto Truman Street, the VW van backfiring when he gave it too much gas.

"About a mile ahead," GT said, "take a right on Duval Street and then look for Eaton Street on the left. The place we're going is just around the corner from there."

Ten minutes later, the old van pulled into a small shopping center and parked in the shade of a big banyan tree on the corner across from the fortuneteller's store.

"We wait here," GT said, peeling two twenties off his new money roll and handing them to Conner. "I saw a sandwich shop around the corner. Go get us something to eat."

After Conner left, Malik asked, "How long we gonna wait?"

"Till either the fortuneteller or our guys get here."

CHAPTER
FORTY-ONE

Airborne once again, the Bell commuter helicopter flew directly toward the sun, now high in the morning sky. The sawgrass on the landscape below gently bent and swayed, waving in the light breeze, a stark contrast to the Miami skyline ahead.

"Did he tell you anything?" Travis's voice asked over the headphones I was wearing. Scott, Germ, and Donnie sat across from me. Bond, Guthrie, and the other three men who I'd never learned the names of stayed behind to wait for another helicopter from Homestead to come and get the bodies and the prisoner.

"Nothing useful," I replied. "Said he didn't know Bradley wasn't accompanying him to the meet until just before they got in the van to leave. He said Bradley didn't even give him a reason, just handed one of his guys the briefcase with the money in it and told them to get back as fast as they could. Has the takedown team learned anything?"

"Brown's wife arrived to open the store at oh seven-thirty hours," Travis replied. "They only live a block away and she was walking. Venomous woman from what Kumar said."

Kumar Sayef is part of Deuce's first team, now reassigned as the Bravo Team leader. A former Delta Force interpreter and interrogator, he's about my age and had been a sergeant first class, until Deuce recruited him. He speaks a number of Middle Eastern languages and dialects.

"We're going straight there," I said. "Donnie says the area behind the gun store is large enough to land a helo."

"If they slipped out after Brown left," Travis said, "they have a three-hour head start. They might have stolen or even rented a car and be as far north as Melbourne or Orlando."

"I don't think so, Colonel. Bradley doesn't strike me as the type to let things go. He brought his own muscle down all the way from Pittsburgh, rented a nine-passenger van for five guys, and arranged to buy guns. Doesn't sound to me like someone who'd just up and change their mind."

"Your daughter's getting worried," Travis said.

"Tell her what you think you can, Colonel. I trust both her and Nick."

"I do too," he replied. "Call me when you're on the ground."

Removing the headphones, I leaned toward Scott. All three men had been listening in. "What am I missing?"

"Her car," Donnie replied.

"What car? The Colonel said they only live a couple blocks away."

"Aye, I heard that. Reckon she also walks to the grocer? Carries everything back in her hands? I been here in the land of opportunity only ten years, mate. But one thing I've noticed for sure is that every married couple has two cars."

The nose of the chopper came up, the pilot slowing and circling to the left. Through the Plexiglas I could see the gun store, easily recognizable by the flashing lights of two cars and a large black van and the number of people outside holding guns.

On the ground again, I trotted quickly around the building toward the group of men in the parking lot. I spotted Kumar coming out of the store and changed direction toward him.

"Find out anything from the wife?" I asked him without preamble.

"She's not talking, Jesse. What about Brown?"

"In a lot of pain. An old back injury got reinjured. Donnie shot him up with enough morphine to deaden the pain and more than enough to loosen his tongue. Said he had no idea that Bradley and Conner weren't coming out there and no clue why they're not still here. Where's the wife's car?"

"I just sent two men to check their house," he said, pointing back toward the chopper. "It's just beyond those trees. No car there and only the husband's monster truck here. However, there are two grease stains on the concrete driveway. Chyrel is checking DMV records now."

Pulling my sat-phone out, I called Travis. "We're here," I said as soon as he answered. "Kumar says there's no second car at their house. Any word from Chyrel on the wife's car?"

"Just got it, should be coming to both you and Kumar, too. Besides the Dodge truck, they also own a sixty-six Volkswagen van converted into a camper."

My phone beeped but, knowing it was the incoming text from Chyrel, I ignored it. "I think it's time to get local law enforcement's help, Colonel."

"Doing that as we speak," he replied as my phone beeped a second time. "I'm putting out an APB on the van, Bradley, and Conner. Did you learn the other guy's name?"

"Brown called him Malik, but said he didn't know the last name."

"Alright, keep me posted."

I closed the phone without checking the text message. Nothing I could do about it here, anyway. *In fact, there wasn't anything I could do about anything here*, I thought. Suddenly, I was overwhelmed with the urge to be somewhere else. Anywhere where I could hold a rod in one hand and a beer in the other. Anywhere near crystal-clear water.

Frustrated, I turned and looked around the lot and building. That's when I noticed Binkowski's van parked in the empty parking lot across the street. The parking lot looked like it could hold twenty cars and, except for the van, it was empty. A big white sign stood by the entrance with XXX written in big red letters. The van stuck out like a sore thumb.

Kumar was talking to two of his men a few feet away. "Kumar, where's Binkowski?"

"He left four hours ago, before the raid. Guthrie asked to be part of your takedown team, so I assigned someone else to the van." He frowned and looked across the street.

"He hasn't checked in since Brown and the other four men left."

Together, we sprinted across the street and into the parking lot. Reaching the van, we both pulled our side-arms and cautiously approached it. A slight gust of wind told me all I needed to know, as the stench of death it carried reached my nostrils.

Kumar stood off to the side, weapon ready. I grabbed the door handle and yanked the door open, instantly bringing up my Sig. A body lay on the floor of the van in a pool of congealed blood. The temperature inside had to be well over a hundred and thirty degrees and the body was bloated, nearly unrecognizable.

Kumar keyed the mic hanging on the front of his body armor. "Get three men over here, now! Cordon off this parking lot, and someone call the sheriff's office and the base coroner."

Turning to me, Kumar sighed, his shoulders falling. I saw the look in his face. I'd had it myself on more than one occasion. "His name was Greg Murray," Kumar said quietly. "Five years with the Rangers. He was only twenty-four years old, married with a two-year-old son. I recruited him myself."

Scott and Donnie came running over with three other men from Kumar's team. "The wife just tried to make a break for it," Scott said. "She made it out the back door, but one of the guys caught her just standing in the parking lot out back. She had a set of keys in her hand."

"We gotta find that van," I said to nobody in particular. Then I remembered the text from Chyrel and the second text notification. *Maybe she found out something,* I thought, pulling my phone out of my pocket.

Looking at the screen, I saw that there were two messages, but only one of them was from Chyrel. The other was a voice mail from Lawrence, which I clicked, then put the phone to my ear.

"Cap'n, yuh say to call if I see dem two bald black mons. Dey just now cross di Stock Island Bridge, headin' into town. A white mon was wit dem."

Two bald black men? I thought. Erik Lowery was dead. Then I remembered. When the gray van had arrived, the man driving it had been tall and black, with a shaved head, just like Bradley and Lowery.

"Scott, you and Donnie are with me." I started to jog across Old Dixie Highway toward the gun store. "Where's Germ?"

"Sitting on the wife," Donnie replied. "What's going on?"

"We have to get to Key West," I shouted back.

The two men raced after me as I dashed around the building. The chopper pilot was leaning against his aircraft, taking advantage of what little shade it offered, as I came running up with my phone in my hand.

"Get her started," I shouted as Travis answered the phone. "Colonel," I said into the phone, "Bradley and Conner are in Key West, probably headed to Dawn McKenna's place. We're headed there now in Nick's chopper. Call Key West PD and let them know. They should be considered armed and are wanted for murdering a DHS agent."

"What?" he shouted. "Who?"

"Greg Murray," I replied, climbing into the copilot's seat.

I ended the call as the blades began turning, the turbine beginning to spool up. Minutes later we were in the air, flying low over the southernmost tip of the Florida mainland. Climbing, I pointed southwest and shouted to the pilot, "Key West! As fast as you can get there."

Flying out over the water of Florida Bay, the long chain of islands stretched out to the hazy horizon far in the distance. The pilot climbed to a thousand feet and leveled off. "We can make Key West airport in about forty minutes."

How could something so easy go so wrong, so fast? I thought.

CHAPTER FORTY-TWO

Shortly after parking in the shade of the banyan tree, a Key West police cruiser pulled up in front of the mystic's shop and a cop got out. He went to the door, tried it and then knocked on the glass. Peering through the window, he then moved around the small converted house, reappearing on the opposite side, looking through the window there.

GT and Malik slid down in their seats when the cop arrived, watching with just their eyes above the dashboard. Finally, the cop went to his car and pulled the radio microphone from the passenger side and spoke into it for a minute. Then he got in the car, drove to the corner and turned left.

"What do you make of that?" Malik asked.

"Means we know she's not here yet, we wait."

Five minutes later, the fortuneteller walked right past in front of the van, carrying a canvas bag loaded with groceries. Even though GT had only seen her for an instant when she'd let Buchannan in, he knew it was her. She actually glanced in the van as she walked past and nodded, before turning and crossing the street. At the door, the woman unlocked it and went inside.

"Okay," GT said. "Let's move."

All three men got out of the van, trotted across the street, and just walked right into the mystic's shop. GT locked the door behind him. He pulled a cheap Glock .45 out that he'd had Brown include in the deal.

Off to the left was a room decorated in red and gold fabrics, a large round table taking up most of the center of it and plush velvet chairs around the walls.

"I'll be just a minute," the woman's voice came from the back of the building. "Just make yourself at home in the parlor."

Pointing to Conner, GT whispered, "Sit over there on the far side of the table."

As Conner made his way over, GT said, "Other side of the door, Malik."

The two black men put their backs to the walls on either side of the door inside the parlor and waited. GT slowly holstered his gun. After a minute, they heard footsteps approaching from the back and the woman stopped in the doorway. "Oh," she said. "You're not Lawrence." Then, stepping toward Conner seated at the table, she smiled and asked, "Are you here for a reading?"

Stepping forward quickly, GT wrapped a strong arm around the woman's waist, pulling her back into him. He covered her mouth with his other hand, his mouth at her ear. "Bet ya didn't see that coming, did ya, fortuneteller?"

The woman struggled against him, but he was far stronger and he simply lifted her by the waist and carried her into the middle of the room. "Now, you be quiet and you might just make it through this. Where's Buchannan live?"

Stepping up next to GT, Malik started to say something, but was interrupted by a metallic clang. Malik simply slumped forward on the table as Conner stood up and started to come around it.

GT spun around, shoving the woman toward Conner. There in the doorway stood the old taxi driver, an aluminum bat in his hands. The man took a powerful swing, which GT quickly ducked under, drawing his gun at the same time. The report of the shot was deafening. The taxi driver continued his spin, the momentum of the swing, along with the big forty-five caliber slug that entered his right shoulder from behind, carrying him completely around. He collapsed onto the floor. The woman screamed, running toward the fallen man.

Conner managed to grab her around the waist and she fought him with a ferocity he hadn't expected in such a small woman. She somehow twisted around in his embrace, her fingernails raking the skin off his face, searching for his eyes. Stepping forward, GT hit her in the back of the head with the butt of the gun and her struggles quickly ceased.

Looking around, GT saw a door in the corner and opened it, revealing a large closet lined with shelves. In the corner was an old upright vacuum cleaner. He grabbed it and yanked the cord loose, tossing it to Conner. "Find something to cut that with, then tie them both up in the closet."

Conner scurried out of the room, headed to the back of the house, where he assumed there'd be a kitchen with knives. When he returned, GT was kneeling over Malik, the man just beginning to groan as GT helped him to his feet.

Conner went to the taxi driver first. The bullet had gone through his upper shoulder cleanly, the wound already starting to congeal. Tying the man's hands behind his back, he went quickly over to the woman. Checking the back of her head, there was a large knot where GT had hit her, but he found only a little blood.

Conner quickly tied her hands behind her, then rolled her over. Pulling her into a sitting position, he was surprised at how little she weighed when he lifted her up onto his shoulder and easily carried her to the closet.

The much larger taxi driver was a different story. Finally, Conner hooked his hands under the man's shoulders and dragged him backward to the closet. Stepping back out, he asked, "What do we do now?"

"Check her purse for a phone," GT said. "Maybe that Buchannan's number is there. We'll text him and say there's trouble and he needs to get here quick."

Conner looked around and spotted a purse on a table by the parlor entry. Looking through it, he pulled her phone out, found her contact list and scrolled through it, but didn't find a Buchannan, nor a Stretch. "Nothing," he said and went back to the purse, looking through the billfold for a business card or something with the man's number on it. Finally, he looked at GT and shrugged. "A bag of weed, lipsticks, and a grocery receipt."

A loud knock came from the front door and GT raised a finger to his lips. Tiptoeing to the window, he took a quick glance outside. It looked like the same police cruiser was again parked outside. This time, the cop didn't go around looking through windows. He just walked back to the police car, got in and drove away.

"We'll wait till the bitch wakes up, then make her text the guy," GT said, plopping down in an overstuffed velvet chair.

Malik gently rubbed a big swollen spot on the side of his head, but the guy had only got him with a glancing blow and he counted himself lucky. Ten minutes later, sitting in a chair across from his boss, who now had his eyes closed, Malik heard a car pull up out front.

"GT, someone's here," Malik whispered.

Getting quickly to his feet, GT went to the door and looked out. He couldn't believe his eyes. They wouldn't have to wait for the woman to wake up after all. He reached down and quietly unlocked the door, then retreated to the parlor, picking up the bat and hiding behind the wall. He motioned Malik and Conner to the other side of the opening and waited.

CHAPTER FORTY-THREE

Just as we were approaching the airport, my phone rang. It was George Hamilton. I pushed the button to accept the call and said, "What'd you find out?"

"She's not in the house. The back door was unlocked and I waited until the local cop arrived and we went in. No sign of her and no sign of a struggle. I sent the cop back over to her shop to check again. He's pulling up now, hold on."

I heard a muffled conversation and then Hamilton came back on. "Not at her shop either. She's just disappeared."

"Is it possible she went for a walk and you missed her?" I asked.

"Possible, like I said, the back door was unlocked and it's only a few feet from the path. But I should have seen her there."

"I just spoke to the taxi driver, Lawrence. He said he usually stops by her shop for coffee about this time and

would be there in just a few minutes. Head to the airport and pick us up."

"Roger that," Hamilton replied.

Minutes later, Hamilton came to a stop in front of the general aviation building and the three of us climbed in. Shaking his hand, I said, "Go to her shop. You can drop me and Scott off there, then you and Donnie can go back to her house. Every cop in town is looking for them and for her. It's just a matter of time."

Minutes later, I was relieved to see Lawrence's cab parked at the curb in front of her place of business. Scott and I climbed out into the blazing heat and I suddenly felt extremely tired. I'd been up most of the night, running on caffeine and adrenaline mostly. The oppressive heat and high humidity just added to my weary feeling.

I opened the door and let Scott go ahead of me. "Dawn?" I shouted. "It's Jesse." Hearing nothing, I motioned Scott to check the back of the house and I stepped sideways into the parlor.

Out of nowhere, an aluminum bat hit me square on my upper left arm. The pain shot up through my shoulder and neck then exploded in my head. I instinctively spun away, only to be caught flush on the jaw by a crashing fist. As I continued to spin in slow motion toward the deck, my eyes caught sight of Chase Conner in the corner of the room.

I landed hard on my injured arm, and a new wave of pain shot through me, spots and swirls fading in and out of my sight as I heard a loud boom. I tried to raise my head up, but the pain was too intense and my head fell back and rolled to the side. Trying to focus, I saw Scott standing in the doorway, a red stain spreading across the left side of his chest.

"Not yet, motherfucker!" I heard a voice yell.

Rough hands grabbed the front of my shirt, pulling me up. A hand grabbed my jaw and turned my head, so that I was looking into GT Bradley's hate-filled eyes.

Seeing his right hand cock back, my mind told my body to move, but nothing happened. Bradley's fist caught me squarely on my left eye. The pain didn't even register as my head bounced off the deck and my vision started to fade to black.

"I'm just gonna cut you up slowly," the man hissed. I felt something cold against the side of my face. It suddenly turned white hot, and a new pain registered in my brain as warm blood trickled down my cheek and neck.

I tried to struggle away, but Bradley pushed me hard to the deck again, crashing the back of my skull on the century-old hardwood. I slowly opened my eyes and saw Bradley, Conner, and the other black man standing over me.

"Not so tough now," Conner said as he viciously kicked me in the ribs, the pain erupting behind my eyes, painting everything a bright red, with white strobe spotlights pinging on and off all around me.

Just as everything began drifting into darkness, my last thought was that I shouldn't be on island time. I should have stopped to look around. I shouldn't be losing my edge. As blackness closed in over me, I heard a crashing noise, as if it came from the far end of a long tunnel. The crash was followed by three deafening explosions. It didn't sound like what I imagined the Pearly Gates opening would be like.

EPILOGUE

Laying in a hammock, the air felt dry and cool on my bare skin. The wind rustled the palms over my head and I knew I was dreaming. I'd had this dream before. Alex came to me in these dreams, telling me it wasn't time to join her. I didn't want to open my eyes and see her again. Or maybe this was my time to join her. Maybe this time, I really was dead. I was ready.

The gentle swaying of the hammock felt good, the soft cool breeze raising goose bumps on my arms. It just felt right. I'd only turned forty-six a couple of months earlier and had spent nearly thirty of those years fighting or preparing to fight against people who threatened our way of life. I'd done enough. I'd given the best years of my life to what I thought was right. To what was just and honorable.

"Are you waking up?" I heard her say. But it wasn't Alex's voice at all. This voice was a little higher-pitched, with just a hint of a Puerto Rican accent. An accent she tried hard to hide, but always came out whenever she was excited or agitated.

I slowly opened my eyes, the rhythmic sound of small waves lapping on a nearby shore giving over to the beeping of a heart monitor. The first thing I saw was Linda's face, hovering over mine.

She smiled. "Enjoy your nap?"

I tried to sit up, but she put her hand on my chest. "Easy, Jesse. The doctor said you'd need to hold still for a couple of hours until the cast sets good and hard."

I looked down at my left arm. There was a dull throbbing sensation there and I had a cast from my wrist to my shoulder.

I flopped my head back. "A broken arm? I've never had a broken bone in my life." Then I remembered what'd happened and tried to rise again. "What about Scott?"

"Right here, Gunny," I heard him say and looked to my right. The heart monitor was hooked to him and he was propped up with a large bandage high on his left shoulder.

"The others?" I asked, not really wanting to know.

"Your taxi-driving friend is in the next room," Eve said, standing on the opposite side of the bed. Nick was with her, a hand resting gently on her shoulder and Alfie snoozing in his hammock.

"Lawrence and Dawn are both fine," Nick said. "Travis and I spoke with them just a few minutes ago. Interesting man."

Looking around the room, I saw Travis and Rusty standing by the door. Rusty stepped up next to Nick. "Kim'll probably be here before they even let you out of here, brother."

"Bradley, his man Malik, and Conner are all three dead," Travis said, with a crooked grin. "Remember Miss McKenna saying her daddy's Mossberg was in the closet? Well, guess where Bradley stashed her?"

I grinned slowly. "You're kidding."

"No," he replied, stepping closer. "She would have got Donnie, too, except he had his badge up when he came through the door. He said the barrel was still smoking and she was standing over you and Lawrence looking like, and I quote, 'a vicious mother from Hell, defending her baby against rabid dingoes.'"

"Will she be okay?" I asked Travis.

"I think so. Seems like a really tough little lady. Donnie got her and Lawrence out and waited for the police. He kept her from giving any statement to the cops until Nick and I got there. The local cops all know her and saw no reason to take her in, anyway."

Looking back up at Linda, I grinned. "Can we unwind now?"

She punched me on the good right arm and smiled.

Two days later, Linda and I, along with Eve and Nick, Kim, and her boyfriend Marty Phillips, a Monroe deputy, Coral and Michal, Travis and nearly all of the men and women under his command attended Greg Murray's funeral service in Valdosta, Georgia, where he was from. Michal was duly impressed with the G5 we flew up in.

It hasn't been determined yet who had actually killed Murray. We assumed it was either Bradley or Malik, but it was still under investigation. An honor guard from his

most recent Army unit was flown down from Fort Bragg to fold the flag and render honors. A large number of his Ranger buddies from Fort Benning came down together in a bus as well.

After the service concluded, I got Travis alone for a minute. "I don't know if you're aware," I began, "but I set up a trust fund some time ago to help the families of local fallen military. In a few days, will you let the widow know that the boy's college tuition is covered? No need for her to know where it came from, though."

"I'll do that, Jesse," he replied. "What are your plans?"

Just then, Linda and my family came and gathered around me, along with Coral and Michal, who was now using the name Bob full-time. Linda took my hand in hers and leaned her head on my good arm.

"I think I'm gonna take some time to myself and just look around a little, Colonel."

THE END

If you'd like to receive my monthly newsletter for specials, book recommendations, and updates on coming books, please sign up on my website:

www.waynestinnett.com

Jesse McDermitt Series
Fallen Out
Fallen Palm
Fallen Hunter
Fallen Pride
Fallen Mangrove
Fallen King
Fallen Honor
Fallen Tide (November, 2015)

Charity Styles Series
Merciless Charity
Ruthless Charity (Winter, 2016)
Heartless Charity (Fall, 2016)

The Gaspar's Revenge Ship's Store is now open. There you can purchase all kinds of swag related to my books.
WWW.GASPARS-REVENGE.COM

AFTERWORD

When I first set out to write my first novel, I had but one goal in mind: to make enough extra money to buy tools to outfit a woodworking shop where I could build canoes, kayaks, small sailboats, and powerboats, the plan being that I could get out of the truck and off the road, to be home with my family. The first two books were published in 2013 and I began to notice that I could actually do more than that. In 2014, I published a third novel and then a shorter prequel to the series and things began to explode.

I'm no longer on the road and I'm able to be home with my family full-time now, thanks to you, my readers. The plan of outfitting the woodworking shop is on hold for a while, though. We're moving to Beaufort, South Carolina, and will be building a whole house around the woodworking shop.

I'd dreamed most of my life about being a novelist. Growing up on the east coast of Florida, I cut my teeth on the works of Ernest Hemingway and John D. MacDonald, then, as a young man, James W. Hall, Carl Hiaasen, and Randy Wayne White, among others. My writing style and characters are a direct reflection of the musings of these and many more great authors.